SEASON OF DESIRE

AN AGE GAP, RUSSIAN BRATVA BILLIONAIRE ROMANCE

LISA CULLEN

© Copyright 2023, by Author Lisa Cullen .

All Rights Reserved.

No part of this publication may be reproduced, distributed or transmitted in any form or by any means including photocopying, recording, or other electronic or mechanical methods except in the case of brief quotations embodied in critical reviews and certain other non commercial uses permitted by copyright law. Unauthorised reproduction or distribution of this work is illegal.

This book is a work of fiction. Names, characters, businesses, places, events, and incidents are either the products of author's imagination or used in a fictitious manner. Any resemblance to actual persons, living or dead, is purely coincidental.

This book is intended for adult readers only. Any sexual activity portrayed in these pages occurs between consenting adults over the age of 18 who are not related by blood.

DESCRIPTION

**I turned him down . . . he bought the entire ballet company.
I still said no . . . he blew hundreds of thousands on a night out for everyone.
I gave in to my lust . . . and he got me *pregnant*.**

His name is Alexei Federov and he is a Russian mob boss.
When he sees me dancing in a ballet performance, he forces his way into my life.

I've never dreamed of a family or finding love. The chance was ripped away from me when my health suffered for my career. All I could ever dream of is dancing.

But when a sultry, passionate night of seduction leads to a baby in my belly, *everything* changes.

I struggle to make my choice, but deep down, I already know . . .

The moment Alexei finds out I'm pregnant, he's going to rip my freedom away from me, and I'll never dance again.

1

ALEXEI

My mom's petite hand rests in the crook of my elbow as I escort her into the opulent Curran Theater for a night of ballet. It's been too long since Maksim, Dimitri, and I took her out for a night to the ballet, and she loves it so much.

And though I fully expect the next three hours to be pure torture, I can't help but grin at the wide smile that stretches across her face. I find the silent storytelling of ballet monotonous and boring, but I endure it because it makes my mother happy and it's a sin for Russians not to like something so deeply rooted in our traditions.

Walking next to me is Maksim, my oldest brother, and his fiancée, Symphony, each dressed to the nines in a tux and a dusty rose cocktail dress that plunges low enough to show off her considerable and too-perky-to-be-real cleavage.

Maksim's fiancée is a swimsuit model with legs for days, firm breasts, and perfectly tamed blonde hair that spills around her face and shoulders and sets off the glow of her golden skin.

His hand rests lightly on the small of her slender back as he guides her through the mob of people in the lobby and toward our exclusive, pricy seats.

"I don't get what the big hype is about," Symphony says.

She wears the scrunched expression of someone who just found dog shit on their shoe, telling me she's less than enthusiastic about tonight, even if it's an excuse for her to show off her expensive wardrobe. And while she hangs a dress better than most, I don't know what my brother sees in her.

She must give a phenomenal blowjob because after trying to get to know her for the past few years, I'm positive her mouth has no other good use.

More often than not, she uses it to complain about or devalue anything that wasn't her idea. But she has Maksim on the hook, and when she loops her arm around his, he gives her an indulgent smile.

"*Swan Lake* is a classic. I promise you'll like it," he says.

To my left, my mother's smile falters slightly, and I bristle. Having successfully raised three challenging boys in my father's Bratva world of cutthroat business, my mother is nothing short of a saint, and no one should be raining on her parade.

I know if Dimitri and his wife, Camille, were here, he'd be knocking Symphony down a peg in a matter of seconds—they've never gotten along. But he's currently at home with a new baby, so it looks like I'm up to bat.

"You didn't have to come," I point out to Symphony drily. "In fact, you still don't. Why not just head home early?"

"Alexei," Maksim warns, his gray eyes flashing.

He has the same imperious look my father used to be so good at, the one that sticks in my mind as my strongest memory of him. Maksim's look now reminds me that, as he's the oldest and, therefore, the head of our family. I'm supposed to show him respect.

I shrug and pull out the tickets to grant us access to our private balcony. The black-suited usher gestures us inside a moment later.

But Symphony's not finished whining. "All I'm saying is it's done, like, every year. Can't they put on a new ballet?"

"It hasn't come to town for the last three years," I state coldly. It's part of why Mom has been looking forward to tonight for over a month.

"The principal has received incredible recognition for her performance. She's new this year, hired just before the end of last season, but from what I've heard, this is a performance everybody will want to see," my mother adds kindly.

"It's one of Mother's favorites," Maksim says, his tone indicating that should be more than enough reason for Symphony to like the ballet.

I realize it's ironic that I would find my brother's fiancée annoying for missing the significance of this ballet when I would rather have stayed home myself—not that I would ever say or do anything to hurt my mother's feelings. But still, she didn't have to punish us with her presence if she wants to vocalize her distaste. And for me, tonight's about treating my mother, not the dancing on stage.

Symphony seems to finally register the foot she's put in her mouth and leans her cheek on Maksim's shoulder. Then she flashes my mom a plastic smile. "Well, if you like it, Mrs. Federov, I'm sure I will too."

Ignoring her pathetic attempt to mend the situation, I turn my shoulders to block her from my mother's view as I help my mom into her seat.

Normally, I can brush off Symphony's juvenile way of getting attention by whining about things. Dimitri's the one who lets her get under his skin.

But in my mind, Maksim has every right to make himself as happy or miserable as he wants to be with his chosen bride. She'd just better not say anything more to offend my mom, or we'll have a problem.

Settling into my seat, I take the opportunity to scope the building's interior, assessing the situation, as I always do, for any potential threats or concerns to look out for. The theater is beautiful, with richly colored walls, intricate gold-painted molding on the ceiling, and arching pillars that surround the stage.

From here, we have the perfect vantage point to see the dancers and also people watch the mass that makes up the audience tonight. It's a full house. This really must be a good performance for the large theater to be sold out this early in the season.

"Thank you for coming out tonight, Alexei," my mom says, patting my knee. "I know how much you hate sitting still for these."

She's not wrong. That restless energy I've had all my life is part of what makes me good at what I do—security for our family, as our business often means making enemies.

"Are you kidding? I wouldn't miss it."

The champagne that's delivered to us a few minutes later is going to make this much more tolerable. At least it will help me stay awake when the music starts to lull me to sleep.

A hush falls over the crowd as the lights dim, and excited murmurs ripples through the theater before fading as the music starts. Sipping my champagne, I settle back, letting my senses travel around the room in the hopes of finding something that might catch my interest.

The curtains open, and a tall, slender ballerina wearing a simple slip of a dress strolls onto the stage with impressive grace. It's the same familiar opening from the classic ballet that we always see—the innocent heroine on a stroll before she's confronted by the villain who turns her into a swan.

But it's different somehow.

Because she catches my attention immediately.

Something in the dancer's movements is so refined, so poised that even when I glance away, her silent steps call my eyes back to her within moments. Her dance is filled with the levity and ease of an innocent girl enjoying a walk around a lake.

The music almost seems to stem from her motion, like she's so deeply intertwined with the notes that her feet bring them to life, rather than the other way around. Her arms are soft and fluid, her legs strong and energetic, her body moving with a flexibility that quickens my pulse.

And then the energy shifts as the villain appears to chase her.

My muscles tense as I watch the familiar scene unfold with new eyes—because I don't like the very real fear in the ballerina's face, the desperation in her movement as she turns to run. They move together, the innocent girl and the villain, in a dance that consumes her, transforming her movements from sweet, soft, and innocent to the sharp and tense leaps and twirls of fear.

How can beauty and terror be so closely intertwined?

Sitting forward in my seat, I start to follow the ballet more closely, intent on the prima ballerina's plight. Then the spell consumes her, transforming her into a breathtaking swan that falls to the ground in despair.

"Incredible, isn't she?" my mom whispers beside me as the curtain falls on the distraught ballerina, leaving me tense. "She's from New York."

My fists clench as I find myself riveted, my body eager to see she's safe even though I know it's only a story. I glance sideways at my mom, forcing myself to relax as I realize my stress is unnecessary. "What?" My eyebrows press into a frown as I realize I wasn't listening.

"The principal. She's from New York. The Tapestry Dance Company hired her as prima above all the talent they have here in the city." Her eyes glint knowingly, like she can see the rapture in my expression.

"I can see why," I murmur, turning back to the stage as the curtain rises once again.

Hardly daring to breathe, I actually pay attention to *Swan Lake* for the first time in my life, ensnared by the ballerina's movements every time she enters the stage.

She's stunning, her body sheer perfection. But it's more than her athletic figure that captivates me. It's the way she uses it like an artist. Her poise, her timing, the curves of her arms and legs like a masterpiece. She holds herself with a dignity that suits the character.

But the emotions on her face enthrall me.

Even from here, I can tell the prima is a stunner. Cream-colored skin that looks as delicate as China contrasts with her full red lips and thickly painted eyes. Her dark hair is pulled back now to make room for her crown of white feathers. And in her sparkling white tutu and bodice, she looks as regal and elegant as the creature she's meant to represent.

I don't dare look away and miss a single moment of her performance. She has me spellbound. I've never seen someone move with such otherworldly grace. She dances just as beautifully with her partners as she does alone, her presence commanding the audience, her singular motions leaving the theater hushed and still.

She tells the classic story with the same scenes and dances I've grown up watching, and yet her performance is entirely different. The emotion flows from the principal into her audience, allowing us to live the love and betrayal, devastation, and elation in Odette's sad story of transformation and hope for freedom.

It's agony as the climactic end sends the prima toppling into a lake hidden behind the stage, her death freeing her from the villain who had so cruelly cursed her in the opening scene. My shoulders tense as she comes on stage with the cast and the audience rises to give her a standing ovation. And there's no doubt in my mind that they're all standing just for her.

Then she takes a final fluid bow, and the curtain falls, stealing her from my view.

That can't be the end. I have to see her again.

For hours, I couldn't take my eyes off a single woman—a challenge I've never faced before—and now I have to meet her. I have to know her name.

"That was simply breathtaking," my mother says, her voice warbling on the brink of tears from the moving performance.

"Yeah," I breathe, my eyes lingering on the stage as my muscles tense.

"You look like you're about to be sick there, Brother," Maksim observes dryly from his seat.

"You know what? Maybe I am," I state distractedly, rising from my chair to push past my brother and his fiancée without another word of explanation.

But I'm on a mission to find her.

The ballerina.

And I intend to make her mine.

2

NADIA

Electric excitement crackles through me as the curtain falls. It doesn't matter that I've been practicing this performance rigorously for a year now. It doesn't matter that this is my fifth performance of *Swan Lake* in front of a packed theater. Knowing I am the prima of the Tapestry Dance Company still fills me with giddy disbelief.

"Incredible, Nadia!" McKenna says as I make my way off stage. "That last number just keeps getting better and better."

I beam as we head back toward the dressing rooms together. "Thanks, McKenna."

I appreciate that the girls have accepted me when most of them have been here for several years now and I came in to take the position they would all want to have. My choice to take the position as prima didn't exactly set me up to make friends, and though I have to admit that it's a bit lonely coming in to take the top spot, I'm okay with that. I've never needed friends. Not at the expense of becoming a principal. And I want to become the best there's ever been.

Still, McKenna's efforts do mean a lot to me—talking to me when most of the girls took longer to warm up to my presence, offering me words of encouragement and friendly smiles.

"The girls and I were talking about going for a drink after we change. Would you like to join?" she offers as the din of the theater fades in the long hallway of dressing rooms.

"Oh, that's so nice of you to invite me, but I'd better not." Landing where I have didn't come from a healthy work-life balance. Becoming a principal has required constant focus, and I can't lose that, even if it means I don't make as many friends.

"Are you sure?" she presses, slowing in front of her own dressing room door.

Her wide brown eyes tell me she wishes I would accept her invitation one of these days, and though I doubt I will, it still softens my resolve just a little.

"Maybe next time," I say, smiling back.

Then I leave her at her door as I continue on to the end of the hall.

Stepping into my dressing room, I take a moment to breathe. Closing my eyes, I inhale deeply and review my performance in my mind, the small details that I could have done better. But I relish the intense elation that comes after a show in which I gave my all. And I know I'll only get better from here.

The performance went well, and I feel like I'm improving with this new company every day. I can't wait for my mom to fly out from New York next week to see me perform the lead. She's always been my best supporter, the person who has loved and protected me, given me every opportunity she could. I've come a long way since we came to America, and I know it will make my mother proud to see me in this role.

Shrugging out of the straps to my leotard, I approach my dressing room table, where my change of clothes sits folded and waiting for me.

A sharp knock alerts me to someone at the door—probably a delivery of flowers, something I've received from admirers every evening since I began performing as principal.

"Come in!" I call, covering my breasts with my bodice as I reach for my makeup bag.

The door clicks open, and movement catches my eye in the mirror above my makeup table, but the person doesn't slip in and out like they usually do. Instead, they pause as the door shuts quietly behind them.

"You can just leave them on the—" I gasp as my eyes find the person in my mirror and focus on the tall, muscular, broad-shouldered man there. He's gorgeous, with laughing gray eyes, dark hair that's cut close to his scalp, and an impressive five-o'clock shadow that accentuates his square jaw. The charcoal-gray suit tailored to fit him perfectly looks like it's of the finest quality.

But what in the hell is he doing in my dressing room?

Clutching my leotard more firmly against my body, I whirl, my heart pounding at his unexpected intrusion. Fear launches me straight into anger as I lash out with my words, my brain working a mile a minute. "What are you doing in here? I thought you were one of the girls delivering flowers. You're not supposed to be here. Get out!"

"I'm sorry, but I can't do that," he says softly. "Not until I know your name."

His deep voice has a hint of a Russian lilt, though he's more fluent in English than I am—impressive, considering my mom always impressed the importance of being able to speak the language of our adoptive homeland when I was growing up.

The familiar accent, combined with his diverting physique and striking features, makes it hard to maintain my anger. But cold and imperious are my best weapons right now if he thinks he's here to take advantage of me. *Where the hell is security? And how did he get past them?*

"You think you can just barge into my dressing room, demanding my name, and expect me to give it to you?" I snap, tipping my chin defiantly. He'd better not think he'll be coming anywhere near me when he's barged so inappropriately into my private room.

"Actually, I was hoping you might say yes to a date," he says casually, taking a step forward.

My eyes flash to his feet then back up to his face, daring him to keep moving forward. I don't care how good-looking he is. I'll knee him in the balls if he tries to touch me. "I don't date strange men who enter my dressing room unannounced," I state icily.

"Alexei Federov." He introduces himself as if only just realizing I might not already know who he is.

Definitely Russian, then, and it gives me a trembling sense of foreboding.

Then he flashes me a charming smile that makes my heart skip a beat. "And you are . . . ?"

I hesitate because I know what kind of man he is just from our brief exchange. He's the kind of man who thinks he owns the world —who thinks he owns me. He's Bratva. No doubt about it. My mother and I fled our homeland over men like him, and yet here I am, half a world away and still unable to escape the Russian mafia.

"Nadia . . . Lukyan." I don't dare take my eyes from him for even a moment. Not that I would want to. I've never seen a man so gorgeous, and even if I won't let him touch me, I can't stop myself from appreciating his appeal.

"See? Now we're no longer strangers," he quips.

And the levity with which he delivers the line catches me by surprise. I laugh, the shock bursting from me with unexpected mirth as his humor disarms me. Despite my better judgment, my shoulders relax slightly. I shouldn't trust him, but for some reason, I'm tempted to. Perhaps it's the glint in his eye that holds far more mischief than malice. But I don't *think* he's here to hurt me.

"Now that we're properly acquainted, will you let me take you on a date?" He takes another careful step forward, as if he thinks he might be able to approach without notice if he does it slowly enough.

"No." My answer is definitive, though my lips still twitch with amusement because, with my lessening fear, I find I enjoy teasing this impressive specimen of a man.

"You know, most girls would sell their souls for a date with me," he brags, sauntering forward, and his lithe movements mimic a predator on the prowl.

I can tell from the hint of silver in his short black hair that he's older than me—maybe in his late thirties or early forties—probably fifteen to twenty years older than my ripe age of twenty-three. And still, he looks entirely formidable, his sheer size something not to be trifled with. His bulging arms could probably snap me in half if he wanted to.

A shiver runs down my spine, and my fear spikes once again as I realize I might have let my guard down too soon. But his playful eyes make it nearly impossible not to fall for his charm.

"Well, I'm not like most girls," I state flatly, adjusting my arms over my breasts to try covering them more efficiently.

I feel intensely vulnerable in front of him now. If I have to fend him off, I will surely give him quite the show.

"I can see that," he says appreciatively, his light-gray eyes scanning up and down my body, the desire in them heating my body with its intensity.

It infuriates me to have someone objectify me so openly, like he could own me with a glance. And at the same time, it makes my heart flutter. But I refuse to let him get the best of me. "Well, perhaps if you want a yes, you should go try one of those other girls because my answer is still no."

My stomach drops as he continues forward, not stopping until he's within feet of me, just shy of triggering my flight response—like he knows just how far he can push my discomfort.

"What will it take to get you to go out with me?" he asks, his voice low and enticing, like this is a business deal he's adamant about closing.

If he wants to make this into a negotiation, he's going to be sorely disappointed. "A lot more than the effort you've put in," I challenge, refusing to drop my eyes as I dare him to give me an offer I can't refuse.

The smile that curls his lips sends my heart into overdrive. It's dangerous and playful all at once, warning me that I just might be in over my head. Adrenaline pounds through my veins, filling me with nervous anticipation. I should be terrified right now. But I'm too overwhelmed by his proximity to think straight.

And then he takes another step, closing the distance to hook a finger beneath my chin. My breath catches in my throat, my lips parting to say something, but I don't know what. And I can't bring myself to make a sound.

"Very well, Nadia Lukyan," he murmurs, his steel-gray eyes peering deep into my soul. "I accept your challenge. But I promise you'll give in to me eventually."

Heart hammering an erratic beat, I force myself to speak. "In your dreams," I breathe. The words sound far more confident than I feel, but they give me the strength to smile, a smirk meant to intimidate—to make him think twice about messing with me.

But it only seems to call his attention to my lips.

His eyes drop, and suddenly, I'm intensely aware that his lips are just inches from mine. An unbidden thought flashes through my head as I wonder what it would be like to kiss him. His lips are full and look soft surrounded by the dark scruff covering his face. And though he's considerably older than I am, I find myself overwhelmingly attracted to him.

I shove the thought down, unwilling to follow through with my inappropriate curiosity. I'm half-naked standing in front of him. We're complete strangers. And I have no clue how dangerous it might be if I try to play this game—how far he might take it if I open that door.

I've never found much time for men in my life. Too many other things have occupied my time and attention. And suddenly, I'm out of my depths, unable to breathe as I wait to see what he'll do to me.

A kiss is inevitable. I can see it as clear as day.

He's going to steal one before he leaves.

And I find I'm not entirely upset by the idea, even though it would be a blatant disregard of my refusal. But the energy crackling between us is more than I can stand, the tension so powerful that it makes me tremble.

For one agonizing moment, his chin tips—like a magnet is drawing his lips closer to mine.

I don't dare move. I don't dare breathe.

Then Alexei's eyes flick back up to mine, the heat of their intensity leaving me a puddle of indecision. And to my astonishment, he releases me, taking a step back to put space between us.

"What . . .?" I breathe, confounded by his behavior.

"I will kiss you, Nadia. But first, I intend to take you on a date." His lips quirk in a crooked smile filled with mischief. Then he gives a slight nod and strides back out of my dressing room without another word.

The air trapped in my lungs releases all at once as I collapse against my makeup table. I don't know what to make of what just happened. I'm speechless. And my heart won't stop pounding as my anticipation lingers far longer than the man who created it.

3

ALEXEI

Sitting in the cluttered office of Henry Lang, the Tapestry Dance Company's owner, I observe him with mild interest. He looks somewhere between frazzled and nervous as he slumps into his chair behind his desk, ten minutes late to our scheduled meeting.

This is going to be an easy deal—far easier than Nadia, I have no doubt. Flummoxed by Nadia's flat-out refusal to date me, I refuse to be discouraged. Instead, I find myself inspired by the challenge she poses. Because as much as she made it sound like she would never date me, I could see the truth in her eyes. She wants me to.

"Mr. Federov, so sorry I'm late," he apologizes, removing a Kleenex from the box on his desk to dab at the perspiration covering his forehead that seems to be growing more prominent as his hairline recedes.

"Not a problem. I requested this appointment to discuss with you the possibility of an investment," I state. Normally, I leave this kind of thing to Dimitri. He's the negotiator. I prefer the action side of our business far more. But in this case, I intend on closing this deal on my own, and I've participated in my brother's negotiations often enough that I know the strategy I intend to take now.

"Investment? Oh, I, uh, don't really have the money to spare for investing in ventures..." he says, paling slightly.

His physical response to my request tells me our family reputation precedes me. He's scared. I smile, my lips curling into an arrogant smirk. Though I'm not here to intimidate him, I do thoroughly enjoy knowing our family has the acumen to keep everyone wondering just what we're capable of.

"Actually, I was hoping I might be able to invest in one of your business ventures—take it off your hands completely, in fact. I assure you, I'm here to negotiate a fair price. One that both of us will find suitable." I lean forward in my chair, resting my elbows on my knees as I maintain eye contact.

"Oh." Lang's eyes widen. "Ooh. Yes, of course. I have many great opportunities for a successful businessman such as yourself to profit from. Which one are you considering?"

"The Tapestry Dance Company. I know you're currently bankrolling the ballet troupe, and as you might know, my mother loves the ballet. I intend to buy it for her as an early birthday present."

"Indeed?" Lang perks up, his eyes brightening as he seems to relax slightly with the conversation's turn. "And how much are you hoping to buy it for?"

"Let's say three million." Based on the company's profits over the last few years, it's a generous offer and one I'm sure would be well worth the investment with Nadia as its principal. She's turned the company's troupe into a sensation overnight.

From the way Lang's eyes bug out of his head, I know he hadn't dreamed I would come out with an offer like that from the starting gates, but I intend to close this deal before I leave the room today. I have more pressing negotiations I want to pursue. With a particularly sharp-tongued prima ballerina.

"Three million dollars?" Lang repeats in disbelief.

"That's what it's worth to me," I state frankly.

Not to mention, it's a drop in the bucket compared to what my family brings in. Even if it did create a loss—which I'm sure it won't, as the company will easily bring in that kind of revenue within the next three to five years—it wouldn't hurt me any.

"It sounds more than fair," he agrees breathlessly.

"Wonderful. I've already taken the liberty of having my lawyers draw up a contract," I state, placing it on the desk before him. "This would entitle me to full ownership of the dance company and its business strategy moving forward. In it, the contract outlines the agreed-upon price, which I can pay in cash as soon as you're ready to sign."

Lang pulls the papers closer, his eyes skimming down the page quickly enough that I'm sure he's not actually reading. He looks far too bewildered to be having a coherent thought at the moment. "I'll need my lawyers to look this over, of course . . ." he breathes, but I can see the glint of greed in his eyes.

"Of course," I agree. "Please, keep it. Have them look it over. I expect you can make your decision by the end of business today?" I rise from my chair, buttoning my suit jacket as I go, allowing my actions to add the pressure of a deadline even if my words are casual, nonchalant.

"Y–Yes, of course. How shall I reach you?"

"I'll have my people reach out to you," I state with a nod. "Pleasure speaking with you, Mr. Lang." Extending my hand across the space between us, I give his a firm shake. Then I turn for the door.

Nadia's ballet company will be mine within the day. I'm confident of it. Then the real fun begins. Stepping through the glass doors of the skyscraper's ground-floor lobby, I walk toward my yellow Ferrari SF90 Stradale. It's parked right where I left it, illegally, along the curb of the Financial District's bustling streets.

The Muni dings as it rolls along its tracks, putting traffic on hold. I slip behind the wheel of my car and bring the motor purring to life. My lips curl into a smile as I think about my brief exchange with Nadia in her dressing room.

The fire in her gaze keeps filling my mind's eye, tempting me to the point of driving me crazy. Buying the ballet is an indulgent choice, but I don't mind being flashy if it means having an excuse to spend more time with Nadia. And I wasn't lying. My mother will love knowing we have a ballet company in the family name.

My brothers, on the other hand, I suspect will be less than enthusiastic.

Pulling into the underground garage of our office building, I park near the elevator and brace myself for what's to come. I haven't told either of them anything about this business venture or what led to it, so I'm sure to enjoy the looks on their faces when I do.

Stepping out of the elevator onto the fiftieth floor of our building, I greet Tanya, our receptionist, with a casual smile. Then I head for Maksim's office, where he and Dimitri sound like they've already begun our weekly meeting in which they discuss the ins and outs of new acquisitions in our family business.

Typically, I'm a bystander, happy to let them dabble with the investing side of things while I ensure everyone stays alive and no one touches what's ours. A job made far easier in some regard because our reputation precedes us. Few people are willing to mess with the Federov brothers.

"Morning, fellas," I greet, letting myself into Maksim's office without knocking and heading for the chair next to Dimitri just on the other side of Maksim's desk.

My two older brothers stop mid-conversation to stare at me as I plop into the chair with a grin, unbuttoning my suit jacket as I make myself comfortable.

"What?" I ask when neither resumes speaking after several seconds.

"You never sit there," Dimitri observes, his expression shifting to suspicious in an instant.

Of my two brothers, Dimitri would be the one to notice something like that. He's always been observant, and he and I are closer—both in age and in our relationship. I love giving Dimitri shit.

Maksim, not as much because the guy can't take a joke. He's all work and no play, seeming to let loose only on occasion. I imagine it's because he had to take on the role of *pakhan* at a very early age.

"Well, I thought I might contribute to the acquisitions conversation this week."

Two sets of eyebrows raise in identical expressions of skepticism.

"What, you don't think I have business sense?" I chide at their looks of disbelief.

"Business sense, yes. An ounce of interest in the field? Not a chance. You whined and moaned nonstop the last few times I made you come along for my meetings," Dimitri reminds me, crossing his arms over his chest.

"So, what's this about?" Maksim asks from the other side of his desk.

"I made an offer to purchase the Tapestry Dance Company," I state, cutting right to the chase.

"The . . . what?" Dimitri asks, stunned.

"You're joking," Maksim says drily.

"Am I?" I counter.

My older brothers share a glance, then the room fills with deep laughter as they both lose it simultaneously.

"Why in God's name would you do that?" Dimitri asks. "You know we only invest in restaurants and clubs. The theater industry is far too volatile for our kind of business ventures."

I shrug. "This bet, I'm willing to put money on. Besides, Mom will be thrilled with the idea. You know how much she loves the ballet."

"Yes, but I'm confident we could afford to buy her season tickets for the rest of her life for less than what you must have had to offer. And who is going to ensure the company stays afloat? You? Or do you plan on hiring a CEO to oversee the business?"

"They already have a perfectly capable manager. I'll keep them on so long as I agree with the business strategy."

"And you made an offer without consulting us? How much did you settle on?"

"Three million," I state.

Maksim's expression tells me the offer would probably be what he would consider the company to be worth, and Dimitri gives an approving nod.

"But we don't need a ballet company. The theater industry is too much work," Maksim states after several seconds of silence.

"Maybe, but I'm making this investment with or without you," I say.

Dimitri studies me carefully, his gray eyes—the signature color we all inherited from our father—speculative. I haven't said anything about Nadia to either of my brothers, and I don't intend to. Not after all the hell I've given them about women over the years.

But even though he wasn't at the ballet, I know he can tell I'm not saying everything that's on my mind.

"I think we should give it a go," Dimitri says after a pause. His eyes shift back to Maksim, who still looks skeptical. "If our baby brother is finally going to back a horse, let's see how good his business sense really is."

After a long silence, Maksim nods. "Fine. You've closed the deal?"

"I will have by the end of today," I state confidently.

And tomorrow, I'll close on Nadia.

4

NADIA

The energy filling the dance studio this morning creates a nice buzz in the air as I settle into a deep stretch, leaning forward onto my thighs as I wrap my hands around my feet. The director's late—not completely unheard of, but pretty rare from what I've experienced over the past year—and several of the girls gossip about what could be keeping him.

"Did you have a nice day off?" McKenna asks, plopping down beside me and offering a broad grin.

Her kinky black curls hang loose around her face today, allowing her dark skin to relax into a softer shape than when she has her hair pulled back into a tight ballet knot. It makes her look closer to her young age of nineteen.

"Yes, I managed to relax a little besides getting errands done. How was yours?" It's impossible not to be friendly with the enthusiastic ballerina. Even I struggle to maintain an arm's length with her.

"Went home for a family dinner last night. That was nice," she says, shrugging before she starts to stretch beside me. "My brother's home from college, so it was great to see him."

I smile politely and shift into the splits to continue my routine.

"Good morning, dancers!" our director calls as he enters the room, beaming with an enthusiasm that tells me his tardiness is not from a flat tire or some other unfortunate event.

A chorus of greetings follows as we all continue to stretch out.

"Sorry I'm late, but I have a very important announcement to make if everyone will gather around."

McKenna and I exchange a glance at the unusual request. Normally, announcements take place as we're stretching so we can move straight into practice once he's done.

Rising out of my stretch, I follow the other dancers as we make a tight circle around our creative director, Stew Lubox. His typically flushed cheeks look exceptionally colorful today, his eyes bright with excitement, and a few of the ballet dancers lean close to murmur as he waits for his big reveal.

"I have some very exciting news," he says. "Our company has been making waves in San Francisco in a big way. And because of that, we've been bought by a wealthy investor! He's already held a meeting with our manager, and it sounds like he's willing to put money in to expand and improve our program. That, my pretties, means good things for us."

Chatter erupts through the room at his statement, and I glance around at the excited faces of my fellow dancers.

"Does that mean new costumes?" Leon asks, practically bouncing with excitement.

"Yes, and bigger productions with more dancers. This is going to take us to the next level in the competitive world of dance!" Stew explains.

The noise escalates as questions fly around the room, each clamoring for attention over the last. Beaming, Stew attempts to bring the noise back down, his hands gesturing to lower the volume.

"I'm letting you all know now that the new owner of Tapestry Dance Company is well known for being a playboy and a considerable partier, so I expect you all to be prepared to participate in more 'team outings', so to speak," he says cheekily.

Several of the girls titter excitedly, whispering behind their hands.

"And I expect everyone to be on their best behavior and willing to entertain our new benefactor. Ladies . . ." he says pointedly, his eyes searching out several of the girls, including me, as he not-so-subtly hints that "entertaining" might include pleasing this new owner in a more . . . intimate way.

My gut wrenches as disgust flares inside me. If he's thinking I should be willing to sleep with this playboy benefactor to keep him happy, he'd better think again. My body's not for sale. I don't care what this mystery owner might expect. And if that's what it takes to stay principal ballerina in this dance company, then I'll find another.

But no one else seems particularly perturbed by his statement. Maybe that's to be expected here. Or maybe everyone else is just so excited about the prospect of expanding the program that they haven't picked up on the hint.

For now, I'll keep my mouth shut and see how things shake out. But I know how twisted this industry can get, and it wouldn't surprise me if this philanthropic playboy bought our ballet just to have access to the cream of the crop when it comes to young, athletic women eager to please their new boss. It wouldn't be the first time.

"Would you all like to meet the new owner?" Stew asks, his eyes gleaming with excitement.

A chorus of approval greets him, and he turns back to the door, opening it as he leans into the hall.

A moment later, he opens the door wide, inviting in the tall stranger.

My heart stops.

It's Alexei Federov.

His name flashes through my mind without a moment's delay. I haven't been able to get it out of my head since this weekend's performance. I haven't been able to get *him* out of my mind since that night.

Tension knots my shoulders as I take in the sight of his towering frame—over six feet for sure. His broad shoulders fill out a black suit today, the wine-red shirt beneath it making him look both distinguished and devilish all at once.

The silence is deafening as the entire troupe is struck dumb momentarily. Then the girls burst into enthusiastic greetings, swarming him as they seem to decide they're more than happy to please our new owner.

A wave of irritation washes through me as Alexei's words from inside my dressing room run through my mind. *Most girls would sell their souls for a date with me.* I find it more than a little disturbing to find it's true. But what's worse is the hint of jealousy with which I watch the scene unfold.

"He's beautiful," McKenna breathes next to me, and when I glance over, her brown eyes are wide with awe.

Despite myself, it makes me laugh. She's so unassuming and innocent, her observation objectively admiring rather than covetous, that I can't help but find it adorable. She's too sweet for her own good.

McKenna laughs with me, her smile bashful as she seems to realize she said her thoughts out loud. And our mirth draws Alexei's attention.

Over the sea of dancers, his intelligent gray eyes find mine, and the mischievous glint there makes my heart stutter. One corner of his lips lifts into a crooked smile, and that smirk says it all. This is his next move in the cat-and-mouse game we've started. And suddenly, I find myself metaphorically trapped between his paws.

"Oh, my God, he's looking at us," McKenna gasps, her voice tinged with horror.

It mirrors the emotion coursing through me as I stand trapped in his iron gaze. Pulse roaring in my ears, I can't shift my eyes from his.

Alexei is dangerous—and not just because I know without a shadow of doubt that my initial instincts were correct. He's definitely Bratva. I've asked around since he came barging into my dressing room.

But more than that, I know he's dangerous because he does something to me that no man has before.

He completely disarms me.

His eyes shift from mine as he takes a moment to address the sea of women before him, expressing his gratitude for their warm welcome, assuring them that we'll all be having a wonderful time together.

Then he slowly makes his way through the group. Each girl hesitates to step aside, as if hoping his movement is meant to bring him closer to them. And the disappointed silence that follows as he breaks away from the group makes my ears ring.

"Oh, shit, he's coming over," McKenna breathes, her hands nervously brushing down her dance skirt as if to smooth the wrinkles from it. "What do we do?"

"Leave it to me," I state boldly, finding my voice as my defiant streak comes out.

Alexei may be gorgeous and charming, but I refuse to let him win this game. I've spent my life running from men like him, conceding my freedom and my happiness to stay safe. And for once, I'm going to stand my ground and keep what's mine.

Plus, I'm really going to enjoy refusing him. I know I should be careful, that men with his kind of power and lack of respect for the law are not to be trifled with. Still, this time, I won't back down or run.

The slow swagger of his purposeful strides makes my stomach tremble, and as McKenna seems on the verge of hyperventilation beside me, I square my shoulders, tipping my chin defiantly as I narrow my eyes at our dangerously appealing new boss.

"Nadia, isn't it?" he says playfully, his eyes dancing as he toys with me.

And though he's pretending to be unsure of my name, the sound of it on his lips makes my heart flutter.

5

ALEXEI

"What, you think owning this ballet company means you've won?" Nadia challenges, cutting right to the chase and completely disregarding my light teasing. "You can't just buy whatever you want," she states, crossing her arms over her chest.

The girl next to her—who looks like she's straight out of high school—gapes openly, her jaw dropping as her eyes shift to look at Nadia, utter disbelief written across her face. Clearly appalled by Nadia's caustic tone, she doesn't seem capable of saying a word. Nadia completely ignores her, glaring daggers at me instead as her lean, muscular arms remain crossed over her chest.

"Clearly, I can," I say, smirking as I lean closer. "I have the money, and no one's told me no yet."

"No?" she counters, her full lips pursing as she cocks an eyebrow in a silent reminder that she has.

Laughter tugs at my lips as I refuse to let her ruffle me. "Well, not for long."

The pride in her smug expression diminishes as she suddenly looks nervous. Then she recovers so quickly I wonder if I even saw the emotion in the first place.

"Yes, well, if this is your attempt to get me to go on a date with you, then you grossly overestimated your powers of persuasion. Because I won't."

"*Nadia,*" the girl beside her breathes in disbelief, her eyes wide with shock.

The prima is clearly not afraid to give me a piece of her mind, and I find her anger amusing because my purchase of the ballet company will only help her and the company itself gain more notoriety.

"That's alright," I say, turning my eyes on the young dancer beside Nadia for the first time. "I'm sure we'll have plenty of time for your principal to warm up to me."

The girl darts her tongue out nervously to wet her lips, then swallows hard as she nods.

"I would like to take everyone out for a celebratory dinner tonight," I state, turning to include the room as I raise my voice. "After rehearsal, of course." I give the director a nod.

He beams in response and claps his hands. "Hear that, everyone? If you had plans tonight, cancel them. We're going out!"

Nadia looks more than a little put out as her eyes flash toward the director, I note. But I don't object to his announcement. She's likely pissed because she did have plans, and I'm not about to give her an easy out. She might not know it yet, but this girl is mine. I've never wanted anyone so badly before.

And her efforts to antagonize me only challenge my competitive side on top of intensifying my attraction toward her. I like her feisty side, and she seems to have a wealth of fire that I can't wait to explore. She doesn't just roll over and concede because of who I am, and I like that.

"I'll plan on picking everyone up here at, say, seven? And dress nice. We're dining in style."

I give Nadia a playful wink, and she glares. Then I head back toward the door. I would have loved to stay and watch her dance. Maybe someday. But today, I have business to attend to. Tonight, though? I plan on thoroughly enjoying myself.

I CAN HEAR the squeals of excitement as the stretch SUVs pull up in front of the dance studio at five minutes to seven. Everyone's wearing their evening best—the male dancers in sleek suits, the women wearing a smorgasbord of dresses, some glittery, others soft satin, all matching some color of the rainbow as they show off the ballerinas' long, athletic legs and trim curves.

I have to admit, the selection of women in this twenty-five-person dance company is quite impressive. But as my eyes land on Nadia in her little black dress, the rest of them fade into the background.

She stands slightly apart from the rest of the girls, her face a mask of polite disinterest as she watches the white stretch SUV park in front of the curb. My driver gets out to open the door for them. As the other girls filter into the cars, sliding along the bench seats, Nadia hangs back.

Her hair is loose tonight, like it was for the first few minutes of the ballet the night I watched her dance. And for the first time, I can see just how thick and dark it really is. The soft waves cascade down to her waist in a black waterfall of spun silk that shines beneath the streetlight.

Her outfit is simple, the black dress modest on top and flaring out at her hips before ending just above her knees. The fabric looks soft and velvety, and from the thin shoulder straps, I can tell she's not wearing a bra with it.

Just thinking about it makes me hard, and I force my eyes down to her feet to distract myself. Her strappy heels are reminiscent of the way a ballerina might lace up her slippers, and the thin, crisscrossing lines accentuate the impressive muscles of her calves.

Elegant, understated, and yet Nadia is by far the sexiest woman here.

Her eyes dart between my SUV and the other, as if debating which one I might be in, and I smirk when her friend from the dance studio beckon her toward mine. I'll have to learn her friend's name. She might make a good ally in this little game Nadia and I have going.

As soon as she steps into the car and looks for the last open seat, Nadia's eyes find mine. It seems everyone is still debating the safety of getting too comfortable with the new owner because the only space open is right next to me.

I flash Nadia a grin and indicate she should take the seat.

After glancing over her shoulder, as if debating whether she has time to change her mind, Nadia resigns herself and settles into the last spot.

As she turns, I catch a glimpse of her dress's open back and am rewarded to find the single strap running over each of her shoulders breaks apart into five thin straps that fan across her back in an enticing pattern before meeting the low waist of the skirt.

Goddamn, the only thing better than seeing Nadia in this dress would be getting to take it off her.

The ride to Pier 39 isn't a long one, and I enjoy the soft brush of Nadia's shoulder against mine every time the limo rounds a corner or hits a rough patch of road. She ignores me studiously the entire time, focusing her attention on the conversation taking place beside her, though she doesn't say a word.

We pull up outside the French restaurant Le Fleur—one my sister-in-law, Dimitri's wife, happens to own and run. She won't be here tonight, as she's still taking maternity leave, but typically, she works as the executive chef, managing the kitchen staff who work behind the elegant restaurant's half wall.

The neat, open-kitchen concept has proven to be a hit in San Francisco, the restaurant's first few months in business proving to be a riotous success. It doesn't hurt that Camille's menu is to die for and her staff are some of the best in the industry.

"Welcome, Alexei," Camille's friend Hannah greets me from the host stand, her smile broadening to one of genuine warmth.

"Hannah," I greet with a wink.

"We have you all set up upstairs," she says, gesturing as she nods a greeting to the rest of the dance troupe behind me. "Let me show you the way."

Always the professional, even though I've eaten here numerous times since it opened and know my way around perfectly fine.

The second floor covers a smaller area, just enough to fit our large group, and it looks down on the main dining room. An open railing shows off the fine chandeliers and hardwood beams exposed along the ceiling.

It's all very French decor, and very fine.

"Nadia, why don't you sit next to our generous benefactor?" the director, Stew Lubox, suggests with a glint in his eye. "As you're principal, I'm sure he would like to hear how you came to us."

The not-so-subtle attempt to place Nadia within my reach is certainly helpful to my plan, and yet, it sets my teeth on edge when he shares a look with me that says blatantly, *She's all yours.* He must have picked up on my interest in her at the studio this morning, though I don't particularly appreciate the undercurrent behind his suggestion.

Nadia seems less than pleased as she plops unceremoniously into the chair beside me, her face an emotionless mask. But I can see the fire in her eyes. She is not happy.

"I hope you know this means you'll be feeding me tonight," I tease, my voice low as I lean closer to her so only she can hear.

Shock flits across her face, and her head snaps in my direction as her anger flashes to the surface, her lips parting as she prepares to give me a piece of her mind. Then she stops short when she sees I'm smiling.

"Or you'll hold the fan to ensure I don't get too hot," I add playfully, pushing the envelope.

"In your dreams," she counters, though the subtle twitch of her lips tells me she can appreciate my humor—especially when it comes at the director's expense.

"Have you ever tried this restaurant before?" I ask as several servers arrive to offer us a fine bottle of Bordeaux.

Nadia shakes her head. "Between practice and my strict diet to maintain the proper figure, I haven't had much inclination to explore the city since I arrived."

"You live in one of the culinary capitals of the world, and you haven't tried our restaurants? People fly from around the country to try this restaurant." Well, at least the original Le Fleur. The location might have changed in the past year, but the truth remains that Camille's cooking has attracted food critics from as far away as Chicago and New York.

"And what makes this restaurant so special?" she counters, quirking her perfectly shaped eyebrow as her green eyes dance.

"Aside from the fact that it belongs to my family?" I tease.

Nadia rolls her eyes, accepting the glass of wine poured for her and taking a delicate sip.

"Hold on. Did you just tell me you haven't explored the city at all?" I ask as the information sinks in for the first time.

"I've been busy," she says defensively.

"For a year?"

"How do you know I've been here a year?" Her eyes narrow with fresh suspicion.

I chuckle. "My mother's a fan." I can still hear her ringing praise after Nadia's performance last weekend, her amazement that someone so new to the role of principal could be so exceptional.

This seems to amuse and even please Nadia, and she falls silent as her lips curl into a subtle smile. She masks it by taking another sip of her wine. Then she turns her attention to the menu, studiously examining it as she ignores me with intent.

I let her be, striking up a conversation with Matteo, one of the lead male dancers who performs the role of Baron von Rothbart—the antagonist. I'm pleased to learn he's far less villainous in real life and considerably more willing to open up to me than the ballerina he dances with on stage.

I do manage to eek a stamp of approval from Nadia when it comes to Le Fleur. Though she keeps her meal light, sticking with the glazed salmon, candied walnut, and Roquefort salad, she does try the duck pate and escargot I order as appetizers for the table.

"I hope you all know how to kick off the ballet slippers," I state at the end of dinner as I pay the bill. "Because we're going clubbing next."

Nadia gives me a sharp look that tells me her plan had been to head home, but I'm not about to let her off that easily. I fully intend to break through the stone-cold wall she has between us before the night is out.

Piling back into the stretch SUVs once more, we head toward Carmelo, and I guide the troupe up to the private VIP balcony. Thrumming club music makes the air pulse, the beat surging through my veins. Bright strobe lights flash across the crowded dance floor. The colorful neon sconces that line the wall are the only other source of light, lending the club a dim, sensual atmosphere.

A bar lines one wall of the main floor, a DJ occupying the stage along the back, his tables glowing with brilliant lights as he bobs his body to the beat. We have our own personal bar in the VIP section, however, which means the troupe of twenty-odd people can enjoy dancing together without getting sucked into the mob below.

Sipping on a gin and tonic, I watch the ballet troupe unwind. Not surprising, they're all quite exceptional at dancing—even with the down-and-dirty version of club music. Nadia's friend has her by the hand as she seems intent on getting the prima ballerina to join in the levity.

And while Nadia's body moves with natural rhythm and grace, I can see she's only dancing to appease her young friend. Setting aside my drink, I approach the two girls. As soon as she realizes I'm there, Nadia's friend stops, her eyes widening like a deer in the headlights.

"What's your name?" I ask the girl, gently clasping her upper arm as I lean close to be heard over the music.

I'm rewarded by the slightest flicker of emotion that passes across Nadia's face. *Could it be jealousy?* I'm tempted to believe so.

"McKenna," she says shyly, her eyes flicking toward Nadia in a silent plea for help.

Though adorable, the girl's far too shy for my taste. I like someone with a little fire and spice. Like Nadia.

"It's nice to meet you, McKenna. Would you mind giving me and your friend here a moment?" I ask, smiling down at her.

"Oh—yeah, sure," she says, her eyes flicking quickly to Nadia for confirmation. Then she flees like her life depends on it.

Turning my attention to Nadia, I'm pleasantly surprised to find she's not glaring at me—not even frowning, in fact. And the dangerous smile that stretches across her face sets my pulse racing.

"Care to dance?" I offer her my hand.

And though she doesn't say a word, this time, I get a yes. Because she places her delicate fingers on my palm. And when I pull her close, setting that hand on my shoulder as I wrap an arm around her waist, she doesn't resist.

She peers up at me through her thick lashes and bites her lip with a coy smile. Then she starts to move. And damn, does she know how. Her hips sway and roll as if taking on a life of their own as her hands roam my chest and arm.

Her dress is soft beneath my palm, the loose skirt accentuating the enticing movement of her hips, and my thumb brushes the skin above the low scoop of her dress's back. Everything about her is irresistible, and before I know it, she's drawing me in, her appeal intoxicating.

Her soft touch fills me with an intense heat, a craving that makes me want her more than ever. And she knows it too. She's doing it on purpose. I can see it in her face—she's taunting me, showing me just what I can't have.

When she turns in my arms to grind her hips back against me, I know this she-devil is going to be the end of me. Because it's suddenly clear that she's intent on driving me insane.

And she knows exactly what she's doing.

6

NADIA

The effort it takes to keep from laughing forms a tight knot in my chest. I roll my hips purposefully back against Alexei. After subjecting myself to an evening I would have much preferred to have spent *not* appeasing my dance company's new owner, I intend on giving him a taste of his own medicine.

If he wants me, then here I am. He can see just how much fun I might be. But that doesn't mean he can have me. And I'm ready to drive him crazy like he has been me.

Peering up at him over my shoulder, I flash a brilliant smile as we move to the beat. I roll my hips provocatively, my skin tingling as I tease him mercilessly. I have to admit I'm having fun. Though I only agreed to dance with Alexei in order to torture him, it feels surprisingly good to be pressed against him.

To my surprise, despite his considerable amount of muscle that led me to believe he would be stiff and limited in his dance skills, Alexei knows how to move. His hips keep up with mine, igniting my curiosity as I wonder just how good a lover he must be.

It sounds like he's not short on practice, and from the way he moves, I suspect he knows exactly what he's doing between the sheets. Still, he doesn't take the opportunity to grind against me like so many men do. He's actually dancing, the contact between us the perfect level of intimacy so that we move effortlessly together.

His strong chest is a solid wall behind me, offering support as I lean into him. His hands rest lightly on my hips, his fingers pressing into my flesh just enough to send a ripple of goosebumps across my neck and arms.

I hate to admit it, but torturing Alexei is starting to turn me on.

I can feel his growing excitement, which fills me with intense satisfaction because I know he wants me. And still, he doesn't instigate anything further, allowing me to stoke his arousal without getting handsy. His self-restraint is far sexier than I thought it could be.

"I think you're more of a club girl than you let on," he observes, leaning close to my ear so he doesn't have to shout over the throbbing music. His breath whispers across my skin, his lips brushing my earlobe for just an instant, as if by accident.

I shiver as my heart flutters, my physical response betraying my intentions to torture him. I'm not supposed to be the one getting excited here, but I can't entirely ignore the wet warmth at the peak of my thighs.

I need a moment of reprieve to collect myself. "What makes you say that?" I ask, spinning in his arms once more to interlace my fingers behind his neck.

His large hands find the small of my back, their warmth searing into my exposed flesh as he keeps them just above my ass. Respectful and yet dangerously close to overly familiar as they linger on the edge of copping a feel.

And when I look up into the silver-gray of his eyes, I find it impossible to look away. He might be a good fifteen years older than me, but I don't know that I've ever seen a man so gorgeous. The chiseled line of his jaw, the proud shape of his full lips, his straight nose and strong, masculine brow. Everything about him screams power and strength and devastating perfection.

Not to mention, his cologne is the perfect balance of leather and spice, subtle and yet mouthwatering in its appeal. In an instant, I find my attraction toward him skyrocketing, shooting past my stubborn streak as a fresh form of emotion overwhelms me.

"Because you know how to dance dirty," he observes, his eyes dancing as his voice rasps from his throat.

My core tightens at the masculine sound, and I rein in my butterflies as I'm suddenly all too aware of just how large and muscular and imposing Alexei truly is. Overcome by how attractive he is, it takes me a moment to recall my question he was answering—why he thinks I'm a club girl. Because really, I'm not. I just like dancing.

"Yes, but can you dance?" I tease, grateful that our movement masks my breathlessness.

With a low, dangerous chuckle, his hands travel up my bare back and along my arms to find my hands. Taking them in his, he steps back, putting space between us as he steps seamlessly into a salsa.

My heart palpitates as he leads like he was born to it, his body moving with the rhythm and comfort of someone who's spent their life dancing. I don't know that I've ever seen something so sexy as a man who knows how to salsa and can surprise me with it.

I can't help myself. A genuine smile splits my face as he moves me around the private dance area, leading me into twirls and testing my own knowledge of Latin ballroom.

"I should think my salsa knowledge would give me a few brownie points," he teases lightly, pulling me close.

"I'll admit it doesn't hurt." Still, I can't give in that easily.

He barged into my dressing room, all but demanded I date him, and when I refused, he made it impossible for me to avoid him by buying the company I work for. I can't just roll over and give him what he wants after all that. Then again, I do find his persistence more appealing than I would like to admit.

I've always had to fight for what I've wanted, and I kind of like that someone's fighting for me for a change. It makes me feel like he might see I have worth beyond my ability as a ballerina. I'm used to admiration for my skill as a dancer. But rarely does that translate to something more.

Usually, it's all too easy to scare off admirers because I don't have the time, and they can find plenty of girls who are easier than me.

In truth, I find Alexei far more charming than I dared believe possible.

He's unlike any Bratva man I've met before.

Strong, powerful, dangerous—entirely capable of simply taking what he wants—and yet his hands haven't strayed once tonight. He might be presumptuous, but somehow, he's still a gentleman.

Moving into a Rumba as the song changes, Alexei pulls me firmly against his body, his arms forming a steel frame. My stomach knots at the feel of his muscular arms holding me close. As our hips move together, I find it shockingly hard to breathe.

His lips are within inches of mine now as he peers down at me, the intensity of his gaze unnerving and exhilarating all at once.

"It seems I tricked you into a date after all," he teases, his low voice rumbling against my chest as our bodies remain locked together.

"This is not a date," I counter. "This is dancing." Though I'll admit that I've given him enough of my attention that, under different circumstances, it could be.

"Are you so sure about that?" he counters, his crooked grin filled with mischief.

"I never said yes, so this isn't a date," I insist, pressing my lips together to keep from smiling as I hold his gaze defiantly.

His eyes dance.

"Well, I've bought you dinner, we've had some nice conversation, and now we're dancing together. That sounds like a date to me. Not to mention, I fully intend to kiss you before the night's out," he warns, his eyes dropping to my lips as his expression intensifies.

My stomach flip-flops, then calms when his gaze lifts to capture mine once more.

A knowing gleam lingers in their gray depths, telling me he saw the unbidden anticipation in my face. I'll never admit it, but I just might want to know what it's like to kiss this Russian gangster who came bursting into my life like an explosion.

"That doesn't make it a date," I say breathlessly, trying to strengthen my resolve. But fending him off is proving a harder challenge than I had anticipated. And not for the reasons I had expected in the first place. "At best, it's a group date."

"I'll take it," he rasps, low and dangerous.

Scarcely daring to breathe, I remain riveted as he guides me in our seductive dance. And just when I think I can't take any more, he guides me into a turn, allowing me a moment to catch my breath as I step away from his intoxicating presence.

We come back together like two magnets snapping into place, and my fingers wrap around his bulging bicep, sending a shiver of appreciation up my spine. How is he so ridiculously strong and at the same time, gentler than any man I've ever danced with?

It sets my body on fire.

"How are you still single?" he murmurs as his hand finds the small of my back and pulls me close.

"Who says I am?" I ask playfully.

"Are you telling me I'm going to have to chase some man out of your life if I want you for my own?"

My heart skips a beat at those words. The possession in them.

He wants to claim me.

And to my utter astonishment, for the first time in my life, I'm not so opposed to the idea.

I gave up the concept of love and a family years ago.

But right now, with Alexei's lips hovering just inches from my own, I find myself yearning to know what it's like to taste that kind of happiness, that intimacy.

Even if it's not for keeps.

"I guess you'll have to kiss me and find out," I dare, peering up at him through my lashes as I scarcely dare to breathe.

Alexei's eyebrow quirks as he tries to translate my veiled invitation.

Then, throwing caution to the wind, he closes the distance between our lips and kisses me.

Electric pleasure crackles through my body, stemming from our point of contact. The feel of his soft lips, adamant as they find mine, and the gentle scratch of his facial hair ignites a fire deep in my belly.

In an instant, all my resistance crumbles as the passion of his kiss blasts through my walls. This connection, this attraction between us, is white-hot and it consumes my soul.

7
ALEXEI

Fire licks through my veins as Nadia melts against me, her arms shifting to wrap around my neck as I pull her against me, deaf to the music as my pulse roars in my ears.

Kissing her brings the sweetest relief after days of agonizing yearning. I've wanted to know what she tastes like since the moment I first saw her. And now that it's finally happening, I'm not disappointed.

Her lips are tart and fruity, just like the champagne she's been drinking, and the way her slim body molds to mine makes me throb with anticipation.

She kisses with as much passion as she dances, the same saucy heat of her temper transforming into a delicious war for control. She's fiery and fun to tease—something I love to do more than anything—and more than that, she knows how to hand out as good as she's dealt.

There's not a shadow of doubt in my mind that this girl is for me.

I don't care if I have to fend off a hundred boyfriends.

But for some reason, I sense that there is no other man. It's like she's been waiting for me. And I don't know how I got so lucky, but I'm not letting this one slip through my fingers.

Parting her lips with my own, I stroke my tongue into her mouth, deepening the kiss. Nadia's tongue tangles with mine. Groaning, I pull her more firmly against my body as I cradle the back of her head with my other hand.

I think I could kiss her forever.

She's sent my body into a frenzy, and I don't know how I managed to resist as long as I have. But now that I've had a taste of her, I'm not sure I can stop.

Just as caught up in the moment, Nadia arches into me, pressing her breasts against my chest so I can feel the taut points of her nipples—confirming that she's, in fact, been without a bra this entire night. Christ, the thought of it makes my cock throb painfully.

The sharp sound of a wolf whistle cuts through our moment of indiscretion, and bursts of giggles and the swelling of an "ooh" makes me smile against her lips. We've been caught making out. I don't care. It fills me with intense satisfaction to know she kissed me back, that my agonizing restraint paid off in the end.

Because she didn't turn me down.

But she pulls back now, blushing profusely as she glances toward her coworkers.

"Want to go somewhere a little more private?" I suggest close to her ear.

Her eyes shift from the tittering dancers to meet mine once more, and she bites her lower lip as she hesitates. Conflict wars across her face as she has a silent, internal debate. Then she nods, the rose color in her creamy cheeks intensifying.

Grinning broadly, I sling my arm around her shoulders, tucking her close to my side and hiding her from view as her dance troupe goes back to their dancing and drinking, forgetting her in an instant.

Guiding her down the stairs and through the crowd of clubgoers to the front door, I give the bouncers a nod as they offer us a double-door exit. The limos still wait for us, parked along the curb just down the street.

Taking her to the nearest one, I open the back door and help her in.

Using my offered hand, she slips inside the vehicle and scoots across the bench to make room for me. Telling the driver to take us to my place, I turn my attention to Nadia a moment later, placing my hand on her thigh.

She leans forward, her fingers combing into my short hair as she resumes our kiss in an instant. Gripping her hips, I pull her closer, and she slides willingly toward me.

All that teasing, all the playing hard to get vanishes in the wake of our attraction, and her lips claim mine with an intense excitement that makes me painfully hard for her. Nadia's intoxicating, her fiery energy translating to a passion that fills me with unbridled lust.

Our tongues tangle in an intimate dance, and Nadia shifts, slinging her leg over mine as she straddles me. I groan into her mouth as she rocks on top of me, grinding against my erection. Gripping her ass firmly, I pull her closer, consuming her lips with ravenous need.

I've never wanted a woman so badly in my life.

I have to have her.

The heady scent of orchids fills my nose as her subtle perfume drives me crazy. Hands traveling up her back, I start to explore her body, captivated by how strong and lean and limber she is. The body of a top athlete. Someone who spends every day pushing it to its limits to create sheer perfection on stage.

"You are so beautiful," I growl, relishing the feel of her silky hair as I tangle my fingers in it.

Nadia moans softly, her hips rolling on top of me as she dry humps me.

"Fuck, I want to be inside you."

Gasping into my mouth, Nadia kisses me more desperately. But she doesn't say anything. If she lets me, I'll fuck her into tomorrow.

The limo pulls to a stop a moment later. The driver clears his throat uncomfortably after we continue to make out for several more seconds.

"We're here, sir," he says stiffly.

Nadia attempts to pull back, but I snarl, following her movement as I refuse to stop kissing her. A warm laugh bubbles from her lips, filling me with a deep satisfaction. Grudgingly, I break our kiss, allowing Nadia to climb off my lap and out of the stretch SUV.

"Thank you, Spencer. You can go back to Carmelo now." He's booked to take the rest of the ballet dancers home when they're ready.

Then I follow Nadia from the car, watching appreciatively as she adjusts her dress to ensure her legs are covered. Her nipples stand out against the soft black fabric, though whether that's from arousal or the crisp San Francisco evening, I can't be sure.

Shrugging out of my blazer, I drape it over her shoulders, and she gives me a look of appreciation.

"This way," I say, placing my hand on the small of her back as I steer her into the lobby.

We stop in front of the elevator bank, and I press the call button as Nadia holds my jacket tightly around her shoulders. My eyes find her emerald gaze, and the heat lingering there fills me with anticipation for the ride up to the top floor.

The doors glide open, and we step inside, the tension between us electric as I wait for the doors to close. Then two more couples follow us inside. Nadia and I share a glance as my shoulders tense.

Her lips curl into a subtle smile as we step toward the back of the elevator, maintaining the few inches that separate us. I seriously debate whether it would be entirely inappropriate to kiss her even with the four other people sharing the confined space.

The elevator carries us up to the third floor, letting the first couple out. Then up to the tenth floor for the second couple. The wait is painstaking, and my hand twitches to touch her. Finally, the second couple exits.

And as soon as the door closes, I'm on her, pressing her against the elevator wall as it finishes carrying us to the penthouse.

Nadia's breathy laugh is melodic and makes me want to kiss her all the more. Forcing her arms over her head, I pin her in place as I lean in to capture her lips, and when the doors open into my apartment, I don't break the kiss.

Instead, I wrap my arms around her waist as I steer her backward into the flat. Her heels click gently against the marble floor, and Nadia wraps her arms around my neck, allowing me to guide her blindly wherever my heart desires.

Making a sharp left down the hallway, I guide her straight toward my bedroom. Now that we're alone, I push my jacket off her shoulders, dropping it behind me as I start to undress her.

Nadia's fingers go to work on my tie, and the satisfying hiss of the fabric as it loosens around my neck makes me all the more eager. Collecting the fabric of her skirt in my hands, I guide it over her hips and up her body.

She pauses her progress on the buttons of my dress shirt long enough to lift her arms, and I finish pulling her dress up over her head a moment later. I groan with appreciation as her modest breasts come into view for the first time, her pert nipples standing out with excitement.

The skimpy lace of her black thong makes my cock throb against the seam of my pants. Taking a moment to admire her soft curves and flat stomach, I look her up and down with deep hunger.

Then her fingers wrap around the edges of my shirt and she pulls me forward to kiss me once again. I love that she's just as excited as I am, just as eager to be with me, even though I must be nearly twice her age—certainly more than a decade older than her, judging by the look of her perky breasts.

Hands exploring the curve of her waist, I make my way around to her ass and palm it, feeling the round firmness of her athletic body. Flinging open my dress shirt, Nadia exposes my chest, her palms gliding up over my pecs to feel them before she guides my shirt off my shoulders and down my arms.

She doesn't even seem to notice as we make it into my dark bedroom and I flick on the lights. I want to see every glorious moment I spend with her because I intend to see just how flexible my ballerina really is.

When the backs of her knees find the bed, I fall on top of her, pressing her into the mattress as I cage her with my arms. Breaths heaving from her lungs, Nadia looks up at me with her mesmerizing gaze as I draw back to see just where she stands on how far we've gone.

The molten desire there sets my body on fire.

"I want to tie you up in knots and fuck you sideways," I state brazenly, but I'll only do it if she actually wants this.

Agonizing as it might be to stop right now, I want to know that when I claim Nadia, she wants me as desperately as I want her. With a coy smile, Nadia nods.

That's all I need.

Growling with appreciation, I kiss her greedily. Hands roaming freely over her soft skin, I cup her breast for the first time, squeezing it gently in my palm. Nadia groans, her back arching as she presses up into me, and her fingers trace the line of my spine, raising goosebumps across my flesh.

Slowly, I kiss my way down her body, starting with her neck and down between her breasts. Lips trailing down the center of her body to her navel, I knead her supple tits with both hands, deeply satisfied to finally feel them for myself. I've been thinking of them ever since I barged into her dressing room, eager to experience the breasts that created such enticing cleavage that day.

Nadia whimpers as I pinch her taut nipples between my fingers and thumbs, rolling them. Her hips rock beneath me, calling attention to the sweet heaven that awaits me. Releasing her breasts, I let my hands travel down the curve of her waist.

Then I hook my fingers around the thin fabric of her panties. Guiding them down over her hips and thighs, I take them off, leaving her entirely naked except for the strappy black shoes that show off her striking legs.

Kneeling on the floor, I hook Nadia's knees over my shoulders, relishing the sharp bite of her heels as they dig into my back. Gripping her thighs, I haul her hips to the edge of the bed. Gasping from the sudden movement, Nadia reaches down to find my head, and her fingers comb into my hair.

Then I lean in to take my first taste of her sexy pink slit.

"Oh, God!" she moans, her thighs tensing as I lick her slick seam, collecting the tangy arousal on my tongue.

I purr appreciatively at just how wet she is for me. Repeating the motion, I'm rewarded as her hips jerk upward, crushing her clit against my lips. I suck it into my mouth, thoroughly enjoying the cry of pleasure that issues from her.

Trembling beneath my hands, Nadia feels like a tight spring about to release, and I wonder how long it's been since she's slept with a man because she's incredibly responsive. Circling her clit with my tongue, I press two fingers inside her pussy at the same time. And before I can even start to ease back out of her, she falls apart around me.

With a cry of pleasure, Nadia jerks and twitches, her pussy pulsing around my fingers as she comes hard. Wet arousal coats my knuckles, and I hum appreciatively at the sight of her breasts rising and falling with violent gasps.

Her eyelids flutter as I rise, allowing her legs to fall over the edge of the bed, her heels finding the floor.

"How long has it been since you've been with a man?" I ask as I head to my nightstand, my curiosity getting the better of me.

Nadia's green eyes land on me as she seems to silently debate whether she's going to merit my question with an answer. Finally, she seems to decide it doesn't bother her if I know. "Three years, give or take?"

Hand on the drawer handle, I pause, my eyebrows raising as I look at her. "How come?"

She shrugs, pulling her feet up onto my bed to remove her shoes before letting them fall to the floor with a clunk. "No one's caught my interest, and I decided ballet was more important."

"And yet you're here with me?" I tease, a grin spreading across my lips as I find it oddly flattering.

Her eyes glint as she falls back into our banter. "I had nothing better to do," she says casually.

I hope she's up for a full night of me, then, because I have a million dirty things I want to do to her. Turning my eyes back to my task at hand, I open the drawer and dig around for a condom.

"*Blyat,*" I hiss as I realize I've used my last one. Maybe I still have some stashed in my bathroom.

"What's wrong?" she asks, cocking her head enticingly as she lets her dark waterfall of hair cascade over her shoulder. With her feet curled under her and her weight resting on one palm, she looks like a mythological mermaid in the midst of a siren song.

"I might be low on condoms. Let me check another spot." I head toward the ensuite bathroom, not daring to suggest we attempt withdrawal as our form of birth control. I'm going to kick myself if I have the perfect girl waiting naked for me on my bed and I'm unprepared.

"You don't need one," she states, shrugging one shoulder.

I pause, staring at her, waiting for an explanation.

Her eyes drop to the bed in a moment of vulnerability. "I found out a few years back that I can't get pregnant. Hormone imbalance," she states, doing her best to sound casual, though I can hear the hint of pain lingering beneath the confession. Then her green eyes lift to meet mine once again. "It's up to you. I mean, I get if you don't want to trust a girl you barely know with that kind of gamble. But there you have it. Now you know my sex history in full."

I'm not sure whether I should try and comfort her, but judging by the way she attempts a joke at the end, I'm guessing this is one of those subjects that fits into the category of "too personal" when casually fucking on a pre-first date.

Instead, I turn to face her as I raise an eyebrow. "I'm clean. I get tested between partners. So, if you don't care, I'm all for going without a raincoat."

Nadia giggles and rolls her eyes at my attempt at levity.

"Did you just roll your eyes at me?" I challenge as her fiery side triggers my urge to dominate her.

"Maybe," she teases coyly. "What are you going to do about it?"

"I might just have to punish you," I state boldly, prowling toward her with predatory excitement.

Nadia's breath catches, and her eyes grow wide as her pupils dilate. I wonder if she's ever been spanked before, but I can tell the thought arouses her.

"You wouldn't dare," she states imperiously, lifting her chin in defiance.

"Oh, no?" I unbuckle my belt slowly, purposefully, and her eyes flick down to watch me.

She swallows hard, her tongue darting out to wet her lips. Then she meets my eyes again.

"Apologize for rolling your eyes at me," I command, snapping the belt tight with a crack.

"I'm sorry for rolling my eyes at you," she says without hesitation.

"Good girl," I praise, stopping at the edge of the bed so she has to look up at me. "Now give me your wrists."

A glimmer of fear flickers in her eyes, and this time, she doesn't obey me so readily. What I won't do to earn the trust she keeps locked away inside her. Though I've only ever touched her with respect—reverence, even—she doesn't seem to think that's enough to see I'm playing.

I wonder what in her past might make her come to such a quick and definitive opinion of me, but I intend to break through those barriers. Here and now, if I can. Letting the belt fall limply at my side, I reach slowly toward Nadia, cupping her delicate chin in my hand.

A shiver ripples through her, making her bare nipples harden deliciously, and I smile.

"You never need to fear me, Nadia. I promise you're going to enjoy this punishment thoroughly. And if you want me to stop at any point, if it ever crosses your line of comfort, I will stop immediately."

"If I just say stop, you'll stop?"

"Unless you'd rather pick a safe word. Sometimes, stop doesn't always mean stop in my world."

"Safe word, as in olly, olly, oxen free?" she asks, and I can't help it. I laugh.

"Yes, that works."

"Okay," she says breathlessly.

"Good. Now, hold out your wrists."

8

NADIA

Heart hammering in my chest, I do as Alexei says, throwing caution to the wind. I find Alexei irresistible. He might be older, dangerous, and now technically my boss, but he's sexy and strong and a fantastic kisser. I want to see what he's like in bed.

What's the worst that could happen? I'm not looking for a relationship, nothing to distract me from ballet, but why not have a little fun? It's been a long time since anyone's made me want them the way Alexei does.

Holding my wrists out to him, I watch as his steel eyes glint with anticipation. Taking his belt, he wraps it around my wrists, trapping my hands as he works the soft leather into an expert knot, incapacitating me.

The exhilaration of putting my safety in his hands gives me an odd high. It's almost like being drunk, only my mind is sharper now, taking in all the details of his fancy apartment. His silk sheets, him.

The colorful ink that covers every inch of his broad, muscular chest and arms depicts a world of fierce beasts and haunting wraiths, each a kind of dark fairy tale told in still motion. But the tattoo that catches my eye most is the quote in Cyrillic that sits at the top of his left pec. *The secret to man's being is not only to live but to have something to live for.*

I was so wrapped up in my desperate need and then my euphoria when he went down on me that I didn't fully register his ink work until we reached the bedroom. And as he cuffs me with his belt, I finally have the opportunity to read the familiar letters of my mother tongue.

"You are a fan of Dostoevsky?" I ask, admiring the curving language that I see so rarely in America. I'm finding the man more fascinating by the minute.

Alexei's eyes flick to mine, his eyebrow quirking. "You know the *Brothers Karamazov*?" he asks in mild surprise.

"What? You think ballerinas don't read?"

"I think you are an enigma I'm dying to make sense of," he breathes.

Then he leans in to kiss me deeply.

Excitement and nervous anticipation zing through me as his strong arms wrap around my body and move me into the center of the bed like I weigh little more than a feather. Compared to his impressive size, I probably do.

Then he guides my hands above my head to hook the belt onto the bars of his headboard. Goosebumps rise across my flesh as his eyes skim down my body, taking in my exposed breasts, my flat stomach, my bare pussy.

One warm palm strokes between my breasts, following the path of his eyes, and I gasp as his fingers just brush my clit before he shifts off the bed. Opening his bedside drawer once again, he hooks a finger around a thin silver chain and raises it slowly, dangling it above me.

"Do you know what these are?" he asks playfully.

I shake my head. They look like miniature versions of the jumper cable clamps you hook up to your battery when you're trying to jump start a car.

Oh, God.

His smile is sinfully sexy as he opens the clamps and teases one of my nipples with the chain linking them. My breath quickens as the cold metal makes my nipple harden, then he carefully pinches the taut nub with a rubber-coated clamp.

Something between a gasp and a shocked laugh bursts from my lips as pain-laced pleasure lances straight to my core. And though my nipple throbs from the intense pressure, I'm still intensely turned on, excitement pooling deep in my belly.

He repeats the same process with my other nipple, and I moan when he gives the chain a light shake, as if testing to ensure they're secure.

Amusement curls his lips as he leans back to admire his handiwork.

"Is this my punishment?" I ask, terrified he might say no and yet dying to learn what he has in mind.

Alexei chuckles, the deep sound rumbling from him like a lower earthquake. "Do you feel punished?" he asks playfully.

I consider his question for a moment. "Not . . . really," I hedge. While the nipple clamps are almost painful and I feel intensely vulnerable with my hands bound, I find I'm less fearful than I thought I might be.

"Good, because this isn't your punishment. Your punishment for rolling your eyes at me is that you're not allowed to come until I say you can."

I swallow hard as I think back to how quickly I came with Alexei's perfect lips wrapped around my clit, his fingers pressing inside me. Maybe that was just because it's been so long since a man's touched me, but I get the sense that it's not the whole story. Alexei's good. Very good. He knows how to kiss. He knows how to go down on a woman. I don't know that I'm going to be capable of waiting for his permission to come once he's inside me.

And then what?

Heart thrumming a frantic beat, I grip the cold metal of his headboard, willing myself to succeed. And when he undoes his pants, stepping out of them a moment later, I know I'm in trouble. He's huge. His erection is far bigger than others I've seen before. I'm not sure I'll be able to take him.

Strong hands grip my knees, slowly spreading my legs as Alexei exposes my pussy, and my breathing quickens as I creep closer to hyperventilation. Alexei groans appreciatively as he takes a moment to admire my slick folds. Running his fingers through my slit, he gathers my arousal and then sucks it from his fingers.

"You taste like heaven," he rasps as he leans over me to claim my lips.

I can taste the tang of my excitement on his tongue, and I find it dangerously sexy to know he likes going down on me. That he enjoys licking my pussy.

His hips shift, and I shiver as he grips his cock to stroke his silken head between my folds. Using my arousal as lube, Alexei lines up with my entrance, and my skin crackles with anticipation.

We're really doing this.

I'm never this reckless or spontaneous. But Alexei makes me feel alive, and I want more.

He gives it to me.

Thrusting inside me forcefully, he penetrates me deeply. I cry out as I'm suddenly so full it's almost painful. And yet it feels torturously good to be claimed, his cock buried deep in my depths.

"Fuck, you're so tight," he groans against my lips, and the agony in his voice makes my excitement spike.

I quiver beneath him as I find myself on the precipice of a second orgasm in a matter of minutes. Alexei rocks inside me without mercy, stretching me to my limits as he drives me wild. I moan with each euphoric thrust. Tingling pleasure reaches my fingers and toes as my muscles tighten with anticipation.

And then the sexy god of a man dips to take the silver chain between his teeth. I gasp, arching up off the bed as he gives a playful tug. Sharp pain is followed by a warm relief as I acclimate to the toy's use, and I shudder as I try to hold off the mounting climax threatening to consume me.

Leaning onto one arm, Alexei takes advantage of the space between me and the bed, snaking his free arm beneath me so he can prop my hips up. And suddenly, the angle with which he pounds inside me is entirely different. It's deeper, more tantalizingly delicious, and his pelvis grinds against my clit with each thrust.

The stimulation is too much. I'm going to come. Oh, God, I'm going to come even though he told me not to. And suddenly, I can see the punishment for what it is. He's set me up to fail. It's excruciating trying to stop myself, to hold off the mounting ecstasy. And at the same time, the level of pleasure he's giving me is mind blowing.

Each time he enters me, his iron length finds that hidden spot that drives me wild, his silken head hammering my G-spot until I'm ready to scream.

He gives another gentle tug of the chain.

My arms jerk violently, trying to take control back because I know I can't hold on any longer. But I'm helpless, entirely at the mercy of my cruel sex god.

"Oh, *fuck*!" I groan, panting in my effort to outlast him.

Alexei drops the chain, a wicked smile curling his gorgeous lips. "Don't come, Nadia. You'll only make it harder on yourself," he warns.

A trickle of fear enters my body, but Alexei's deep voice holds it at bay. *You never need to fear me . . . I promise you're going to enjoy this punishment thoroughly.* So far, he hasn't been wrong, and despite my mother's careful upbringing, I find I'm terribly close to trusting him.

Reaching between us, Alexei gently removes one nipple clamp, easing the pressure off my taut nub, and the relief is positively sinful. I gasp with it, my chest heaving. Then he does the same to my other nipple.

Hot, throbbing agony pounds into my suddenly overly sensitive nipples, and just the chain slithering across them makes me cry out.

Then, with a dangerous smile, Alexei dips to claim one breast with his mouth, the other breast with his free hand.

I lose it.

Screaming as my orgasm rips through me with hurricane force, I explode around Alexei's cock. Walls spasming, gripping his massive girth like it's the sole thing keeping me rooted to earth, I come hard.

Alexei groans, the vibration rippling against my tender nipple, and that only intensifies my release. Clit throbbing, pussy milking his rock-hard cock, all I can think about is the mind-numbing euphoria.

Every inch of me trembles with the all-consuming pleasure, the sinfully pleasurable agony. In the back of my mind, I know he's going to punish me for not obeying him. But right now, I can't bring myself to care.

Gasping and twitching beneath Alexei's strong, impressive body, I slowly come down from my high, the bone-deep contentment loosening my muscles as I breathe forcefully.

Alexei growls, releasing my nipple with a pop as he raises his head to look down at me. "You disobeyed me," he says, his deep voice dangerous.

"I'm sorry," I breathe, my heart fluttering at the unspoken threat in his tone.

"You will be," he warns as he pulls out of me.

A shiver races down my spine as I watch him with bated breath.

His hands move slowly down my body, massaging and exploring me as he goes. And when he reaches my ankles, a devilish grin spreads across his face. His eyes flick up to meet mine, daring me to say something as he grips my legs firmly.

And then he spins me. I gasp as my world lurches, and suddenly, I'm on my stomach. The leather of my makeshift handcuffs bites into my wrists, just enough to send a jolt down to my core.

Alexei's strong hands massage their way back up my legs, making my pussy throb with anticipation. And when he reaches my hips, he grips them, lifting my body off the bed and onto my knees.

My back muscles quiver to keep me balanced in the position that's not quite kneeling, nor am I on all fours. A moment later, Alexei's hands are at the headboard, his strong chest warming my back as he adjusts the belt, loosening it just enough that I can rest my arms on the mattress. Still, I'm tied to the bed.

Alexei sucks a sharp breath between his teeth as his hands travel down my stretched arms, over my shoulders, and along the planes of my bare back.

"You are a beauty," he praises, taking the time to circle the dimples of my back.

Then his hands grip my ass firmly, appreciating the way it sticks up in the air, putting me on full display for him. Turning my head, I look over my shoulder at him. My heart stutters at the broad, muscular cut of his shoulders, the way his ripped chest tapers into a trim waist with a full-on six-pack.

Resting my temple on my outstretched arm, I watch him closely, the way his gray eyes shine with appreciation as his hands run over my round ass, petting and massaging my soft skin. His fingers trace the seam of my ass, coming close to my folds without actually touching me.

The teasing caress is torture.

Then one hand comes down hard across my flesh. I squeal at the sharp sting that warms my skin, and my eyes squeeze closed. Then warm anticipation pools in my belly as his hand returns to stroke and massage my abused flesh.

I've never been spanked before, but it's shockingly arousing.

"Bad girls get spanked," Alexei explains calmly, his hands continuing to stroke and massage me. "This is what happens when you come without permission. Do you understand me?"

Whimpering, I nod.

Then his hand comes down hard on my other cheek. I gasp, the air leaving my lungs all at once as the biting pain crackles up my spine, followed by an intense pleasure.

"You will answer me with words, Nadia," he commands.

"Yes, I understand," I gasp, looking over my shoulder at him once more.

Still, he spanks me again.

I groan as the pain makes my pussy throb, and fresh arousal coats my folds.

"Yes, sir," he corrects.

"Yes, I understand . . . sir," I say, glaring at him defiantly.

I'm torn between rebellion over being spanked like a disobedient child and admitting the intense pleasure his punishment brings. I don't want to hand over my control, to give him the power of commanding my obedience, and at the same time, I secretly want him to spank me again.

Alexei arches a brow, his proud look imperious. He brings his palm down on my other ass cheek, evening the score. "That's for your attitude," he warns as I moan lasciviously.

Then he grips my ass cheeks, spreading them and exposing my pussy.

"I think you like being a naughty girl," he observes playfully, his fingers stroking through my folds and making me gasp as he flicks my clit.

I can't help it. My hips roll back at the sinfully delicious touch. Alexei laughs darkly.

A moment later, his silken cockhead glides between my folds, gathering my wet cum on his tip. Then he presses inside my entrance.

"Oh, God," I mewl as he penetrates me from behind.

Again, his thick girth stretches me impossibly, pushing me to my limits as my walls spasm around him. He goes slowly this time, seeming to understand how intensely stimulated I am from his punishment.

And somehow, the tantalizing new pace is agonizing. I can barely breathe as the zinging pleasure steals the air from my lungs. Moaning, I rock back, straining against the belt around my wrists as I eagerly seek relief.

Alexei's fingers press firmly into the bend of my hips, his grip strong and commanding as he constricts my movement.

"You want more, *igrushka*?" he taunts me, his pet name hinting that I'm just his plaything to tease and torment with pleasure.

But I'm so turned on, I don't care. "Yes," I moan, my hips rolling as he slowly spears me with his cock.

His hand comes down hard across my ass cheeks, and I squeal, jerking from the unexpected blow.

"Now answer me properly," he says, his voice rough with arousal.

"Yes, sir," I whimper, my walls pulsing around his hard length.

"Good girl," he praises, his hand massaging away the stinging blow.

Then, as if to reward me, he increases his pace. Hips rocking forward, he slides in and out of me, steadily growing more adamant in his thrusts. The friction is divine, and his thick head presses against my G-spot every time he pushes inside me.

I'm going to come again.

Panting with the effort to hold out, I bite my arm, using the pain to refocus my attention, to help me wait just a little longer.

"Shall I let you come, *igrushka*?" he purrs, his deep voice driving me wild.

"Please, sir," I plead.

One strong hand glides up my back, bracing against me as he presses me into the bed. And as he shoves inside me, my agonizingly tender nipples brush against the silk bed sheets. I shudder at the delicious torture.

And then, Alexei reaches around my hip with his other hand, his fingers finding my clit.

"*Blyat!*" I gasp. I don't think I've ever cursed this much in my life. But I can't help myself. It's taking every ounce of my considerable self-control to wait for his permission.

"Beg me to let you come," he commands, his voice rich and sinfully sexy.

"Please, please, please," I pant, shuddering beneath his expert touch. "Oh, God, please let me come, sir."[1]

I never realized submission could be so liberating, so arousing. But I'm overcome with desire, my pulse hammering through my veins as it carries euphoria out to the tips of my fingers and toes.

"Come with me, Nadia."

Like a trigger, the sound of my name leaving his lips launches me over the edge. Screaming with my release, I slam back against him. It's agonizing ecstasy, the way he fills me so completely. As my walls clamp down around him like a vise, hot cum explodes inside me.

Alexei grunts, his hips jerking forward erratically as we come at the same time.

Holy hell, it feels good, taking all of him as he fills me with his seed. His cock pulses, releasing several bursts as I throb around his hard length, milking him powerfully. And all the while, my clit flutters beneath his fingers. Electric pleasure zings through my body every time he circles the tiny bundle of nerves.

Goosebumps erupt across my back and shoulders as I relax completely, my muscles unwinding as I find a contentment I've never known before, a satisfaction that turns me into a puddle.

Alexei's warm chest covers my back, and soft lips tickle the nape of my neck after he brushes my long hair away from the flaming flesh.

"I think I might have to keep you here all night," he promises darkly, his soft voice making it sound that much more thrillingly ominous.

"Do your worst," I warn, turning my head to look at him over my shoulder.

A wicked smile stretches across his chiseled face, and as he reaches beneath me to cup my modest breasts, he leans in to kiss me passionately.

This is going to be a long night, I can already tell, and I'm going to enjoy every minute of it thoroughly.

9

ALEXEI

Early-morning sun trickles through my picture window, rousing me just a few hours after Nadia and I finally went to sleep. I should have closed the blackout curtains, but by the time we collapsed on the bed together, spent, I was too exhausted to think of it.

Fiery doesn't even begin to describe my fierce Russian vixen. She's insatiable, responsive, and entirely too much fun. I don't know that there is such a thing as enough when it comes to Nadia and sex, but I certainly did my part in exploring that point last night.

Conceding to the fact that I'm awake after only a few short hours, I roll onto my side, my hand traveling over the soft sheets to find her soft curves. But she's not there. With a groan, I force my eyelids open to find her standing at the foot of the bed, slipping into her delicate lace thong.

"Where do you think you're going?" I ask playfully, propping myself up on my elbows as I watch her lithe dancer's body move across the floor.

Stooping, she collects her strappy heels, then stands to face me. Covering her perfect breasts with one arm, Nadia scoops her hair over her shoulder to cover herself, giving her a semblance of modesty.

"The studio. I have rehearsal," she says simply.

Then she turns toward the door.

"When can I take you on a real date?" I ask, stopping her in her tracks.

I can't help but admire her gorgeous ass, still on full display. I love those two dimples at the small of her back, peeking out just above the lace of her panties.

Nadia turns, her eyebrow arching as she gives me an imperious look. "Never."

"Oh, come on. You had fun. Admit it. So why won't you let me take you out?" I've never had to work so hard for a girl in my life. Especially after we've already fucked.

Normally, it's the other way around. I enjoy the chase, the game, but follow-through isn't my forte. And yet, with Nadia, I can't seem to satiate my hunger.

"Last night was fun," she concedes, "but ballet is what I live for. I'm finally where I need to be. I can't afford to let anything distract me. And dating you would be a distraction," she states bluntly.

Sliding off the bed, I dip to snatch up my boxer briefs and haul them on. "So, that's it? You're actually going to turn me into a one-night stand? Were you even going to say goodbye?"

Biting her lip, Nadia's eyes drop to the floor momentarily. Then she strengthens her resolve and meets my gaze once more. "I don't usually do this kind of thing."

"What kind of thing?" I press, striding forward to close the distance between us.

But Nadia doesn't allow it. As I approach, she backs into the hall, glancing down it as her eyes search for her abandoned dress. "The whole relationship thing. Sex, even. I gave up on that years ago. Now, ballet is the only thing that matters to me."

"Why can't you have both?" I ask, her reasoning baffling to me.

Nadia scoops up her dress and slips it on over her head in one fluid movement, hiding her perfect body from me. "I just . . . can't. Okay, Alexei? Leave it alone."

"Come on. One date. At least let me try to change your mind," I negotiate.

Closing the distance between us, I capture her wrist and turn her to face me before she can reach the front door. Nadia's green eyes peer up at me with a gravity that gives me pause, but I refuse to let her go. Not until we've at least finished discussing this.

"If last night didn't change my mind, nothing will," she states frankly.

And though I know there's a compliment hidden in there somewhere, it's a massive blow.

Nadia searches my face as I stand mute, unsure of what to say to that. Still, her rejection only makes me want her more.

Sighing, Nadia steps toward me, rising onto her toes as she closes the distance between our lips. The kiss is soft and sensual and lingering, her warm mouth pressed to mine as if to seal our fate, closing the book on us in an instant.

My hands find her hips, and I snake my arms around her, pulling her close as I refuse to take no for an answer. Deepening the kiss, I relish the sensation of her body melting against mine. She's saying we're done, but her body tells me otherwise.

Her shoes click softly in her hand as she wraps her arms around my neck, kissing me back with euphoric delight. Breathing in deeply through my nose, I persuade her with my lips because my words aren't enough.

And for an instant, I actually think it might work.

Then Nadia draws back, breaking our kiss as she sinks back onto the flats of her feet.

"Goodbye, Alexei," she breathes.

Her hands run down my arms as if to memorize the feel of them around her waist. She steps out of them a moment later and turns to press the call button on the elevator. It dings open, and I watch mutely as she steps inside and turns.

I move to follow her but hesitate as her expression closes, her face wiping clean of emotion, as if she's left it all here with me. The doors slide silently closed, leaving me to stare at the silver reflection of my stunned face.

What the hell just happened?

I've never had a girl walk out on me like that before. It's beyond confusing.

But more than that, I find the rejection to be far more painful than I could have anticipated. The sense of loss opens a deep chasm in my chest, a place I hadn't even realized I'd reserved for Nadia.

It's strange to think, but I genuinely like Nadia—more than just physically—even from the short amount of time I've known her. She's smart and daring and driven. She's not afraid to speak her mind or say what she needs. She's unlike any girl I've ever known, and I find her entirely too appealing.

But what hurts most of all is that I think we could actually have a unique connection, something deeper, longer lasting. If only she would open up to the possibility.

At a loss, I stare at the elevator door for a long time. I can't chase her down now. Making her late for practice won't help my case in any way. But I'm not ready to let her go.

I will take Nadia on a date, come hell or high water.

This can't possibly be it.

Sighing, I comb my hand through my hair and scrub the back of my neck. I don't know what my next move is going to be, but I'll think of something. Until then, I might as well get a jump start on my day. Time for the gym.

10

NADIA

Freshly showered and wearing an appropriate outfit for rehearsal, I hike my bag higher onto my shoulder as I head into the studio. It took me longer to get an Uber than I had anticipated, so I'm almost late, but I wasn't about to go back up to Alexei's apartment and ask him for a ride.

The image of his face flashes before my mind's eye, his confusion and mild frustration as I left him standing in his entryway. Guilt triggers in my gut. I feel bad about how bluntly I turned him down, and a hint of regret niggles at the back of my mind.

Did I make the wrong decision?

I've never felt this level of attraction to someone before. Most of the time, it's easy to forget, to stop thinking about the person and move on. But not with Alexei. I can't seem to get him out of my head.

Giving up relationships never seemed like that much of a sacrifice before him. But after the unforgettable night we spent together, I wonder if I might not be able to have both a relationship and dance, like he said.

Forcing the notion from my head, I silently scold myself. Men don't want women like me. They want someone who can be a wife to them, someone who will someday carry their children. Not a washed-up ballerina who has nothing to give beyond a fun time between the sheets.

No, Alexei would tire of me eventually and want to find someone he can start a life with.

I need to keep my head clear and remind myself of that fact to spare myself the pain.

"There she is," Candace says as I step through the door, and her playful tone combined with her ugly smirk tells me I'm in for a hard time. Her blonde hair is pulled up into a tight bun that stretches her features into something of a leer, accentuating the glare of her blue eyes.

"The girl of the hour . . ." Lina, her curly-haired sidekick, pipes up. "Or should I say night?"

"Where did you and *Alexei Federov* slip off to last night?" Candace prods, her voice caressing Alexei's name with worshipful appreciation.

"Did you sleep with him?" Matteo asks, his voice tinged with jealousy.

I'm confident he'd been hoping Alexei might be gay. He'd talked him up plenty last night.

Heat floods my cheeks at the barrage of attention, and I press my lips into a thin line as I head to the side of the room to drop my bag at the foot of the wall mirror.

Candace gasps. "Oh, my God, she *did*. Look at the blush!"

"I don't see how it's any of your business," I state coldly, my defenses flying up.

I know it looks bad—entirely unprofessional—to be sleeping with the company owner. Not to mention he's considerably older than I am. I never should have indulged myself. But his charm and persistence made it impossible to keep the big picture in my head.

Add a few glasses of champagne on top, and I never stood a chance.

Still, I can't bring myself to regret it.

My night with Alexei was one of the hottest nights of my life. I've never even considered BDSM before in my near-nonexistent sex life.

And though he barely had me dip my toes last night, I think I could easily get addicted to Alexei's form of playful punishment.

"Defensive and moody, I'd say they definitely did the deed," Lina singsongs.

"And either it wasn't good or it was just that good and it turns out our hunky new owner didn't want to carry it on into today," Candace prods. "Did he boot you from the bed after he finished?"

"Leave her alone, guys," McKenna cuts in, her voice impressively authoritative for one of the youngest members of our troupe.

"Oh, come on. We're just teasing," Matteo insists, but his expression shifts to apologetic as he sees my discomfort for the first time. "We're only giving you a hard time because we wish *we'd* caught Hotty McHot's eye."

Candace and Lina giggle.

"He's not *wrong*," Lina concedes. "I think any of us would want *that* Russian mob boss for a sugar daddy."

The offhand comment jars me as she so casually confirms my feeling about him the night he barged into my dressing room—he's Bratva and therefore dangerous.

"Those are just rumors, Lina," Candace says.

"No, I have a cousin who told me it's the truth. He and his brothers are definitely mafia."

I don't bother correcting her on the name. Mafia is Italian. Bratva is Russian. But I remain quiet as I consider that fact.

McKenna seems to notice my distress and loops her arm through mine, pulling me away from their ribbing. "Seriously, don't worry about them," she says as she takes me to a quieter corner where we can stretch. "It's no one's business who you spend the night with. Not that I would blame you if you did sleep with Mr. Federov. He's gorgeous. Besides, it's not like you're sleeping your way to the top or anything. You were already principal when he bought Tapestry."

"Thanks, McKenna," I say softly, giving her a grateful smile.

It still makes me uncomfortable to know my coworkers have taken such an interest in what happened between me and Alexei—

and that he is, in fact, Bratva—but it does feel gratifying to know they can't question my merit as the principal ballerina over it.

Turning my attention to my stretches, I bite back a groan as my muscles ache from the grueling workout they got last night. As a professional dancer, I'm used to tired muscles, but this particular set I'm not used to using, and the deep, throbbing tightness brings Alexei to my mind once again.

Heat fills my body as I recall the positions he bent me into, the expertise with which he pushed me to my limits, never sending me over the edge. Just thinking about it intoxicates me.

Closing my eyes, I try to regain control of my body.

I use the routine of my stretches to help center me, but it also awakens in me a deep yearning. And once again, I'm doubting whether I made the right choice.

It's always been crystal clear to me before now. If I can't have a family, then I want to ensure my legacy in some other way. I want to be the best ballerina this world has ever seen. Then, even if I don't have children to remember me, I won't be forgotten.

That's my dream, to make the world remember my name.

But is it so wrong to enjoy Alexei while I can?

I don't know that I can risk it.

As much as I love being with him—and I do. I have a weak spot for him. I know it already.

But what I can't afford is to let that distract me because I know how this will end, him ready to start a family and me heartbroken because I've fallen for him.

Strengthening my resolve, I do my best to push Alexei from my mind. Instead, I distract myself by turning my attention to McKenna.

"How late did you stay out last night?" I ask.

"Oh, not too late. A few other girls and I left probably around eleven. Can you believe he rented limos for us? I've never been in one before." McKenna smiles with innocent joy as she props her heel on the barre and leans into a deep stretch.

"No? Well, you'd better get used to it. At least in New York, they were a necessity when we went to fundraisers."

"Either way, I have a feeling we'll be seeing more of them now that Alexei is around, don't you think?"

"Oh?" I ask, hiding the way my stomach flutters at the mention of his name.

"He's kind of flashy, isn't he?" she points out with a giggle.

Now that she mentions it, flashy is a good word. He did buy our dance company just to make a point. And the poor guy didn't even get the date he's been demanding of me since the moment he invaded my dressing room.

I refuse to let the guilt rise within me again.

"Ladies! Gentlemen!" Stew calls, bursting through the door a moment later. He beams, seeming entirely pleased with himself. "Did we all have a wonderful evening last night?"

A chorus of giggles and agreement echo back to him.

"What did I tell you about our new owner?" Then his eyes shift to me, and he gives me a knowing smile. "Nadia. What an impression you've made on him. Keep it up, and we just might get a theater built in our honor."

Humiliation floods through me as my skin heats once again, this time making me grind my teeth. *Prick.* Gaining the title of principal is a solid reason for moving across the country and away from my mother, but I'm not so sure I would have jumped at the opportunity if I'd known my new director would be such a misogynist.

Then again, that's the name of the game. Ballet is a rigged industry. It uses our youth, wringing us for all our potential until there's nothing left. Then it tosses us aside, usually around our mid-thirties. I intend to climb to the top before it grinds me down to dust.

Then, maybe I can open my own dance studio. Make it a haven for dancers where they won't be expected to grovel at the feet of our patrons. In the year I've gotten to know him, Stew has managed to stop just shy of demanding we give our benefactors blow jobs. But after yesterday, I wouldn't be surprised if it hasn't crossed his mind.

Still, I don't think I would pick another path in life than dance.

It doesn't matter if I'm rehearsing, performing, or having fun putting together my own choreography. I love the creative passion it requires. I only wish it weren't so cutthroat.

An interesting word to pop into my head. Once again, I'm reminded of Alexei. His world isn't much different from mine in that way. Cutthroat. As a Bratva, his brotherhood would either be the best, or they would be chewed up and spat out. It leaves no room for weakness.

And yet, he's so quick to play, so willing to laugh. He hasn't let his circumstances turn him into the typical cold, brooding brutes who have to purchase a bride because they lack the humanity to win one over.

I find I like the way Alexei teases me more than I ought to.

And best of all, I love the way he lets me tease him back.

"Now," Stew says, clapping his hands as he calls us to order, "let's see how well you all perform after a night of drinking and revelry, shall we?"

11

ALEXEI

"You're going again?" Dimitri asks, leaning against the doorframe to my bedroom, his arms crossed and a look of baffled disbelief quirking his brows.

"Why do you sound so surprised?" I ask from my place in front of my standing mirror as I tie a Windsor knot in my silver-and-black tie.

"Um, because I believe the last time we spoke about the ballet, your exact words were, 'I would rather stick bamboo shoots under my fingernails than go to one of those frou-frou snooze-fests'," Dimitri says flatly. "And now you're going to the same show for a second time in the same season. Did Mom guilt-trip you into it? I'm surprised she didn't even ask me this time."

I give my brother a sideways glance before focusing on straightening my tie.

"Okay, what?" he demands, shoving off the doorframe and dropping his arms to enter my room. He plops onto my bed, his gray eyes —so similar to mine—staring me down in the mirror.

"Mom's not going," I confess.

Dimitri gawks, his disbelief evident on his face, a silent demand for an explanation hovering on his lips. "Are you taking a date?" he presses when I'm not immediately forthcoming. "I mean, even if you decided to buy the ballet company, I don't see you all of a sudden becoming a ballet aficionado."

Sighing because I know he's not going to let me off without an explanation, I turn to face my brother. "I have a thing for the prima."

Dimitri's laugh fills the room as his head tips back in full-on mirth. "Okay, now I get it."

I roll my eyes, knowing he doesn't have a clue. And suddenly, I recall all those jabs I took at him when he told me about Camille for the first time. I'd teased him relentlessly for finally finding a girl, sure that I would never suffer the same fate.

And here I am, panting after a girl who isn't the least bit interested in a date with me beyond our one night together.

Dimitri's perceptive gaze reads my face like an open book, and his smile shifts as he grows intrigued. "Wait, like this isn't your usual hit-it-and-quit-it type thing?"

Again, I remain silent, my shoulders tensing as I sense the karma I'm about to receive.

Instead, he gives a knowing smirk. And says nothing.

"What?" I demand.

"You like her," he observes.

"That's what I said," I grumble, pulling my suit coat off its hanger and shrugging it on.

"No. I mean you *really* like her."

Rolling my eyes again, I flick off the light to my bathroom and make my way toward my bedroom door, silently telling Dimitri he's overstayed his welcome.

A dark chuckle rumbles behind me as I turn off the light on him as well and he follows me toward my penthouse elevator.

"Well, isn't this the shoe on the other foot?" he points out.

"I'm sure I'll be over her in a week," I state.

But even as the words leave my mouth, I know I'm lying. I don't want to admit it, but my brother's right. Before Nadia, I never would have gone to the ballet for any woman but my mother. And now, I have a front row seat for the show tonight. Because I intend to keep asking until she grants me that date.

As we step onto the elevator, Dimitri gives the self-satisfied grin of an older brother who's never going to let me live this down.

I'M SO close to the stage that I can see the ballerinas' expressions as the curtain rises on the opening act. After our dinner and night of clubbing, I recognize most of the dancers on sight. Nadia's friend, in particular, with her russet skin and petite form, stands out because of her megawatt smile. She's almost too happy to be in character, and yet, her dancing is perfectly on point.

But each of the talented performers fades into the background as soon as Nadia makes her way on stage. I watch her every move, fascinated about what makes her so striking on stage, curious about what caught my eye the first night I saw her.

The porcelain of her skin makes her almost glow in the stage's brilliant spotlight, like a China doll too delicate to hold. Her movement is flawless, her slim, muscular body timed perfectly to the music, but it's something more than that.

Her expression is not the suspicious, guarded look she's leveled on me every time I've entered a room. It captures the emotions of the innocent and unsuspecting heroine she's performing. And yet, I find that can't be it either.

Because when it comes down to it, I prefer Nadia's sharp edges, her quick wit and cautious skepticism, over the naive young woman she's playing now.

No, the thing that draws me in, the undeniable appeal, is something outside the range of human sight. It's an invisible aura that surrounds her, almost humming with her single-minded determination, her laser focus and unshakeable conviction. I can almost taste it, and as I drink her in, I find it intoxicating.

The scene transforms into the one in which Matteo—looking villainous once again as the Baron von Rothbart—turns Nadia into a swan. This time, I'm close enough to get a full dose of the anxiety on her face in the moments before she's cursed.

And though I know it's a performance, her distress nearly pulls me out of my chair.

Then her transformation is complete, and I watch, spellbound, as she floats across the stage like a beautiful white bird. At this distance, I can see any misstep, each wobble the dancers make.

But not Nadia.

She's as weightless as a feather whispering across the stage, her feet and arms moving so effortlessly in time with the music that it makes my pulse quicken. She is sheer perfection, and I'm riveted.

The scene comes to an end, Nadia settling into an artistic pose. And just before the curtain closes on her debut swan dance, her green eyes skim the crowd. For an instant, she seems to soak up the raucous applause, breathing in the audience's wordless praise. Then her gaze shifts, her eyes finding me in the sea of people, as if she can sense me watching her.

And before I can identify the expression on her face, the curtain falls.

Heart pounding, I stare at the painted tapestry showcasing a moonlit lake. The music swells and transitions in the pit before me. With rapt attention, my breath trapped in my chest, I wait for Act Two to begin.

The seconds feel like hours, and when the curtain rises once again, it's to reveal the iconic flight of the swans leading up to Prince Siegfried's hunting scene. As a swan once again, Nadia guides the other cursed ballerinas as they fly like a flock around the prince.

Spinning and dipping, Nadia's arms curve in spectacular arches to demonstrate her avian flight. She moves across the stage with an ethereal grace, her white ballerina outfit twinkling with sequins and gemstones that catch the light.

As she twirls, I can't help feeling that she's dancing for me.

Because while my eyes never leave her striking form, her gaze continues to find me. One turn after another.

Body vibrating with tension, I follow her movements like a hawk. I'm filled with a craving that no amount of watching can satiate, and as her figure shifts and twists, bending and flexing in athletic and yet soft and dangerously enticingly feminine ways, her gaze dares me to take her.

I intend to do just that.

The hint of a smirk tugs at the corners of my lips as I recall how furious she was with me for bursting into her dressing room after the first performance I watched. I wonder if she'll see it coming this time and if she'll dare to send me away again.

Her entrancing solo transitions into a duet as the curly blond-haired male dancer, whose name I believe is Ethan, joins her as Prince Siegfried. Dressed in a lavish embroidered velvet brocade and tights that look painted on, he takes Nadia gently by the waist, spotting her as her seductive dance grows more intense, her positions more challenging.

And still, even as she dances with him, her eyes return to me.

One leg held high in the air, Nadia arches her back, curving around Ethan as he turns her in a circle like a music-box ballerina trapped on her platform. Inexplicable jealousy flares up in me at the male dancer's fortune.

He gets to touch her every night, soak up the beauty of her movement, and feel the iron strength she harnesses into the most delicate performance I've ever seen.

But tonight, she dances for me.

She barely seems to register him as they move together, her hands finding his in transitions rather than her gaze acknowledging his presence. And while she remains attuned perfectly to the music, her dance as passionate and captivating as ever, her emerald eyes seek me with an alluring persistence that ignites my soul.

Tonight, she won't refuse me. I won't let her. I'm taking Nadia on a date—even if I have to drag her.

Electricity crackles across the stage, flowing between us with supercharged tension. Pulse pounding, I barely manage to stay in my seat when all I want to do is take her from the male dancer's hold and carry her to a hidden corner of the theater.

Nadia leaps off the stage as if taking flight, Ethan guiding her higher into the air as she performs for him and me simultaneously.

She floats back to the ground like a cloud might settle over a mountain.

The scene ends with the music fading into silence, and Nadia settles into a rigorous pose as if it were nothing more than a casual stance. When the packed house erupts in exuberant applause, her eyes find mine with an intensity that makes my body throb.

I can see her desire reflected back at me, a look of promise that tells me she wants me as desperately as I crave her. And I intend to give her exactly what she wants. When she finally agrees to a date with me, she'll know all the juicy benefits of saying yes to me.

12

NADIA

Alexei's intense gray eyes make my heart flutter erratically. Every time I look at him, he's watching me with predatory intensity. And though I don't miss a beat, my body taking over the performance I know in every cell of my being, I'm far more affected by his gaze than I will ever admit.

Seeing him in the front row tonight both unnerves and exhilarates me.

I know he's not here just because he enjoys the ballet.

I can see it in the way he remains fixed on me.

He's here for me.

And while I hate to acknowledge it, that sends a thrill of anticipation through my body.

Memories of our night together flash through my mind even as I move across the stage, my body heating under the ferocity of his steely gaze.

He has a kind of obsessive energy that makes my pulse stutter, and though I know I need to focus on dancing, I can't help but glance his way, again and again.

I find myself daring him to follow through with the silent promise he telepaths across the stage. I know he wants me, and I want him too, with a shocking desperation.

It's all I can do to make it through the performance because every time I look out into the dark sea of people who have come to watch me, all I can see now is him.

I hardly note the standing ovation when it's finally time to take our bows. Now that my performance is done, I force myself to smile and dip into a deep curtsy, lowering my head so I won't seek him in the crowd once again.

Then, blessedly, the curtain closes.

"Everything alright?" Matteo asks as we make our way backstage. He snags a towel from the chairs waiting there, wiping his brow.

"Yeah, fine." *Do I look as distracted as I've been all evening?* I hope not. I'm sure that wouldn't go over well for the rest of the full house who came to see the performance tonight.

"I only ask because you nearly missed that last lift transition. You've never been off before," he points out.

My skin warms. "Sorry. It won't happen again." I don't offer an explanation. I would rather not say exactly what was on my mind at the time, and lying seems rather excessive.

"Don't worry about it. Just thought I'd ask."

"Thanks for the concern, but I'm fine." Collecting my water bottle, I head back to the dressing rooms, my body thrumming with anticipation.

Will he be waiting for me?

I don't dare let myself hope. It's far too risky of an emotion.

Still, as I open my door to an empty dressing room, my heart sinks just a little.

Releasing the breath I hadn't realized I was holding, I step inside and shut the door. Then I make my way to the makeup table to remove my feather crown. It takes countless bobby pins, and I drop them each into their container with a soft click, focusing on my task rather than the disappointment tightening my stomach.

Releasing my hair from its tight bun, I run my fingers through my thick black locks, loosening it as I massage circulation back into my scalp with a quiet groan. Then I withdraw a makeup wipe from its package and get to work removing the dramatic black, white, and silver paint from my face.

As I use up my third wipe to remove the last of the black paint from around my eyes, a soft click sounds behind me. My heart jumps into my throat at the sound, and I resist the urge to spin and see who's entered.

Instead, I toss the wipe in the trash before slowly turning to find Alexei standing in front of the closed door, his hand lingering on the handle behind him.

"Hi," I say, doing my best to keep my tone steady and nonchalant.

An amused grin tugs at the corners of his lips. "Hi."

Then he strides across the room, closing the distance between us without hesitation.

My breath catches as his hands find my hips, his tall, muscular body curving around mine. Electricity sparks across my skin at the sudden contact, Alexei cutting right to the chase—no mincing words, no foreplay.

I suppose the performance was buildup enough.

My body is already throbbing with excitement, my pulse roaring in my ears. The way he watched me through the entire performance has me craving his masterful touch, yearning for another taste of his intoxicating attention.

And when his lips find mine, my heart stops.

His strong arms wrap around my waist, pulling me firmly against his chest. My arms travel up around his neck in response. I don't care if I seem easy or desperate. I've never ached for someone like I do Alexei. And though I'm not looking for a relationship, I won't say no to the kind of sex he delivers.

That level of satisfaction is addicting.

His tongue traces the seam of my lips, stroking between them as I grant him access. We dance together in a passionate kiss. The stiff tulle of my tutu feels like an obstacle between us, the hard fabric resisting the pressure of his hips as he backs me against my makeup table.

As he pins me there, his hands travel up my waist to my shoulder blades, his strong fingers finding my bare skin. Their warmth against my sweat-cooled flesh sends goosebumps rippling across my skin.

Nipples hardening against the shell of my bodice, I suddenly feel too confined, eager to be released from my ribbed cage. As if reading my thoughts, Alexei's hands travel back down to the top of the lined fabric, his fingers searching for the hooks hidden beneath a thin panel.

With practiced ease, he releases each latch, making my pulse quicken as he strips me with a care that tells me he knows just how many hours went into creating my costume. A wave of appreciation washes through me at his silent show of respect to my art.

And then the well-shaped top releases, allowing a wave of cool air to wash across my chest and stomach. I shrug out of the straps, letting the bodice slide down my arms. I set it aside, not bothering to look at where it goes as my thoughts are consumed by his strong palm finding my modest breasts.

Alexei swallows my gasp at the intense arousal that sears through me at his calloused hands brushing across my sensitive flesh. He groans appreciatively, his fingers pinching and teasing my nipples as his other hand splays across the small of my back, holding me close.

Eager to feel more of his skin against mine, I shove at his suit jacket, dragging it off his shoulders and onto the floor. Next goes his tie, and my heart pounds as I think of the ways he could tie me up with the soft slip of fabric if we were in his bedroom once again.

I doubt he'll have that opportunity in the sparse furnishings of my dressing room.

But that doesn't slow him down.

As I whip the tie out from his collar and get to work on the buttons of his shirt, Alexei finds the hooks of my tutu. The desperation with which we undress each other is exhilarating, the way his tongue continues to tangle with mine, his lips eager and demanding.

Heart pounding, I step out of my tutu as he shoves it down my hips and thighs. Wearing nothing but my thin tights and ballet shoes now, I stand before him as he leans back to admire me openly.

The flaps of his shirt hang loose, exposing several inches of his ink-colored chest. My fingers itch to touch the rippling muscles beneath, but Alexei kneels before me before I can move.

Stomach tightening as his face hovers inches away from the peak of my thighs, I follow his lead as he grasps my hips and guides me back onto the makeup table. Then his hands roam down my fabric-clad legs to the lace of my slippers.

Watching him stooping before me, my foot resting on his knee as he removes my shoe, gives me an intoxicating sense of power. The gesture is almost supplicating—if he weren't taking me like he knows without a shadow of doubt that I want him.

In an instant, my slippers are on the floor, my tights following within seconds. I gasp as his hands grip my knees and spread them wide. Then his lips close around my clit as he dives straight in.

Shocked by the intensity of my instantaneous spike in arousal, I forget to monitor the groan that escapes me, and my body quivers as I lose myself in a haze of lust. His tongue flicks out to circle my clit. My hips rock, lifting off the table as my toes find the floor once again in my sudden need.

Alexei's fingers dig into my flesh in response, taking control of my body as he holds me exactly where he wants me.

"Oh, God!" I whimper as my walls tighten, twitching with my building anticipation.

Alexei growls appreciatively, the vibration sending excitement jolting into my core. Then he nips the tiny bundle of nerves, the shocking assault launching me into an orgasm before I even know it's coming.

Crying out, I tremble violently as my clit flutters, my pussy spasming with release that sends warm relief flooding to the tips of my fingers and toes. Gasping, I brace against the table with my palms, my arms trembling as my chest heaves.

A satisfied purr rumbles from Alexei, the sound low and enticing. Then he releases my clit with a gentle *Pop*. A wicked smile plays across his lips as he rises from his knees, his gray eyes finding mine.

Flushed in the wake of my orgasm, I watch helplessly as he

unbuckles his belt and opens his pants, withdrawing his cock. Starved of the tantalizing view of his godlike body, I focus on the impressive size of his erection, my core tightening with fresh anticipation.

"You want this?" he teases, stroking his cock as he catches me staring.

Breathless, I nod, unsure I'll be able to speak.

"Where do you want it?" he presses, stalking toward me with fire in his gaze.

"Buried in my pussy," I murmur, my chest tightening, my nipples hard enough to cut glass.

Alexei's hand cups the back of my head as he kisses me deeply, his tongue stroking inside my mouth. He tastes tangy, my cum lingering on his lips, and I groan at the memory of his lips on my clit. His hard cock presses firmly against my body, teasing me with what's to come.

Then his strong arms hoist me off the makeup table, turning me in one fluid motion to face the mirror. The sight of him looming behind me, his eyes brilliant with unbridled lust, makes my heart flutter. And when his arms wrap around me, his hands exploring the flat planes of my stomach, my eyelids flutter.

His cock presses adamantly between my ass cheeks as he grinds against me, one hand traveling up to cup my breast as the other reaches down to cup my pussy. My clit fires off zaps of electric euphoria as his fingers circle it gently, and I roll my hips, tempting him to fill my wet hole.

Watching him grope me is almost as arousing as the feel of his hands on me, and the intense heat in his molten gaze makes me tremble. Leaning in, he captures the lobe of my ear between his teeth and nibbles, drawing a gasp from me as my body pulses with need.

Then the hand kneading my breast slowly makes its way up my chest. A knot forms in my stomach as his fingers wrap around my throat, his expression dangerous. Panic flits through me at the threatening hold, and as his grip tightens, restricting the oxygen to my brain, my ears start to ring.

Terror mingles with a darker excitement as I find I'm not entirely suffocating—just enough to leave me gasping. And as my face flushes from the gentle strangulation, I watch with fascination. I can feel the measured restraint in his grip, know that he could tighten his hold and kill me if he wanted.

Instead, his eyes find mine, and in their dark depths, I can see his promise of immeasurable satisfaction. Relinquishing control to him, I keep my palms flat against the makeup table as he guides his cock between my thighs.

His silken head slides along the wet seam of my pussy lips, pushing between my folds as he finds my entrance. He shoves inside me with one powerful thrust.

Throat partially obstructed, I grunt rather than moan. My pleasure from being so entirely stretched and filled leaves me almost lightheaded—and I'm sure the oxygen deprivation only intensifies it.

Agonizing ecstasy pounds through my veins, culminating at the tips of his fingers around my throat. It's intensely disturbing to realize how exciting it is to be choked while Alexei fucks me. And then I realize, this is his way of tying me up when he has no tools but his own body.

He's taking control, commanding my body to obey him even as he demands my pleasure.

And from the intensity of his silver gaze, I know he's liking this just as much as I am.

Chest pressed firmly against my back, his large, muscular body enveloping my lean frame, he thrusts inside me forcefully, fucking me against my makeup table as he holds my eyes with the burning reflected in his.

My breasts bounce lightly with each forward thrust, and his hand tightens ever so slightly around my neck to hold me in place as he fucks me roughly. It's the most seductively violent sex I've ever had. Though, in the back of my mind, a small voice warns me that we're walking a dangerous line, I don't care.

My body is going wild with heady excitement.

The ringing in my ears turns into a dull roar as my face reddens further, the veins in my forehead beginning to stand out against my skin, and still, my arousal climbs until I feel I might scream. If I don't pass out first.

"You're so fucking sexy," Alexei rasps in Russian, our native tongue, like a fine liquor washing through my body.

My pussy tightens around the iron rod of his cock, and my eyes sink closed momentarily as pleasure consumes me. But I want to watch every second of him claiming my body, manipulating it with masterful ease. So I force my lids open once again, even as the corners of my vision start to dim.

His fingers press more adamantly against my clit as he drives his hips forward, pounding me against the table. I whimper, unable to make a sound louder than that with my air restricted.

"Come for me, Nadia," he commands, his finger circling the tiny button of my clit as he drives mercilessly inside me, his cockhead finding my G-spot again and again.

And I can't disobey. With a strangled cry, I orgasm, my pussy clamping around his erection like a vise. At the same time, his hold on my throat releases, his forearm taking the weight of my chest as I fall forward, suddenly dizzy with the force of my release.

The relief that washes through me is magnified exponentially as blood rushes back to my brain, and I suck in deep gasps of air. My clit twitches, my walls throbbing violently around his cock, and the heady surge of adrenaline leaves me weak at the knees.

Slowly, Alexei allows me to sink forward onto the makeup table, his cock continuing to rock in and out of me as he bends me over the surface. My cheek finds the cool glass of the mirror, and I lean against it, my breath fogging the reflection.

I brace my hand against it, my all-consuming euphoria leaving me fascinated by the sight of him shoving inside me. His free hand shifts to the small of my back, pinning me to the table as his other fingers continue to flick and tease my clit without mercy.

And though I'm still basking in the aftershocks of my second orgasm, I can feel my body starting to build with anticipation once more.

13

ALEXEI

Like a drug, Nadia has me addicted. Her eager response isn't the weak acceptance of a girl relinquishing her will to me but one of a woman knowing exactly what she wants. And she wants me to make her come like before.

I'm more than up for the challenge. We might not have the same number of gadgets I keep at home, but this girl likes it rough, and I plan on giving it to her.

The intensity of her orgasm after the strangulation play was so hard I nearly lost it. As lean and petite as Nadia is, she's the strongest woman I've ever been with. In every way. And I fucking love it.

The way her body comes to life at my touch, it makes me want to bury myself inside her every second of the day. As her emerald eyes watch me in the mirror over her fogging breath, I can see the insatiable lust there.

Though I'm brutalizing her tight little pussy, she's ready for more.

That we're fucking one door down from the rest of the cast only makes this more exciting. I went for the strangulation play because I doubt she wants them to hear her, and she was less than quiet when I went down on her.

Now, she looks so thoroughly used, I don't think she has the strength to scream. But from the way her legs tremble as she tips her hips for me, I know she's ready for another release.

"You like it when I bend you over a table?" I tease.

"Yes," she moans, her breaths gasping between her full red lips.

Running my hand over her full, round ass, I admire her soft skin, the way her flesh remains firm beneath my fingers. Then I give her a sharp spank. Nadia squeals, her hips jerking as her pussy clamps down around my cock.

"What was that for?" she gasps, and I can hear the arousal in her voice.

"For teasing me."

A small furrow forms between her brows, showing her confusion, and I spank her again playfully.

"You were up on stage giving me fuck-me eyes all night," I growl.

And to my intense satisfaction, she actually smiles. She *was* teasing me. In front of a sold-out house, she was silently telling me she wanted me to fuck her.

This girl is going to be the death of me.

"You naughty little slut," I groan appreciatively, thrusting inside her with punishing force.

Nadia moans lasciviously, her hips rolling as she stimulates her clit against my fingers. Following the defined muscles of her back, I guide my free palm up her spine to the nape of her neck and tangle my fingers into the thick locks of her raven hair.

I give a gentle tug, forcing her back into an arch, and Nadia gasps, her fingers splaying on the mirror as she tilts her head back, exposing the gorgeous curve of her neck.

"I ought to punish you properly for that," I threaten. "But I guess we'll have to make do with what we have on hand."

Then I pinch her clit between my fingers, rolling it mercilessly.

The string of Russian curses that spews from her lips makes my cock throb. The girl swears like a sailor, and somehow, knowing this prima ballerina has that kind of vocabulary only makes me want her more.

Her muscles vibrate as she strains to remain quiet, but I can tell she's dangerously close to a third orgasm already.

"Don't you come until I say," I warn darkly, and Nadia shudders violently.

"Please," she gasps, her pussy tightening as I drive forward into her G-spot, continuing to torture her clit with violent pleasure. The perfect balance of pain and ecstasy. "Oh, God, please let me come," she moans more urgently this time.

"I do like it when you beg," I muse.

"Fuck, please, Alexei!" she whimpers, and my cock throbs at the breathy way she says my name.

"Say it again," I command.

"Please, I want to come." Her eyes press closed as she focuses all her energy on holding off her impending release. But I can feel the swollen tightness of her pussy. She's so close that every thrust borders on painful, it feels so sinfully good.

"No, say my name," I growl. I know I'm going to let her come because I can't hold on any longer. She's so goddamn sexy, it's driving me insane.

"*Alexei,*" she moans, the sound almost whiney as she bucks and shudders beneath me.

"Come with me, Nadia," I command, and at the same time, I release her hair to grip her hip as I drive my cock home.

Her walls grip me, pulling my cock deeper inside her depths before falling apart around my throbbing girth. The sheer pleasure of her ecstasy launches me into my own release.

As she milks me, her pussy throbbing in time with her twitching clit, I pour my seed deep inside her, filling her until it drips from her pink slit. The aftershocks of her orgasm continue to throb around my cock long after I've finished, and I keep my cock buried inside her until the last of them slowly fade away.

Nadia pants, her eyes glazed with a satisfaction that tells me she loves it when I fuck her just as much as I love being inside her. Easing out of her, I tuck myself back into my pants and start to dress.

She, on the other hand, pulls out the chair for her makeup table and slumps into it, her muscles seeming to need the support. I can hardly blame her. She just put on a world-class performance. And then she let me fuck her sideways.

Her green eyes watch me in the mirror, and somehow, I find that more thrilling. The way they seem to glint with frustration as I button my shirt and tuck it back into my slacks. This girl has a sex drive that could bring me to ruin. God, but I love it.

"I have to say, watching you on stage, it gives me a world of new ideas when it comes to exploring just how flexible you are," I tease, leaning in to give her taut nipple a light squeeze.

Nadia swallows hard, her eyes fluttering closed as she licks her lips. But she doesn't say anything.

"So, about our date..." I press playfully.

Her eyes snap open, and Nadia rotates in her chair, her eyes meeting mine directly now. In their striking depths, I can see a steely defiance.

"What date?" she asks coolly, reaching across the makeup table to grab a pair of bright-red silk panties.

Bending, she slips them on before doing the same with a pair of black, skin-tight jeans.

"The date you're going to let me take you on now that I've given you a few days to miss me."

Nadia's laughter is light, her lips pressing together in an amused smile as she stands to don a black bra. Then comes the oversized cashmere sweater that hides her modest breasts and trim waist.

Combing her hair free of the sweater's collar, she turns to face me fully. "I told you, we are *not* going on a date."

Her tone borders on exasperation, and she plants her hands on her hips as she levels me with a cool gaze.

Closing the distance between us, I brush a strand of her silky hair behind her ear and run my fingers along the line of her jaw. "You can't say no to me forever," I murmur, feeling the hint of frustration settling in the pit of my stomach.

"I can and I will," she says boldly.

My temper flickers to life at the taunting pleasure in her eyes. She's toying with me. And getting a rise out of it. In an instant, the humor evaporates from me. *She'll fuck me more than once, but she won't let me buy her a meal?* I don't like being someone's plaything, and right now, it feels like that's all I am to her. *Is she fucking me because she thinks she's got me on a string?*

Anger flaring in my chest, I invade her space as my smile falls away. Doubt flickers across Nadia's face as I glare down at her, my nostrils flaring. When she takes a step back, I follow her, backing her against the dressing room wall.

"You don't say no to me fucking you, but you don't want to get to know me, is that it?" I demand, my voice dropping into a hiss.

"I told you I don't want a relationship. You're the one who fucked me anyway," she counters, tipping her chin defiantly.

White-hot fury rips through me as she tries to turn this back on me. The first girl I have genuine feelings for, and she just wants to see how far she can yank my chain. Gripping her shoulders, I shove her back against the wall, leaning in so my face is mere inches from hers.

"You need to make up your fucking mind because I don't like being jerked around. And from where I stand, it seems like you're getting off on toying with me. Do you want to see what happens to people who mess with me?"

Genuine fear flickers across Nadia's face for the first time, and my temper dies as I realize I let my frustration get the better of me. No man should ever lay his hand on a woman, no matter how infuriating she might be.

I hate seeing the way she looks at me now, like all the trust and rapport I built with her has vanished in an instant, gone with my momentary outburst. Guilt riddles me.

Releasing her shoulders like I might something scalding, I step away. I wrestle to regain control of myself, putting space between us as I watch her closely. She eyes me suspiciously, and I feel absolutely awful.

I can't stand that I scared her. Overcome by remorse and self-loathing, I turn, snatching my suit coat off the floor and making a beeline for the door. Without a word, I leave her there, silently chastising myself for losing my temper so thoroughly over our cat-and-mouse game.

14

NADIA

I still can't make sense of what happened with Alexei. After a sleepless night, I'm determined not to think about him or the knot of fear and regret that tightens my stomach every time I focus on those last moments before he stormed from my dressing room.

I can't think about it because tonight, my mom's in the audience. She flew in from New York on a plane that got in with just enough time for her to make the show. As I dance across the stage, I can see her beaming up at me, her face glowing with pride.

It's an immense weight off my shoulders to get to perform for her, and I can't wait to see her after the show. In a world where I refuse to get close to many people, my mom is my one exception, and I've missed her more than words could express.

Security already knows to let her backstage after the performance, and as the final curtain falls, I'm practically giddy with excitement.

I don't wait for my fellow cast members or take my time heading back to the dressing rooms tonight. Instead, I race backstage and wait with bated breath in the hallway for my mom.

"You're looking mighty happy tonight." McKenna beams as she walks past me toward the dressing rooms.

I can't help but smile. "My mom's in town," I confess.

McKenna nods knowingly, her expression soft and warm. "How long's it been?"

"Since I saw her last?"

She nods.

"Nearly a year. This is her first visit." I fight the urge to bounce on the balls of my feet and glance toward the burly security guard standing guard near the hallway entrance. No sign of her yet.

"Wow. No wonder you're smiling. Have fun with her! I'll see you tomorrow."

"See you," I agree, attempting not to sound distracted, but I don't entirely succeed.

A moment later, I catch sight of my mom's dark shock of hair. It frames her face in a soft chin-length bob. A distinguished lock of white stands out at her right temple, her signature Mallen streak making her look older than her mid-forties.

But her blue eyes are as sharp as ever, the spark of love and affection in them apparent as she rounds the corner and spots me waiting for her.

"Mama," I greet, closing the distance between us to give her a fierce hug.

I have several inches on her now, but she still pulls me close, holding me like I'm her baby girl, and I can hear the emotion in her voice as she says, "Oh, I've missed you."

"I've missed you too," I whisper, blinking away the tears that sting my eyes.

"You were spectacular, darling. I can hardly believe it, but I think you've gotten even better since you moved across the country. I'm so proud of you."

"Thanks, Mom. I've been practicing a lot."

She releases me, stepping back to grip my shoulders so she can get a good look at me. "Are you losing weight?"

Worry tinges her voice, and I smile indulgently. It used to drive me crazy, the way she fussed over me. But after a year without her, I even miss that.

"I'm fine, Mom. I promise. If anything, I've gained a few pounds."

It's been a long time since I had to see a doctor about the impact my dancing has had on my body. Still, I know it's never far from my mom's mind.

Cupping my cheeks affectionately, she gives me a warm smile. "Good. Now, show me to your dressing room. I want to hear all about the fun adventures you've been withholding from me during our phone conversations."

I laugh. "I would never withhold something from you," I promise, showing her back to my dressing room. "You, on the other hand, need to tell me all about the new place you're renting."

My mom steps into my dressing room and looks around at the simple furnishings, her smile widening at the sight of the intricately patterned Japanese folding wall I'll use to change behind when I know others are going to be in and out of my room.

"First things first, tell me about your performances. I haven't gotten the chance to speak to you much since opening night."

"They're going really well. We've been nearly sold out every night. And either Californians are far easier to please than New Yorkers, or I'd say we're giving a good show because tonight was not our first standing ovation. We've had one every night."

Mom gasps, her jaw dropping, and it fills me with a deep pride to see her awed excitement.

"That's wonderful. And speaking as a completely objective third party," she jokes, "I would say it's the latter."

Smiling, I settle into my makeup chair and start to remove my makeup. Like she's done so many times in the past, my mom gets to work taking the bobby pins from my hair. Her delicate touch fills me with a warm affection, and I soak up the maternal love, locking it in my heart and storing it away for those times when I miss her most.

She gives my scalp a gentle rub once my hair is finally loose around my shoulders, and I hum appreciatively.

"So, this new place you're moving to, you said it's closer to work?"

I prompt, meeting her gaze in the mirror before I finish wiping away my makeup.

"Oh, it's such a sweet little spot. You'll have to come see—"

A soft rap on the door cuts my mom short, and she turns instinctually, glancing over her shoulder.

"Come in," I call.

The door swings open, and my heart leaps into my throat as Alexei's broad shoulders fill the frame. In his large hand is a bouquet of exceptional beauty, the riot of colors blending in a medley of intriguing shapes and appealing accents. I can smell their fragrance all the way from my makeup chair. But his contrite expression is what melts my heart.

He hasn't said a word to me since last night, but I can tell that he doesn't like the way he left things purely by the boyish apology written across his face. His eyes find mine immediately, their silver intense. Then they flick toward my mom, mild surprise registering a moment later.

"Hi," Alexei says, hesitating in the doorway, and it brings to mind the way I greeted him last time.

But of more note is the way he seems to be waiting for my invitation to enter, something he's never expected before, and whether it's because someone's in here with me now or because he knows he messed up yesterday, I can't say. But so far, he's done just about everything he can to apologize without saying it explicitly.

"Hi," I respond, my eyes darting toward my mom as well.

"Who is this handsome man lingering in your door? Aren't you going to come in?" Mom says, a smile splitting her face.

"May I?" His eyes shift between us before landing on mine.

"Yeah. Yes. Mom, this is Alexei. He, um, owns the Tapestry Dance Company. Alexei, this is my mom."

"It's an honor to meet you, Ms. Lukyan," he says, entering the room fully to offer her his hand.

She places her hand in his, and his thick palm swallows hers completely.

"You raised a wonderful and very talented daughter."

Mom beams as she looks back at me, pride written across her features. "I like to think so. So, you're the reason my daughter moved across the country?"

"Ah, well, no. I only recently acquired Tapestry Dance. In fact, it was your daughter who inspired me to do so."

"Really? But you own other dance companies?" Mom asks, her voice intrigued.

Alexei chuckles. "Actually, no. My family has more to do with banking and business acquisitions—primarily in the restaurant industry. But my mother loves the ballet, and after watching Nadia dance, I've come to appreciate why."

The look my mother sends me over her shoulder tells me she's more than a little impressed by the man whose eye I've caught. Her eyebrows rise in amazement as her jaw drops without opening her mouth.

Before I can react, she turns back to face Alexei. "And you brought my daughter flowers?"

"I did," he confirms, his eyes finding mine.

Stepping lightly across the room, I accept them from him with a murmured word of thanks.

He hesitates then, seeming to want to say something to me but not in front of my mother. I'm torn between enjoying his mild discomfort and wanting to release him from his apparent guilt because while he hasn't said the words exactly, I find I appreciate his actions so much more when it comes to an apology.

My mom seems to pick up on the silent exchange between us, and her lips quirk in a knowing grin. "Since I just got into town, my daughter and I were planning on a late dinner after the show. Have you eaten, Alexei?"

"No, I haven't," he says, turning his attention back to my mom. "But San Francisco has a number of wonderful restaurants open late, and as my family is familiar with the industry, I'm happy to recommend one."

"In that case, why don't you join us?" she presses, her eyes dancing as she glances at me sidelong.

She must really like him if she's willing to share her time with me on her first night here after we haven't seen each other in so long. I doubt she would be quite so taken with him if she knew the nitty gritty of what his business really is. Not that I could ever tell her because she's definitely picked up on our connection.

My nerves spike as I think about sharing a dinner with my mom and the guy I've fucked casually several times now.

"I'm sure he has plenty more important things to do with his time, Mom," I insist, my pulse thrumming.

"No, no. I would be honored. If I'm not imposing. I'm sure you ladies have plenty to catch up on, and I wouldn't want to get in the way." His gray eyes shift between us once again, and I have to say, I find watching him with my mom unexpectedly disarming.

For all his Alpha male bravado and presumption that has put me on my guard, I find this new side of him alarmingly irresistible. Suddenly, it seems to shed new light on the burst of anger I experienced from him last night. He might be incredibly charming, but underneath his persistence, he might not be just a player caught up in the chase.

At least, I hope not because my mom has clearly taken a shine to him.

As soon as I think it, she says, "We insist. Right, Nadia?"

"Right," I agree, and the single word sets butterflies loose in my stomach.

15

ALEXEI

"This view is wonderful," Nadia's mom says, her thick Russian accent making me think of both my own mother and home. She looks out the glass wall of windows cut in pie-shaped wedges to make it resemble a clock face as she admires the twinkling city lights.

"It's one of the main reasons we acquired Sky View," I say, setting down my glass of wine to follow her gaze.

"I can see why." Ms. Lukyan turns to smile at me, and I can see where Nadia gets her good looks.

Her mom has the same high cheekbones and full lips, the same perfectly shaped brows that give away her emotions almost without her realizing it. And though Ms. Lukyan's eyes are closer to a sapphire blue, whereas her daughter's are that astonishing shade of green, they still hold the same intriguing light.

I can tell she and Nadia are very close. I've never seen Nadia as open and comfortable as she is with her mother, even if she keeps casting nervous glances between us like she thinks I might spew what Nadia and I have been doing together lately.

I haven't even told *my* family. I'm almost offended that she would think me capable of saying something to her mother, of all people.

But I see tonight as a golden opportunity because I want to get to know Nadia better, and she's making that nearly impossible.

Her mother, on the other hand, seems more than willing to share about her daughter. I plan on taking full advantage of that.

"So, tell me, Ms. Lukyan, where are you and Nadia originally from? And what brought you to America?"

"We lived in St. Petersburg until Nadia was thirteen," she says, her smile turning nostalgic. "We left just a few years after her father died. It was hard to survive there without him, and we were fortunate enough to have the opportunity to travel to America. My aunt lived here and insisted we stay with her in New York."

I sense an underlying story behind her comment about the challenges of surviving in St. Petersburg without Nadia's father, but I don't press the matter. She seems like an open woman, and if she cared to share, she would have.

"And what do you do in New York?"

"I clean rooms in the Hyatt."

A modest job at a nice hotel, but it tells me Nadia's mom is a hard worker if she can afford to live in New York on a maid's salary.

"And do you still live with family?" I inquire, intrigued by the life Nadia grew up in.

From the corner of my eye, I can see Nadia watching me, her expression as closed and guarded as ever. She sips her wine with deliberation, remaining quiet as she listens to our exchange like she's unsure of my motivation for talking to her mother.

If she would accept a date from me, she would know. I want to understand her.

"No, Nadia's great aunt died just a few years after we moved to New York. Cancer."

"I'm sorry to hear that," I sympathize.

Nadia's mom gives a soft smile. "Thank you. But tell me, where is your family from? No, wait—let me guess."

"Mom's very good at identifying accents," Nadia says with pride, finally seeming to settle into the evening, her suspicion subsiding.

Her mom glows, giving Nadia a warm smile.

"Oh, I like this game." I focus intently on Ms. Lukyan, intrigued by whether she'll be able to spot where my family is from when I left Russia at age nine. My accent isn't nearly as strong as the rest of my family's—even Dimitri's, who is only four years my senior. Interlacing my fingers, I rest them on the table. "Do you need me to say something?" I ask, curious about how she might do it.

Nadia's mom narrows her eyes, her expression turning to one of deep concentration. "You're going to be tricky. You must have come to America when you were young."

I nod, smiling.

"Give me something brief in Russian," she requests, tilting her head slightly.

"*Priyatno provesti vremya s vami oboimi,*" I say, telling her it's a pleasure to spend time with them.

Her lips curl with pleasure, but rather than respond to my comment, she thinks a moment.

Her concentration is interrupted as our food arrives, and the server sets each plate gently before us. With a polite thank you, Nadia picks up her fork and stabs a few leaves of her salad onto it along with a piece of chicken.

After a performance, I would think she would need more sustenance than that. Then again, I'm well aware of the stringent diets ballerinas are known for putting themselves on to maintain their physiques.

Her mom, on the other hand, has a dish of stroganoff, which she works at politely as she considers me. Trying to remain patient, I dig into my own dinner of lamb medallions.

"I think you are from Moscow," her mother says finally, and I quirk an eyebrow.

"You have a gift," I admit with a nod.

She gives a soft laugh, then points down to her food. "I haven't had stroganoff this good in years."

"I'm happy to hear it." The Sky View is one of my favorite restaurants my family owns—and not just for the scenery. "But tell me, Ms. Lukyan, what was Nadia like growing up?"

"She's always been a good girl," Nadia's mom says, reaching over to give her daughter's hand a squeeze.

Nadia softens, her expression loving as she meets her mother's eyes.

"In Russia, she was full of energy and excitement. She's always been a natural dancer and fell in love with ballet as soon as her father and I introduced her to it. But by the time we moved to America, times were tough. She spent most of her energy outside of school and dance working part-time jobs to help me make ends meet. She went and got one as soon as someone would hire her, and many summers, she worked two or three jobs in order to save up money for dance. She's always been a hard worker. I think that's why she's so career driven now," Ms. Lukyan says solemnly.

"You provided," Nadia said adamantly. "I just hated seeing you working your hands to the bone."

"Yes, well, you're a good girl. And you take care of your mama." Then she turns to me again. "I'm happy for Nadia that she's getting recognition for her talent. But I do miss having my daughter around."

"I can imagine," I state.

Their deep love for each other is so apparent it fills my chest with warmth. In many ways, Nadia's mom reminds me of my own. Loving, affectionate, entirely dedicated to her child. It doesn't hurt that she sounds like she's from my home, and I find myself perfectly at ease in her company.

"So tell me, Alexei, do you bring flowers to all your dancers after their shows?" Ms. Lukyan asks, her eyes glinting as she pops a bite of stroganoff into her mouth and chews.

I laugh. "Actually, this is a first," I confess without elaborating.

My attempt at an apology for my abhorrent behavior last night might have been upended from the unexpected presence of Nadia's mom, but I get the sense that taking the time to have dinner with them as a family might go further than a simple bouquet and a handful of words.

I've never seen Nadia so at ease. It gives her a softer edge that I find dangerously appealing.

"Mom, do not go there," she chides, her tone lovingly scolding.

Her mom gives another warm laugh before raising her hands in defeat. "I wasn't going anywhere. I'm sitting right here, enjoying this fabulous dinner."

Releasing a low chuckle, I take a drink of cabernet, enjoying the exchange and ready to settle back and watch them together.

It's easy to be a part of the small family dinner. The Lukyan girls have a unique dynamic that's playful and affectionate, and while they fall into easy conversation, I watch the tension evaporate from Nadia completely.

Their topics range from the new apartment her mom just moved into—which I glean from a subtle comment that she can afford thanks to the money Nadia insists on sending her—to how much of San Francisco Nadia has experienced. None of it, I gather.

Which I intend on changing when she finally lets me take her on a date.

After tonight, my determination is renewed.

I was right to think of this as a golden opportunity. If this is what it means to be a part of Nadia's inner circle, I want to find a way to be there. I don't care how long it takes or what effort it requires because I'm falling for Nadia, and I'm willing to keep breaking down her walls if it means I get to call her mine someday.

The girls choose to forgo dessert, and when the bill comes, I send my card with our server before either has the opportunity to reach for it.

"You can't pay for dinner," Ms. Lukyan insists. "We invited you. It's my treat."

"I insist," I state. "I've been hoping to buy Nadia dinner for some time now, so I intend to take whatever opportunity I can find." I give her mother a playful wink, and the radiant smile she returns tells me she fully supports my intentions.

Now, hopefully, with her stamp of approval, Nadia might be easier to persuade.

16

NADIA

Mom's three-day visit is over far too quickly, and as I stand inside the front doors of the San Francisco airport, giving her a fierce hug, I don't ever want to let her go.

"You're sure you have to leave?" I press, trying my best to keep my tone teasing.

"Believe me, I would stay longer if work would let me," she says.

Giving me an extra-tight squeeze, she releases me and steps back. Hiking her purse higher on her shoulder, she assesses me thoughtfully. "I have a few more minutes before I need to go through security. Would you like to sit?"

She gestures to the line of chairs off to the side of the check-in counters.

"Sure," I agree because I sense she has something she actually wants to say to me.

Rolling her small carry-on behind her, Mom leads the way, settling into a chair off to the side to give us a bit more privacy. She smiles as I take the chair next to her, turning so I can face her.

"I'm so happy to see you've found a nice situation, *Malyshka*," she says, her smile warm. "You seem good, and that puts my mind at ease when I don't get to see you every day. It's been hard having you so far away."

"I know. I miss you. Talking on the phone just isn't the same," I say sadly. "But I am good, and I'm glad you are too. Maybe once this show is over, I can fly out and spend a few days with you."

"I would love that," she agrees enthusiastically.

A silence settles between us momentarily, and my mom cups my cheek then chucks my chin. "I am worried about your being out here alone. Have you made any friends yet? You haven't mentioned any, and you didn't introduce me to anyone."

"I'm busy, Mom. Besides, I'm friendly enough with my coworkers. We've . . . spent time together outside work." It's not a complete lie. I did go to dinner and clubbing with them that night Alexei insisted on taking everyone out.

My mom raises her eyebrow skeptically.

"I'll try harder," I promise, knowing full well that she'll worry if I don't.

"What about your ballet company owner, Alexei?"

Heat floods my cheeks as she strikes right at the heart of the matter, bringing up the one person I'm deliberately trying *not* to form a relationship with. A man who's making it painstakingly hard to avoid.

Her searching gaze reads my embarrassment with the sharp insight of a mom who is also my best friend. "You can't push people away forever, Nadia," she says gently.

"I'm not," I insist, though in Alexei's case, I don't think it's entirely unreasonable to keep him at arm's length.

"He seems like a good man," she says.

If only she knew. I'm sure my mom wouldn't say such a thing if she knew Alexei and his brothers are at the head of a Russian Bratva. Not that I would ever tell her. A Bratva leader is exactly what drove us from Russia in the first place.

While I was too young to fully understand at the time, I know now that the older man who offered my mom a wealth of money when I was just thirteen years old was trying to buy me. For what purpose, my mom would never say, but I have a good guess. And as he was the head of a powerful and dangerous Bratva, it wasn't like she could simply turn him down.

So, in a desperate attempt to keep me safe, we fled as far from him as we could get.

It would crush her to know I've fallen into the lap of another Bratva man.

While Alexei seems nothing like the formidable pervert who wanted me as a child, I know it would terrify her to learn what he really is.

But I'm not leaving San Francisco. I refuse to run again. So instead, I just nod. Alexei *does* seem like a good man. As good as a man with criminal ties could possibly be. And he's dangerously sexy. Which is why I need to stay away from him.

Sighing, my mom seems to read my conviction in my face. "All I'm saying is you might give him a chance. He clearly has feelings for you. Strong enough feelings that he would not only endure a night entertaining your mother but would take the time to try and get to know you through my eyes. Not every guy would do that without some kind of investment on your part first."

"But that's just the thing, Mom. He might want to get to know me, but once he *does* know me, he won't want to stick around. So it doesn't matter." I'm shocked to realize how painful the admission is. I don't think I could say it out loud to anyone but my mom.

"Of course he will," she insists, taking my hand.

"Mom, I can't have kids. You know that. So why would I try and start a family? It will only lead to pain. Alexei will want children someday and will leave me for a woman who can give him that." I blink back the tears that sting my eyes and try to hold my mom's gaze.

"Nadia, children are wonderful, but they're not the end all, be all of the world. You're special. You're good and kind and passionate. You can find love and happiness without children. And if Alexei wants them, why couldn't you adopt?"

She makes it sound so simple, but I know it's not that easy. Men like the thought of having their own children to carry on their legacy.

I've had that specific conversation with enough guys to know for certain that they don't necessarily feel the urge to raise someone else's child.

And besides, as good a guy as Alexei seems to be, I suspect his interest is far more focused on the chase than actually getting to know me. I've given him nothing exceptionally appealing. So the only thing holding his interest is my refusal.

Knowing that makes me sadder than I had thought it might. Especially after watching him at dinner with my mom. He's incredibly charming and charismatic. I can't deny it. Not everyone can win my mom over—especially when she thinks they're interested in me. Her standards have always been nearly as high as mine.

Still, I appreciate my mom's support, and I know she's just looking out for me.

"You're right," I concede, giving her a small smile.

"Oh, *Malyshka*, just promise me you'll think about it, okay? I don't want you to be alone forever."

"I'm not alone. I have you," I tease, nudging her with my shoulder.

My mom smiles sadly. "And I'm here for you. But we both know I won't always be here, and I would love to see you happy and with people who care about you."

"If you're talking about dying, that's a long way off, so just knock it off. Besides, I'm pretty sure you're going to live forever," I state authoritatively.

Chuckling, my mom combs a lock of hair behind my ear. Then her eyes flick up to the clock to our left. "I'd better get going."

"Let me know when you land safe?"

"I will." Mom stands, and when I join her, she pulls me in for another good hug.

"Love you, Mom."

"I love you too, Nadia." She plants a kiss on my cheek, then collects her bags and heads to the check-in counter.

I watch her go, and when she gets in line, she turns and gives me a small wave.

Maybe she's right. Maybe I need to start putting myself out there.

If I don't take the risk of getting hurt, I'll never know what I could be missing out on.

Of course, the only man I've found attractive since arriving in San Francisco has to be one not only tied to a Bratva but also my boss and closer to my mom's age than my own. But when I think of searching for someone to connect to, he's the only one I'm the least bit interested in.

And while my instincts tell me that Alexei could be a dangerous choice, the fact that he has my mom's stamp of approval means a lot. And she's right. He did spend an entire evening getting to know me through her—because I've been so hard-headed that I haven't allowed him to get close to me. Perhaps it's time to change that.

With newfound determination, I head out of the airport.

It's time to take a risk and see where things might lead.

17

ALEXEI

It's nearly ten o'clock at night when the doorman to my building calls up to my penthouse apartment, and I answer with mild surprise, curious why they might be contacting me at this hour.

"There's a young lady here to see you, sir," the doorman says over the phone. "She says her name is Nadia Lukyan."

Astounded that she actually sought me out, I say, "Send her up."

As I hang up, I frown at my phone. I'm not quite sure what to make of it. After having dinner with Nadia and her mom several nights ago, I determined that I would leave them in peace to spend their few days of quality time together.

But I anticipated picking up the chase once more, since her mom would be gone by the morning. So having Nadia show up tonight leaves me both off balance and pleasantly surprised.

I'm waiting by the elevator doors when they finally ding open, and Nadia stands startled in the small lift as our eyes meet.

"Hi," I greet her, my lips curling with amusement.

"Hi," she says, releasing her breath as her shoulders relax visibly.

"This is rather unexpected," I observe mildly. "How can I help you, Nadia?"

"I'll go on a date with you," she blurts, stepping out of the elevator and stopping mere feet in front of me. Her green eyes meet mine with a deep intensity, and beneath their sharp focus is a vulnerability that sets my pulse racing.

It took a lot of courage for her to come here. I can see it, though she's doing her best to hide the fact.

"It's a bit late at night to start a date," I point out, going for levity to try and put her at ease.

But I slowly close the distance between us, unwilling to let this rare opportunity slip through my fingers. Because I get the feeling that it's not just me Nadia says no to. After speaking with her mom at dinner the other night, I don't think Nadia says yes to anybody.

"We can start dating tomorrow," she reasons.

Then she moves forward, rising onto her toes at the same time as she kisses me.

Electric heat ripples through me at the unexpected contact, and as she throws her arms around my neck, my chest swells with deep emotion. Her kiss is passionate and open, and I can feel the meaning behind it.

Before, her kisses were fiery and carefree and enticing, but now, they're all that and so much more. Because she's giving herself to me. It's not demanding or frantic. Her lips are welcoming.

Wrapping my arms around her, I pull Nadia close, arching her back as I bend over her. Consumed by her touch and excited by her bold action, I find my attraction toward her throbbing through my veins.

She melts against my chest, her fingers combing into my hair as she clings to me. Tasting her deeply, I blindly guide her deeper into my house, unwilling to remove my lips from hers to look where I'm going.

Nadia seems more than willing, and when I hoist her up off the ground, she wraps her legs around my waist, letting me carry her wherever I please.

Growling with excitement, I carry her toward the bedroom, my cock already rock-hard and throbbing to be inside her.

Nadia gasps as her back finds the wall to the right of my hallway, and I take full advantage of the opportunity to press her firmly against it, grinding my erection into the apex of her thighs.

Consuming her lips with insatiable greed, I deepen the kiss, and Nadia responds just as fervently. The heat between us is on a whole new level, and I don't know what drove Nadia to this point, but I want to worship whatever force drove her toward me.

Because I got a yes from Nadia, and that knowledge fills me with deep satisfaction. It makes me want to pound my chest and take her somewhere that I can show all the world she said yes to me.

"Fuck me," Nadia breathes against my lips, her breasts pressing adamantly into my chest as she nearly pants with need.

"I'm going to fuck you within an inch of your life," I promise her, redoubling my effort to get her to the bedroom.

Firmly gripping her ass, I carry her down the hallway and into my room.

She squeals as I throw her bodily onto the bed, leaving her airborne for a split second. As she bounces there, her arms flying wide to help her get her bearings, her emerald eyes peer up at me with unbridled excitement.

"Take your clothes off," I command, unbuttoning my shirt at the same time.

Her eyes follow my fingers down my blue dress shirt, and she licks her lips as I shrug out of it a moment later, rewarding her with the sight of my body, which I withheld from her the last time we were together.

I love the way her eyes soak up my chest hungrily. Their intensity grows, and she quickly reaches down to grip the hem of her sweater and haul it up over her head. The scalloped edge of her sage-green lace bra makes it look like two shells perfectly cupping the precious pearls of her breasts, and a rumbling growl of appreciation issues from my chest.

Biting her lip in a coy look of anticipation, Nadia goes to work on her jeans, unbuttoning them and hoisting her hips off the bed to shove the thick fabric and her panties down over her ass and legs in one go. I do the same with my slacks, stepping out of my shoes at the same time.

Her bra is the last thing to go, and as soon as she's gloriously bare before me, I lean in.

Then I'm on her, gripping her ankles as I haul her toward the edge of the bed and closer to me.

Nadia gasps, releasing her lip from her teeth as they part in a sensual O shape.

"One of these days, I want to know what those sexy lips feel like wrapped around my cock," I say darkly, brushing my thumb over the bottom one. "But right now, I have something else in mind."

She swallows forcefully, her green eyes going wide, and I smirk as I bend down to grab my bondage rope from beneath the bed.

"What are you . . .?" Her voice trails off as her eyes land on the silky finger-thick strand I wrap around her delicate ankle.

"Give me your hand," I command, holding mine palm up to indicate which one I want.

Nadia obeys, her movement hesitant yet trusting. Her soft fingers press lightly against my palm, and I wrap my fingers around hers before guiding them down to her foot. I lash her wrist to her ankle and relish the way it automatically spreads her legs.

Then I repeat the process on her other side.

Her breathing escalates, her pert breasts rising and falling with increasing speed as I incapacitate her, and yet, she doesn't tell me to stop.

"You remember your safe word?" I tease, glancing up to meet her eyes.

A smile splits her striking features. "Wasn't it something like olly-olly-oxen-free?"

"Good," I praise. Then I grip her thighs firmly and pull her the rest of the way to me.

Hips resting on the edge of the mattress, Nadia lies exposed and waiting, her thighs spread from the way I've tied her up.

"Mmm," I moan appreciatively. "You know the best part of bondage play?" I ask, smiling wickedly.

"What?" she asks breathily.

"I get to touch you all I want, however I want, and you can't stop me."

Her eyes flash with smoldering heat, and I hold them as I stroke my fingers along her slit just to prove my point.

Nadia shudders violently, her gaze burning into mine. "What are you going to do to me?" she asks, her voice low and sultry.

"I think I'll tease you a little," I say playfully.

Then I slide my fingers between her folds, running them back and forth as I feel her growing wetter by the second. Once her juices are thoroughly coating my fingers, I start to flick her clit with the tip of my finger.

Nadia groans, her eyes fluttering shut as her fingers twitch convulsively against her bonds.

"You like that?" I purr, relishing the way her cheeks flush and her nipples harden.

"Yes," she gasps, her back arching.

"What about this?" I ask, reaching with my other hand to pinch the taut pebble of her breast.

Air rushes sharply between her teeth. "Mmm, yes," she confirms, squirming beneath me.

Giving her nipple a light tug, I release it and grab the base of my cock. Then I slide its head along the seam of her slit, thoroughly enjoying the view as a pearl of precum spreads along her pussy lips.

"Oh, God," Nadia moans, her knees trembling.

I tap her clit with the tip of my cock, letting its heavy girth slap against her sensitive nerve bundle and making her twitch.

"You want me to fuck you, Nadia?" I ask.

"Yes," she whimpers, shifting impatiently.

"Like this?" I ease my cockhead inside her entrance, relishing the way she tightens around my girth.

"Yes," she mewls, her breath hitching as her muscles flex.

I press forward slowly, feeling every inch of her warm, wet depths as I ease inside her. The view is glorious, watching the way her pussy stretches to accommodate me, her athletic body twitching and writhing as Nadia craves more.

But I'm loving this slow, pleasure-inducing torture because I know it's going to make her come that much harder. And while I can see the frustration building in her movements, I can't wait to hear her screams of euphoria by the time I'm done with her.

Gripping Nadia's knees, I spread her thighs farther, showcasing her swollen clit and glistening folds. I feel her eyes on me as I watch my cock vanish inside her tight hole once again. Claiming her body so intimately fills me with intense satisfaction, and feeling the way her walls throb around my cock tells me she likes it just as much.

I want all of Nadia. I want to keep her for my own. And I plan on showing her the best day of her life tomorrow. Because I don't think I ever want to stop fucking her, and she might just be the only woman I'll ever want to fuck again.

My eyes flick up to meet hers, and the ravenous hunger in her gaze sets my skin on fire.

"Enjoying the view?" I tease, pushing inside her up to the hilt and pausing there.

"You have no idea," she breathes.

I reward her by pressing my thumb to her clit.

"Fuck!" She gasps, her head falling back as her eyes roll into her head.

"Oh, I plan to," I promise darkly, rocking inside her at a steady rhythm now.

18

NADIA

I love the way Alexei teases me. In truth, he's earned the excessive confidence with which he pursues me. Because he doesn't just talk the talk. He walks the walk, and it's insane how effortlessly he can drive me crazy.

He's teasing me, bringing me just up to the edge of my release and holding me there until I'm on the verge of screaming. And then, as I'm just about to topple over the precipice, he stops.

"*Please*," I moan, frustration in my voice as he tortures me for a third time. But begging isn't going to help me this time. I've already tried.

And yet, my body is humming with arousal, every fiber of my being attuned to Alexei's movement, his gorgeous body, the way he touches me.

"Please what?" he asks innocently, leaning in to nibble my pebbled nipple.

"Please let me come," I beg, gasping as a jolt of desire crackles through my core, making my clit twitch dangerously.

Alexei moans, the low sound causing my heart to flutter.

Then his lips travel slowly up from my breast, pressing kisses along my chest, my sternum, my collarbones, then up my neck. They brush lightly against my lobe.

"Infuriating isn't it?" he murmurs. "The wait."

Is he . . . teaching me a lesson? He's not actually torturing me for turning him down so many times, is he?

I turn my head to meet his gaze, and the molten silver of his eyes takes my breath away.

"But you've shown me something very valuable, Nadia," he breathes.

And then he kisses me.

My mind goes blank as I'm lost in the passion of his lips, the way he captures my breath as his mouth claims mine. His hips rock, his cock pressing adamantly inside me as his tongue strokes between my teeth, tasting me deeply.

And in an instant, all the frustration transforms into an intoxicating anticipation. He's not teasing me now. He's worshiping my body, the way he grinds forward against my clit, sending sparks of pleasure flickering across my skin, his thick girth sliding in and out of me, finding that hidden spot that drives me wild.

After all that agonizing temptation, the sheer euphoria of relief leaves me trembling uncontrollably.

"God, you feel like heaven," Alexei breathes, his fingers combing into my hair as his strong arms frame my shoulders and face.

"Don't stop," I plead, my need so powerful I feel as though I might explode if he doesn't let me come this time.

Alexei's lips slant over mine once more, his fingers curling as he pulls gently at the roots of my hair. I gasp into his mouth, unable to move an inch with how thoroughly he's bound me. Somehow, that makes it all the more thrilling.

I feel sinfully dirty for loving the way he owns me. At the same time, it's almost empowering to turn over all control to him. I trust him, at least with my body, and it's addictive, this vulnerability that allows me to simply revel in his expert touch.

Breaking our kiss, Alexei pulls away just enough to look at me, and my eyes flutter open automatically.

"I'll let you come now, Nadia. And I want you to look at me the entire time."

I shudder violently beneath him. The intimacy of his request is terrifying, and yet, I want to try it. I'm so close to coming, and I want it desperately. I'll do anything if he'll give me relief.

"Okay," I breathe, nodding.

He gives a low, rumbling purr, and his hips roll more forcefully, stimulating my clit as he drives deep inside me.

My lips part, my breath catching in my throat as I hover on the brink, in momentary agony as my body prepares to be tortured once again. Only this time, he doesn't stop.

"Come for me, Nadia," he commands, thrusting powerfully, and I obey immediately.

Crying out, I explode around his rock-hard erection, my pussy throbbing with such intense force that my vision starts to swim. I've never come so hard in my life. The orgasm rips through me like a tidal wave, leaving tingling relief in its wake.

Clit twitching, my walls milking his cock with iron force, I peer deep into his silver gaze. Intense emotion swells inside my chest as our sex transforms into something far more meaningful than it has before.

It terrifies me.

At the same time, excitement blossoms low in my stomach.

If this is the kind of connection that forms when you love someone, it might just be worth the risk. And while I won't just put my career on the backburner to pursue something I imagine will end up being temporary, for the first time, I'm willing to lower my guard enough to see where things go from here.

"Good girl," Alexei praises, his low voice enticing.

For a moment, I think he might be approving of my revelation. But he can't possibly have read my thoughts in my eyes. *Could he?*

"You're so fucking sexy, Nadia. I could watch you come a thousand times."

I shiver at the delicious prospect. A slow and devilish smile spreads across his lips at my response. It's then that I realize he's stilled inside me, his hard cock buried up to the hilt in my depths.

He leans in, and my eyelids sink closed as he kisses me passionately, his tongue tantalizing as it tangles with my own. Then he pulls away, breaking the kiss as his cock slowly slides out of me.

I moan at the aching hollowness that settles deep inside my belly.

"Don't worry, love. I'm not nearly done with you," he promises, and though the term of endearment falls casually from his lips, it strikes right to my core.

Lungs freezing in my chest, I lie mute and motionless as my heart pounds a mile a minute against my ribs. Thankfully, Alexei doesn't seem to notice the power his words have over me as he turns his focus to the knots binding my wrists.

It takes me several moments to regain my composure, and I watch him with fascination, taking him in with fresh eyes. Alexei is gorgeous—I knew that the moment I laid eyes on him. But until now, I never realized just how devastatingly handsome he really is.

The strong angles of his face are so intensely masculine, as is the stubble that shades his jaw and chin. His proud brow is a perfect contrast to his emotional eyes that tell me exactly what he's thinking. And those lips, full and soft—the only soft feature of his body—are pure magic.

His rippling arms and chest are something else to behold. He's as chiseled as the David, his smooth skin bulging, veins standing out against his flesh because he's all muscle and strength. The tattoos only seem to accentuate his manly physique.

Sharp gray eyes flick up from his work as he releases my hand, and they catch me admiring him. A smug smile tugs at the corners of his lips before he turns his gaze to my other hand.

"Do you spend much time on boats?" I ask playfully.

Cocking an eyebrow, Alexei continues to free me. "Why do you ask?" he hedges.

"Because you seem to be very good at knots."

He chuckles, the sound washing over me and making my stomach tremble.

"My family does own a yacht, actually, now that you mention it. We've been sailing the bay since we were kids."

"I believe it," I tease.

Then, as my hands and feet are finally freed, something he said comes flashing back to me. "What did I show you?" I ask, my brows furrowing as he drops the rope on the floor and turns his attention back to me.

"Hmm?" he asks as his strong arm snakes beneath my back and he guides me farther onto the bed.

I follow his lead, sliding back until my head finds a pillow, and Alexei settles on top of me, his hips spreading my thighs once again.

"You said I showed you something valuable. Earlier. After you finally stopped torturing me."

Alexei's rumbling chuckle vibrates through my chest as he leans in to nip playfully at my lower lip. "You taught me that the wait makes the reward exponentially more meaningful."

My breath catches as my heart skips a beat. Of all the things I expected him to say, that was not it. But it impacts me deeply, and a wave of emotion floods my chest. The comparison is so vivid that I'm left speechless in the wake of his revelation.

I can see now, the intense frustration that I felt—the feeling that I might just go insane if he didn't bring me some relief—it's the same reason he lost his temper with me in the dressing room. *And then the culmination of an orgasm that nearly made me short circuit? Does that mean my agreeing to go on a date brought him the kind of pleasure that he just gave me?*

I can see it in his eyes now.

And his happiness echoes within me.

This game I thought we were playing... it just became something more real than I ever would have believed.

Leaning in, Alexei kisses me with a tenderness that sets my pulse racing. He shifts on top of me, his cock finding my entrance once again, and this time as he eases inside me, an intense heat floods my body.

This isn't just fucking anymore.

We haven't even had our first date, but I can feel the subtle difference.

Sex like this is far more meaningful.

And as terrifying as I might find it, it's also exceedingly invigorating.

Goosebumps explode across my flesh as my nerves light on fire. I can feel every scintillating inch of Alexei not just filling me up, but fulfilling me.

And when he groans with appreciation, I shudder beneath him.

This connection is unlike anything I've ever known before, and I want more. Alexei rocks on top of me, his slow and intimate motions all the more stimulating.

Whimpering, I cling to him, my fingers finding the rods of muscle that line his spine. Our tongues tangle in a fierce knot, and I'm intoxicated by his all-consuming presence, the overwhelming attraction that makes my head spin.

It doesn't matter that we've only just started to have sex again. I'm so close to an orgasm I can't even think straight. This time, I don't beg. Somehow, I know we're not playing that game. He's not going to punish me if I come without permission.

But I feel, instinctively, that he's right there with me.

The thick iron of his cock as he slides in and out of my wet pussy tells me he's fighting hard to hold back. To come with me.

"Oh, God, I'm coming," I gasp against his lips.

Alexei groans, his kiss searing as he presses inside me more adamantly.

And as the first wave of euphoria hits me, I feel him burst deep in my depths. Swallowing my cry of ecstasy, Alexei claims my mouth and pussy simultaneously. Hot cum fills me up as my walls grip him, milking every last drop with excruciating pleasure.

We tremble together, our breaths shuddering as we refuse to come up for air. I don't know that I've ever felt anything so vulnerable and intimate as this.

It's scary, putting myself out there, and yet no one's ever made me feel so safe.

Alexei stills, his cock buried deep inside me, and we gasp in sync as I soak up the deep satisfaction that settles in my belly.

"That. Was. Amazing," he rasps, resting his forehead against mine as we breathe heavily.

I nod, unable to say a word as I take stock of my body.

Tingling pleasure leaves my fingers and toes almost numb, and my clit twitches at the slightest of Alexei's movements. My core tightens around him as he slowly withdraws from my body.

When he rolls onto the bed, collapsing beside me, my legs fall open, blissfully limp.

Gradually, my heart rate slows, my breathing calming along with it, and I fling an arm up over my head as I stare at his white ceiling.

"What made you change your mind?" Alexei asks after several long moments of silence.

I turn to meet his eyes as he rolls onto his side, propping his head on his palm so he can look at me.

"Hmm?" I ask, my brain still foggy with lust.

He chuckles, his gray eyes dancing. "Why did you decide you'll go on a date with me?" he presses.

A lazy grin spreads across my face. "Because I figure anyone who can make me come like that deserves at least *one* date," I tease.

He quirks an eyebrow, his expression telling me he's not buying it. Considering I told him yes before we had sex, I guess it is rather unbelievable.

"Is it bad to say that winning my mom over goes a long way?"

Alexei chuckles. "Probably. But you're in luck because I happen to be a mama's boy, which means I know the power a woman like your mom can wield over your decisions."

"You, a mama's boy?" I ask skeptically.

He shrugs. "Hey, my mom is the only reason I went to your ballet in the first place."

"So it's her fault," I tease.

Alexei's eyes flash dangerously, and he pinches my chin between his thumb and finger, tipping my lips toward him. "You'd better watch that pretty little mouth of yours," he threatens softly. "Or I'll show you what happens to naughty girls who talk back to me."

Humming, I scoot closer to him until my body's pressed against his warm chest. "Promises, promises," I breathe.

And as our lips meet, I know this is going to be a long and steamy night.

19

ALEXEI

Sunlight peers through the window of my bedroom, the light soft and golden as the morning bursts over San Francisco in silent celebration. After a late night with Nadia, I don't want to give up on sleep just yet.

But I know it's time to start my day. Breathing in deeply, I can still smell her floral perfume on my pillow, and my cock twitches at the intoxicating scent. I open my eyes, and a smile tugs at my lips.

Nadia's still sleeping soundly, her head sharing my pillow, her body soft and warm against my chest. The simple gesture—knowing she's not up and out the door, ready to forget all about me now that she's sexually satisfied—excites me.

It feels like we're taking baby steps in the right direction.

I take a moment to study her face, so soft and innocent in sleep. She looks younger now, the constant pressure of her life not tightening her shoulders. Pulling her more firmly against my chest, I press a kiss to the curve of her neck. Nadia hums, nuzzling the pillow, but she doesn't wake.

Her raven hair falls in soft waves across the pillow, a stark contrast to her delicate pale skin. She's breathtaking.

I still can't believe she came to my apartment last night. That she said yes to a date. Finally. And without further coercion. I should send her mother flowers because, while Nadia didn't say it explicitly, I get the distinct impression that her mother told her to give me a chance.

But right now, I want to reward the girl sleeping soundly in my bed.

Slowly easing my arm from around her waist, I slip beneath the covers and guide her legs open. Nadia stirs, murmuring something as she rolls onto her back, and for a moment, I think I've woken her.

Then she quiets once again.

I smile, lowering my shoulders between her thighs, and gently kiss my way from the inside of her knee up her leg. A soft gasp issues from her lips as my tongue strokes between her folds for the first time, and her hips twitch beneath my palms.

I do it again, and Nadia moans.

Then she goes quiet.

Even as she still appears to sleep, her body responds to me, her folds growing slick with arousal as I lap along her seam and flick her clit with the tip of my tongue.

"Mmm, Alexei," she murmurs, shifting under the sheets as I wrap my lips around the tiny bundle of nerves.

For a moment, I'm sure she's awake. But when I pause, so does she, her legs relaxing once again. I'm sorely tempted to smile, but I remain intent on my task, lightly sucking on her clit as I gently hold her thighs.

When she twitches again, mumbling something sensually, I wonder if she's dreaming of me. I hope so. I want her to say my name again in her sleep. But I'm also enjoying myself far too much to stop what I'm doing.

Nadia's pussy tastes entirely too good, tangy and arousing, making me hard as a rock. I release her with a gentle pop to stroke my tongue between her folds once more, and this time, she groans more intensely.

A moment later, the sheets vanish from over my head and Nadia looks down at me with sleepy eyes, her expression entirely too appealing. Lips parted in mild surprise, she flutters her heavy eyelids, and a languid smile stretches across her face.

"Mmm, I want to wake up like this every day," she moans, her hips rolling seductively.

I chuckle low and soft, continuing to worship her clit with my mouth.

Nadia gasps, her head falling back as her fingers comb into my hair, her nails lightly scraping across my scalp. Just the right balance of enticing and painful. When I dip my tongue inside her dripping entrance, she gives a soft cry of ecstasy.

Then her hands travel around my head, exploring until they find my jaw. Gently curling her fingers around my jawbone, Nadia pulls me softly up her body.

I obey, thoroughly enjoying the gentle command.

I pause to place kisses on her stomach, her breasts, her chest as I crawl. Nadia hooks her heels behind my hips as I finally reach her face.

"Good morning," she murmurs, her hands curving around my neck as she pulls me firmly against her lips.

"Mmm," I hum appreciatively as she deepens the kiss, her tongue slipping into my mouth for a slow and seductive taste.

"Hmm, tangy," she murmurs, her lips curving into a smile.

And God, but it turns me on to know she's appreciating her own sinfully delicious flavor.

Suddenly ravenous, I delve my tongue between her lips. At the same time, I grind against her with my hips, pressing my erection against her flat stomach to show her just how much I want her.

One of Nadia's hands travels down my chest, her touch light as she traces the line of my abs. Then her fingers wrap around my cock. I groan, my hips thrusting of their own volition, and her grip tightens as she strokes my length several times.

Then she guides it toward her entrance.

Watching her take charge is entirely too hot. As soon as my cockhead finds her wet warmth, I shove inside her, my need so intense I can't hold back.

Nadia gasps, her breasts arching up into my chest, her taut nipples teasing my skin.

I love being inside her, no condom to dull the sinfully exquisite sensation of her tight, wet depths. Her legs tense around my hips, her heels pressing lightly against the small of my back as she urges me to take her.

And I do, pounding forcefully inside her with deliberate thrusts. I keep a slow, steady pace, easing out of her before ramming back inside, burying myself deep in her pussy as my pelvis finds her clit with each penetration.

Nadia takes me greedily, her euphoric gasps vanishing inside my mouth as we get lost in each other's pleasure.

I can feel her reaching climax before long, her walls tightening around my girth as she edges closer to the precipice. And today, I don't want to control her. I want to see just how many times she can come before I do.

Watching her last night, seeing her eyes dilate when she found her release, it was earth-shattering. It nearly made me lose my mind. And now, all I can think about is exploring just how wild and untamed my fiery Russian ballerina can be.

She's certainly confident and eager enough that she's willing to show me when it's time to fuck.

I swallow her cry as Nadia orgasms powerfully, her pussy gripping me like a vise, urging me to fill her with my seed. But not yet. I want to stay buried inside her far longer.

She whimpers as I continue to pound inside her, drawing out her climax as I grind against her clit. And when she collapses limply against the mattress, I shift our position.

Slipping my arm beneath her hips, I lift her at the same time as I rise onto my knees, bringing her ass off the bed as I kneel.

Nadia gasps, her eyes flying open as her hands brace against the sheets. From this new angle, I proceed to penetrate her even more deeply. Her toes curl as she balances on them, her back straight and taut, her breasts bouncing lightly.

I relish the intense lust on her face.

"Play with your nipples," I command, and my cock throbs when she palms her breasts, squeezing the supple flesh between her fingers.

Her thumbs and fingers lightly pinch and roll the dark tips, and her eyelids flutter closed, hiding her eyes from me.

With my free hand, I mirror her motion as I take her clit between my thumb and finger. Nadia cries out as I tease the tiny bean, and moments later, she unravels in my arms a second time.

Her hips jerk convulsively as her clit twitches beneath my thumb, and I nearly lose it this time, my balls tightening as my cock throbs with the need for release. Grinding my teeth, I grunt as I hold on by a thread.

When her aftershocks slowly start to subside, I don't know that I'm going to last much longer.

Easing her hips back onto the bed, I pause a moment, letting my hands roam down her muscular legs until I find her ankles.

Then I slowly raise them, first one, then the other as I guide her feet up over her head. I fucking love how flexible Nadia is. Even with her knees up by her breasts, her thighs spread wide to put her pussy on full display, she looks perfectly at ease. Ready for a proper pounding.

Her hooded eyes dilate as she watches me, and my gaze rakes down her firm, athletic body, stopping to admire the sight of my cock buried up to the hilt in her tight pussy.

"You're so fucking perfect," I groan, pinning her ankles above her head as I start to rock inside her from this new angle.

She feels impossibly tight as I keep her folded in half, her walls fluttering around my hard length as I fuck her hard. The mewls of pleasure that grunt from her every time I thrust make the base of my spine tingle.

"Fuck, I'm coming!" she gasps, her head tipping back as her jaw drops in a silent scream.

She's so stunning, I don't know how she can possibly be real. As her walls grip me forcefully, I find my own release, shoving deep inside her as I pour burst after burst of hot cum deep inside her pussy.

Nadia gasps, near hyperventilating as her orgasm seems to consume her completely. Trembling like a leaf, she jerks and twitches beneath me, making my pulse roar in my ears. And only after she slumps back onto the bed, her muscles giving in completely, do I slowly guide her legs back down beside me.

Leaning in, I press a chaste kiss to her lips, then I ease out of her and climb off the bed.

"Where are you going?" she asks sleepily, her thighs falling limply open.

"To shower. Care to join me?"

She hums appreciatively, then sits up as if suddenly realizing something. "I promised Matteo I would come in early to work on one of our lifts. What time is it?" She glances at the clock sitting on my bedside table, and her shoulders actually slump just a little, revealing her disappointment. "Raincheck?" she offers, her eyes skimming my body longingly.

"Alright. But you're not leaving without telling me when you're free for our date."

"I'm off tomorrow," she suggests, her cheeks flushing a delicate pink.

"Good. I'll pick you up at ten."

"In the morning?" she asks incredulously.

I chuckle. "Yes. Is that a problem?"

"Um, no, I guess not. I just thought . . . you know. I dunno . . . dinner and a movie? I guess I've never done a day date before."

"Don't worry. I still intend to buy you dinner. But I have big plans in store for you. And some of them will require daylight."

"Okay, now I'm intrigued," she says, her green eyes sparking.

"Good. Then you won't back out. You'll just have to text me your address and be ready for me in the morning."

"I won't back out," she promises gently, her expression softening as she holds my gaze.

I grin. "Good. Shall I walk you out?"

"Mmm, while I would thoroughly appreciate that, I'm not so sure your doorman wants to see your ass," she teases, sliding out of bed and stooping to find her clothes.

"I can get dressed, you know."

"No need. I know the way." Nadia pads toward me and, rising onto her tiptoes, presses a kiss to my cheek. "See you tomorrow."

"I wouldn't miss it."

20

NADIA

Alexei looks dangerously sexy with his wrist slung casually over the steering wheel of his white Corvette. The rich red-leather interior is as bold a statement as everything about Alexei. McKenna's right, "flashy" is the perfect word for him.

He doesn't do anything halfway, and I find that's something I really like about him.

He's not afraid to be who he wants to be.

"Where are you taking me?" I ask, turning my eyes toward the steep road that he weaves down at a frightening pace. The hills of San Francisco feel all the more dramatic at this speed, and I swallow hard to try and keep my heart from jumping out of my throat.

"Well, from what I've gathered, you haven't treated yourself to what this great city has to offer. So today, we're going sightseeing."

"Really?"

Alexei flashes me a smile. "Yes, really. What were you expecting?"

"I honestly had no idea. But not something so . . . normal," I confess and giggle.

He snorts, whipping his car around a turn and leaving my stomach somewhere a block behind us. "Well, seeing as you won't take the time yourself, I thought I might show you a few reasons to love living in the Bay Area . . . besides getting to spend time with me, of course."

Fighting the urge to roll my eyes, I laugh. "Hey, I know this spot," I say, peering out the window as he finally pulls up next to the curb and parks.

"This is Pier 39."

"Your French restaurant is just over there," I realize, pointing.

"Technically, my sister-in-law's restaurant. But yes. Le Fleur." He steps out of the car and rounds the front to offer me a hand.

I take it, letting him pull me from the passenger seat. Rather than releasing me once I'm on my feet, he intertwines our fingers as he swings my door closed.

"How many siblings do you have?" I ask. I recall Lina saying something about Alexei and his brothers, but suddenly, I realize I know little more than that about his family.

"Two brothers. Both older," he says as he guides me between the colorfully painted two-story buildings and onto the pier itself.

"So you're the baby?" I confirm.

"Yes."

"Now I see why you're a mama's boy," I tease.

He smirks, glancing at me from the corner of his eye.

"And you and your brothers all run this family business together . . . of banking and acquiring restaurants." I tread lightly around the subject, not sure whether I want to dig too far into the truth of the matter. I don't know that he would tell me even if I asked outright, and I can't say that I'm ready to confirm that he and his brothers are at the head of a Bratva, anyway.

"I mostly handle the security aspect. My brothers care much more about the money and investments." He shrugs.

Interesting. By security, I wonder if that means he's the muscle sent in to ensure they get paid. But somehow, he doesn't strike me as the type. He's too . . . likable. Then again, most sociopaths are. That doesn't make him any less dangerous.

"And your brothers are both married?" I ask.

"One is. He and his wife—Camille, who owns Le Fleur—just had a baby."

The warmth in his voice makes my chest tighten painfully, and I watch him from the corner of my eye as we continue to walk.

"That's so exciting," I say, trying to keep a note of enthusiasm in my voice.

"My brother certainly seems happy."

His comment catches my ear unexpectedly, making me wonder if he might not actually be less inclined to have kids and, therefore, a better fit for me than I had dared to believe. *Because then he won't be disappointed when we can't have them down the road.*

If we go down that road, that is.

"You don't like being an uncle?" I tease, not daring to approach the subject head on.

Alexei laughs. "It's not that. I mean, obviously, I'm cut out to be the cool uncle his kid's going to love most. I just never really saw my brother as the marrying type—let alone the whole white picket fence and two-point-five kids deal."

I open my mouth to dig into his statement a little further, but the oddest sound captures my attention. Frowning, I turn my head in its direction.

Beside me, Alexei picks up the pace, pulling me toward the strange noise that I'm now starting to assume is our first destination.

As we round the corner of the building, I gasp. More sea lions than I can count sunbathe on long stretches of platform, their unique call suddenly recognizable now that I see what they are.

"Pretty cool, huh?" Alexei asks, and when I glance up at him, he's watching me with a boyish smile.

"I had no idea this was here."

"That's because you need to get out more," he teases.

"Apparently," I concede, turning my gaze back toward the big-bellied beasts.

We stay and watch for a long stretch of time, Alexei finding a wealth of patience as I can't seem to get enough of the animals' adorable behavior. They squabble and snuggle just like any human might, going about their business without a second thought concerning their rapt audience.

Next is a drive across the Golden Gate Bridge with a brief tour around Sausalito. Then back into the city for a late lunch—or early dinner. Rather than another fancy restaurant, Alexei takes me for street food, stopping at a small trattoria-type place that serves to-go soups in sourdough bread bowls.

"You have to try the clam chowder," he insists as we wait in line.

And by this point in the day, I know I can't say otherwise. His choice of entertainment has left me flushed with excitement, the permanent smile making my cheeks ache because I'm never this happy.

But between all the unexpected surprises and the near constant banter that keeps me on my toes, this might make one of the top ten best days of my life. Though the date is not yet over, I'm confident it's the best one I've ever been on.

Ten minutes later, each with a clam chowder bread bowl in hand, Alexei and I make our way down the path toward Golden Gate Park.

The sun hangs low in the sky, casting an ethereal pinkish-purple glow across the sky that makes the bay look almost otherworldly.

"Shall we sit?" he suggests as we come upon an empty bench in a quiet stretch of the park.

"Sure," I agree, settling onto the cool metal and taking my first bite of soup. "Mmm," I moan appreciatively.

"Good, right?" he asks.

"Mm-hmm." Especially after the busy day we've had. And though I know I shouldn't indulge in something so rich and fatty when we're midseason at the ballet, I can't help but cheat—if just for today.

"Tell me more about your family," I request as we sit close together, watching the sun sink slowly into the water and turning the waves a brilliant gold.

"What do you want to know?" he asks, his posture relaxed and open.

"Do you talk with your brothers often?"

"At least once a week. Though we all share office space, so it's typically more like once a day."

"And what are they like?" I ask. Growing up, I'd always wanted siblings, and I'm curious about Alexei's.

"Maksim, my oldest brother, is a natural leader. He took on the role of head of the family at a pretty young age. Unfortunately, that makes him overly serious a good amount of the time."

I smile, my lips pressing together as I meet Alexei's eye.

He chuckles. "Very unlike me," he agrees, voicing my unspoken opinion.

"Dimitri's the middle child. He's smart and outspoken and entirely too much fun to tease. He and I used to fight a lot as kids. But now, I'd say of my two brothers, he and I get along best."

"Are you and your brothers close, then?"

"We have to be," he says and chuckles. "Our mom would knock our heads together if we ever stopped getting along."

I laugh. "She sounds like a good mom."

"Your mom actually reminds me of her. I bet they would get along well."

"You think it's because they have similar backgrounds? Coming over from Russia?"

Alexei studies me for a moment. "Could be," he agrees. "They're both certainly forces to be reckoned with, I would say." His tone takes on a ferocity that reveals his deep loyalty to his mom.

And I like how protectively he speaks about his family—his brothers, his mom. He's dedicated to them in a way I wouldn't normally associate with Bratva men. The ones I met from my childhood in Russia were always cold and calculating and brutal, not a single one as emotionally grounded and open as Alexei's proven to be.

Setting aside my meal, I turn my eyes back to the beautiful scenery before us. Alexei does the same, his arm curving around my shoulders as he pulls me close. The simple gesture fills me with warmth.

"Thank you for the perfect date," I murmur, smiling softly.

"You aren't disappointed that I didn't fly you off to Carmel or pamper you with a shopping spree?" he asks lightly, his tone playful.

I giggle, the sound somewhat foreign to me. I've never been a bubbly girl, but something about Alexei brings it out in me. "It's actually nice to see you *can* be normal," I tease.

"I'm pretty sure there's a compliment buried somewhere in that statement," he says.

As our eyes meet, a spark of excitement ignites in my belly. In truth, it was a compliment of sorts. Because I've never met anyone like Alexei.

Perhaps it's our considerable age difference, but I find he has a strength of personality, a confidence in who he is that no man around my age seems to possess. I find it extremely sexy.

Today, it was nice to see that he has that same unique flair and wit, even when we're doing something as ordinary as walking the pier or driving around town. He doesn't need to constantly be showing off —buying ballet companies or taking the entire cast clubbing—just so he can impress me.

While I'm confident that's why he did those things, it's significant that he can be as fun and charming when we're eating street food on a park bench as he is when we're dining with my mom at a Michelin Star restaurant.

His silver gaze searches my face as if reading the emotions that somersault through me, and his quiet intrigue sets my heart racing. I've never wanted to kiss him so badly as I do now, and without allowing myself to overthink it, I lean in, closing the distance between us.

Our lips meet in a shower of sparks that take my breath away. The overpowering chemistry between us bursts to life as my body fills with intense heat. Our lips move together, parting simultaneously as our tongues collide in a passionate dance.

And suddenly, it's all I can do not to straddle him right here on this park bench as we make out desperately. I don't think I can wait until we get back to his place before I have sex with him.

21

ALEXEI

Nadia tastes even more delicious knowing that she kissed me. This chemistry between us is powerfully compelling, the magnetism an overwhelming pull for me, and I love that, now that she's allowing it, it seems she's just as affected by the intense compulsion driving us together.

Her fingers rake into my hair, her fingertips pressing adamantly against the nape of my neck as she kisses me with a fiery determination that makes my pulse pound. I'm hard in a matter of moments, ready to fill her up as I find her intoxicatingly irresistible.

Our bodies turn automatically toward each other, our knees pressing together as my hand finds her hip. I pull her closer, needing more, and Nadia groans.

"Take me back to your place?" she breathes against my lips.

She doesn't have to ask me twice.

Though it's nearly painful to pull away from her, I break our kiss and peer deep into her mesmerizing green eyes. Then I rise, bringing her to her feet at the same time.

We quickly collect our spent bread bowls, tossing them in the trash on our way to the Golden Gate Park's car lot. I interlace our fingers as we walk, and Nadia glances down at our kissing palms, her cheeks flushing and adorable pink.

I wonder just how many times a man has held her hand.

I bet I could count it with my remaining free fingers.

We don't say another word as we make our way to the car.

Tension crackles between us, charging the air with an electric energy that makes my pulse race with anticipation. I can feel the excitement rolling off Nadia, and it turns me on like I can't believe.

I reach the passenger-side door and open it for her, holding it at the top edge as I keep her hand in mine until she's settled on my red leather seat. She looks up at me with an intense look, her eyes warning me that she might not have the patience to wait until we get home.

And damn if that doesn't make my cock throb.

Closing the door firmly, I make my way around to the driver's seat and slip inside my sports car. I don't even have time to press the button and start the engine. Nadia's fingers wrap around the front of my shirt and pull me closer.

Our lips meet halfway, above the center console, and I cradle her head, combing my fingers into her raven locks as I deepen the kiss. God, I want to please her all night long.

I crave Nadia like an addiction, thinking of her constantly when I'm not in her presence and unable to resist when she's near. Erection pressing adamantly against the zipper of my pants, I adjust myself as it starts to grow painful.

And that seems to redirect my beautiful ballerina's attention.

Our lips part as she glances toward my hip movement, and a moment later, her hand lands solidly on the bulge threatening to rip right through my slacks.

I groan, clenching my jaw as the feel of her fingers wrapping around my hard girth makes my cock throb. A soft gasp escapes Nadia's lips, and she slowly strokes me on top of the fabric, defining my pulsing length.

Her other hand joins the fun, her fingers deftly working the buckle and button of my pants. Then she carefully guides the zipper down to avoid catching me as she unveils my boxer briefs.

Tongue darting out to wet her lips, Nadia keeps her eyes trained on my lap, and it excites me to see the ravenous hunger in her stunning gaze. This girl is unlike anything I've ever known before—passionate, erotic, and insatiable. And despite her apparent trepidation when it comes to commitment, she's fearless in bed.

Her fingers get to work, hooking around the waist of my pants as she shows me what she wants, trying to pull them down over my hips. But in the car, it's a tricky angle, and I lift my hips as I help her.

Shoving my pants and boxers down to my knees, I release my swollen, aching cock. It stands impressively, rock-hard as I envision what she has in mind for me while we're still parked in the Golden Gate parking lot.

Nadia doesn't seem to mind.

Instead, she shifts, climbing onto her knees in the passenger seat so she can lean over the console and wrap her lips around my mushroom tip. Air hisses between my teeth at the exquisite sensation of her warm, wet mouth enveloping my cockhead.

My head drops back against the car's headrest as I groan with the sudden and intense wave of need. Nadia hums, extracting a jolt of pleasure from deep within my core. My cock twitches against her soft, exploring tongue.

Slowly, Nadia lowers her head into my lap, taking me into her mouth inch by tantalizing inch.

"*Fuck*," I groan as my pulse pounds in my hard length, swelling it even further.

I'm so hard and excited, I could shoot my load in a matter of moments. But I won't. I want to enjoy this sinful pleasure to the utmost. Bringing my palms to rest on the crown of Nadia's head, I collect her thick, wavy locks, getting them out of her way so she can maneuver more easily.

I gather them firmly in one hand then run my other slowly down her back and around the soft curve of her full ass, exploring her perfection as her hips press urgently into the air. As she sucks me off at a slow, deliberate pace, I knead one ass cheek before giving her a playful spank.

Nadia's squeal tapers into a moan that vibrates deliciously around my cockhead, and I suck a sharp breath in through my teeth as I fight to hang on a bit longer. Then her hips roll, inviting me to punish her again.

"You like it when I spank you, naughty girl?" I tease, kneading her other ass cheek.

Keeping my cock firmly inside her mouth, she hums a confirmation that makes my balls tighten dangerously. I bring my hand down once again, the sharp sound cracking through the car with a deliciously crisp snap.

Nadia's hips buck, and the responding groan that echoes deep from her body lights my veins on fire. I never knew a person could be this sexy. As she takes my considerable length, my cockhead pressing against the back of her throat, I think I just might explode with the intensity of my arousal.

A string of Russian curses issues from my lips as my hips start to thrust of their own volition. Nadia breathes through the punishing rhythm, her muscles lean and tense as she braces, allowing me to gently fuck her mouth.

Fingers tightening around her thick black locks, I grit my teeth with the effort to pace myself. When Nadia gags, her body jerking beneath my palm, I force my fingers to release her hair.

Nadia leans back to suck a deep breath in through her nose, but she keeps her lips wrapped around the tip of my cock, seeming ready to go for a second round. A moment later, she does, taking control of the pace once again as she guides her lips up and down my throbbing erection.

Feeling my pulse hammering through my hard length, I turn my attention to Nadia's jeans. Flicking open the button, I guide her zipper down, then shift my palm to work my fingers beneath the waistband of her panties.

Nadia shivers against my hand as I make my way toward the peak of her thighs, and the slick arousal I find there nearly sends me over the edge.

"Fuck, you're so wet for me," I groan with appreciation.

Nadia whimpers, her head pausing its motion as I start to stroke her silken slit. She trembles, her hips rolling as I press inside her entrance, and her walls tighten forcefully around the sudden penetration.

Gasping, her throat tightening around my cockhead, Nadia seems entirely consumed by her own excitement. I finger her more stridently, grinding the heel of my palm against her clit as I slide my fingers in and out of her wet depths.

Fucking hell, I'm so turned on it's painful. My cock twitches against Nadia's tongue, eager for more attention, and she gets the silent signal. Her motion resumes, her tongue gliding along the thick vein along my base.

At this rate, if she keeps using her mouth the way she is right now, I'm going to come in no time. My need to feel her tight pussy around my throbbing girth is overwhelming.

Fingers tightening in her hair once more, I stop Nadia's blowjob, gently easing myself from her mouth as I guide her head away from my lap. She releases my tip with a quiet *Pop* and moans as I continue to press inside her with two fingers.

"Not good?" she asks, her green eyes searching my face.

"On the contrary," I rasp, teasing her clit until she gasps deliciously. "Too good. I don't want to come in your mouth."

"Why not?" she asks, her voice breathy and sultry.

My cock twitches in response.

"Because I want to come here," I say, fingering her pointedly.

Nadia groans, her hips rocking back against me, and her eyes flutter closed.

I'll take that as a yes.

Moving my seat back and lowering it as far as it will go, I make room for Nadia. Then, only after I'm ready for her do I ease my fingers out of her wet pussy so I can remove her jeans. She helps me, surprisingly dexterous in the confined space as she shoves the fabric down past her knees and feet.

Naked from the waist down, she doesn't hesitate to climb across the console to straddle me. It feels like I'm a teenager again, but I love how insatiable and daring Nadia is with her sexuality.

"You are the sexiest woman I've ever met," I growl, gripping her hips firmly to steady her as she settles on top of me.

She bites her lip seductively, her green eyes finding mine with a smoldering intensity. Then her slender fingers wrap around my hard length, still moist from being inside her mouth, and she lifts her hips to guide me toward her entrance.

Easing down onto my iron rod of an erection, Nadia moans lasciviously. Her pussy tightens, sending a jolt of pleasure crackling up my spine. I grips her hips compulsively, my fingers digging into her supple flesh as I find myself dangerously close to release.

Then she slowly starts to rock on top of me. Using my body to stimulate her clit, she grinds against me as I ease in and out of her divine depths. I let her ride, exploring her body as she does. Hands roaming up beneath her sweater, I can feel the wet perspiration slicking her skin, and I want to taste its salty goodness.

In one swift motion, I take Nadia's top and whip it up over her shoulders and head, tossing it into the back seat. She breathes heavily, her arousal intensifying visibly as her nipples press against the lace enclosing them.

Leaning up off my reclined seat, I cup one breast with my palm, tuck the lace fabric beneath the soft swell, and capture the taut nub between my teeth. Nadia gasps, her hips rocking more forcefully as she tightens around me.

As I gently tease the hard flesh with my tongue, Nadia begins to ride me more passionately. One hand flies up to brace against the roof of my car as she rolls her hips with desperate need.

Wrapping an arm around her waist, I help support her as I release her nipple with a sharp *Pop*. Then I lick the soft flesh between her breasts, relishing the salty taste of her sweat.

"Oh, fuck!" she gasps, shivering violently as she rides me hard, and her pussy explodes around me.

I love the way she throbs and grips my cock, her body demanding I fill her with my seed.

I can't hold back any longer. The hot, desperate, entirely spontaneous car sex nearly makes me lose my mind, and I wrap my arms around Nadia's slender back, gripping her shoulders as I shove my hips upward, slamming inside her.

As she continues to pulse around me, my orgasm hits me like a freight train. Pouring cum deep in her depths, I grunt, my breathing heavy as black dots dance behind my eyes from the intensity of my pleasure.

Our motions slow and ebb as we gasp together, Nadia's breasts pressing, warm and firm, against my chest.

22

NADIA

I can't believe we just had sex in Alexei's car. I've never done something so racy, and it sends a thrill through my body. My walls twitch excitedly around his thick length as we cling to each other, breathing heavily from the heady relief and unexpected exertion.

A shared laugh bounces between us as I suddenly feel juvenile, like a teenager trying to hide her relationship from her parents. Alexei's molten silver eyes dance with his laughter, his sexy mouth spreading into a wicked grin.

"I think I could get used to this," he says, his deep voice vibrating through my body and making my clit twitch deliciously.

Leaning in, I brush a light kiss across his lips. "What, car sex? Or dates with me?"

"Both," he says simply, his strong hands sliding down my back to rest lightly on my hips.

The simple response makes my heart flutter.

Then I glance toward the foggy driver's side window as I consider the world outside for the first time. It's dark enough now, and the windows are tinted, so I doubt anyone can see us. But I wouldn't be surprised if I had the car rocking at one point in my eagerness.

"Shall I take you back to my place now?" Alexei suggests playfully, and I hear the echo of my original request from when we were kissing on the park bench.

"Yes, please," I murmur, my cheeks flushing.

Easing off him, I clamber back into the passenger seat and retrieve my pants and panties from the floor. I dress quickly as Alexei simply tucks himself away and buckles his slacks before starting the car.

I slip back into my sweater as he pulls out of the parking spot, and I'm buckled in by the time we leave the lot. Deep contentment blossoms in my belly as he races across town, and I find my all-consuming relief so relaxing that I can't bring myself to feel anxious about our speed.

"Do you always drive like this?" I ask, my voice still dreamy with the lingering haze of my lust.

"If I can help it," Alexei teases.

I laugh and let my eyes sink closed to retain the intense relaxation unwinding my muscles.

A warm hand grips my knee momentarily, giving me an affectionate, reassuring squeeze before vanishing to rest on the gear shift once more. I smile without opening my eyes, a hum of contentment issuing from my chest.

We pull into Alexei's parking garage a few minutes later, and as I rouse myself from my intensely relaxed state, he slips from his seat and rounds the car to open my door. Our hands find each other on our way to the elevators, and a giddy excitement blossoms in my belly.

I'm not used to so many public displays of affection, and I find them shockingly addictive. The more I touch Alexei, the more I want to, and this compulsion, I know, was part of what terrified me from the start.

I feel so far out of my control that it unsettles me. But the more I allow myself to explore this connection, the more I want to know where it might lead.

As we step into the elevator, Alexei and I find ourselves alone. He leans against the mirrored back wall, pulling me close as he traps my hands behind my back, keeping our fingers interlaced. His posture is one of complete ease, and I can't help but smile as I look up into his warm, playful gaze.

"What?" I ask, my pulse thrumming as I suddenly feel vulnerable under the heat of his appraisal.

"You certainly are talented, aren't you, Nadia?" His tone is teasing.

I arch an eyebrow, silently questioning his meaning.

"Not only are you the best ballet dancer I've ever seen—and despite my personal feelings for the art, I've seen a considerable number of performances—but you know how to give a blowjob better than any girl I've ever been with."

"And no doubt, that list is quite extensive," I probe gently. No man can have the moves Alexei does without considerable experience. Still, I note the flicker of jealousy that ignites in my chest.

It's a foreign feeling for me.

"Is that jealousy I detect?" he jokes. "Coming from the woman I practically had to coerce to go on a date with me?"

"Practically?" I question skeptically. "I was starting to wonder if you might not kidnap me outright."

"The thought did cross my mind," he says playfully, but the hint of danger that darkens his tone sends a shiver down my spine.

I wonder if he might not actually be telling the truth.

"Well then, I suppose it's good that I changed my mind."

Alexei hums his approval and leans in slowly to capture my lips. By the time the elevator doors ding open, I'm so lost in his kiss that I don't even notice. He guides me gently backward into his penthouse, his large hands encircling my waist.

I don't know where we're going until I feel the cold press of granite against my back. Then Alexei leans down to hoist my hips up onto his kitchen counter. My legs spread to accommodate him as he keeps me close, and I wrap my arms around his broad, muscular shoulders, splaying my fingers over the thick, corded muscles of his back.

"Wine?" he offers between kisses.

It takes a moment for the question to register, and when it does, I give a gentle nod.

He steps back, breaking our kiss to open a bottle, but as soon as his warmth leaves me, I want him back. Snatching the front of his shirt, I pull him toward me, demanding another kiss.

A low, rumbling chuckle reverberates through his body and into mine as Alexei's arms wrap around me once again. I trap him with my legs, holding him prisoner against my body as I hook my feet behind him.

Then I let my hands travel slowly down his chiseled chest and rippling abs. When I find the hem of his Henley shirt, I pull it up, exposing the delicious contours of his torso. Alexei lets me strip him, raising his arms to make it easier as I guide his shirt over his head. I toss it aside, only allowing the space of a moment before I reclaim his lips.

I can tell he likes the way I crave him, and that makes me bold, almost greedy as I demand his attention. My fingers travel softly over his exposed flesh, relishing the astonishing strength of his body. No one should be this powerful. His muscles feel tense and nearly vibrating with potential, the potential to undo me in an instant.

He takes his time undressing me now, working my shirt playfully up over my curves and head. Then his fingers unhook my bra, releasing my breasts to give him free reign. Strong hands guide me back onto the cold countertop.

I gasp as goosebumps erupt across my flesh at the contrasting temperature, and my back arches at the sudden shock. Growling approval, Alexei leans over me to capture a hardened nipple between his teeth. I cry out as he bites down softly.

"Are you ready for me, love?" he murmurs against my skin, his hands kneading my breasts as he shifts from one nipple to the other.

"Yes," I gasp, reaching above me to find purchase against the smooth slab of granite above my head.

Only then do I realize he's set me on a massive island that fills the center of his kitchen. The black stone beneath me is the color of onyx with small glimmering freckles of colorful mica.

Then my surroundings vanish once again as Alexei starts to hiss his way down my stomach to the top of my jeans. Looking down the length of my body at him, I admire the way his masculine face caresses my skin so gently. The contrast of his five-o'clock shadow tickling across my flesh sends sparks of pleasure dancing through my body.

He looks magnificent, his shoulder muscles rippling and bunching beneath his colorful tattoos as he undoes my jeans and guides them with my panties down over my hips, my thighs, my feet. Then he brushes a soft, chaste kiss across my bare clit.

I gasp, back rising up off the counter as a jolt of euphoria bursts through me. Christ, but my body responds to the slightest attention Alexei gives me. He doesn't stop there, though. After flashing me a wolfish smile, he runs his tongue along my slit, collecting my juices like one might a dripping popsicle.

Moaning with the overpowering lust that washes through me, I fight the urge to grab him by the hair and crush his lips against my clit. A moment later, he does it for me.

Hiking each of my legs over his shoulders, Alexei grants himself full access to my pussy, and he starts to lick and suck my throbbing sex with a tantalizing appetite.

"I could eat you up," he rasps, hot breath whispering across my pulsing clit as his eyes meet mine in a firework of heat.

An ironic statement, as we're in his kitchen. But somehow, that makes the offer that much more enticing. Then, before I can respond, he sucks my clit into his warm mouth and starts to circle the sensitive nub with his tongue.

"Oh, fuck!" I scream as an orgasm rips through me a moment later, the release catching me by surprise as he launches me over the edge without warning. A long, low moan escapes me as my clit throbs and pulses with the intensity of my relief, my core tightening as my body seeks something to grip and pull inside me.

A moment later, I hear the sound of a zipper sliding open, the heavy thump of a belt hitting the floor. Strong hands grip my hips, lifting me effortlessly off the smooth surface of the counter.

Alexei turns me, bending me over the hard surface in one fluid motion, and my cheek finds the glassy surface, warmed from my body heat, as my palms press eagerly against the counter.

His cockhead finds my slick entrance a moment later, and he shoves inside me without warning. A bestial grunt resonates inside my bones as Alexei pauses, buried inside me to the hilt, and I quiver with anticipation as he stretches me intoxicatingly.

"You drive me crazy. Do you know that?" he growls, his voice hoarse with arousal.

My pussy answers for me, gripping his hard length as my own excitement overwhelms me.

"Give me your hands," Alexei commands, and when I do, he crosses my wrists at the base of my back, trapping them there together with one sure hand.

The other finds its way to my hair, fingers combing into my thick locks and tangling as he grabs a handful. Then he pounds inside me with relentless force. My body screams with pleasure as the sharp flicker of pain releases a flood of adrenaline into my veins.

I pant against the counter, relishing the punishing pace as Alexei demands my pleasure. The purposeful tug he gives the roots of my hair only intensifies my arousal. His hands disallow the natural rock of my body as he hammers inside my pussy, filling me so completely as he drives his cockhead into my G-spot.

"Oh-fuck-oh-God!" I mewl, pinching my eyes closed as the heat of my excitement lights my body on fire. I'm so close to coming, but this time, I want to wait until he lets me. I want to obey his every command. Still, I'm dangerously close, and he's torturing my body so expertly that I don't know how long I can hold off.

"Come for me, love," Alexei rasps, his voice straining.

And I do, with glorious verve, falling apart around him as I relish the way he owns my body so completely. Pussy pulsing, I milk him forcefully, gripping his cock like a vise. My walls beg him to sink deeper into my depths, to fill me with his cum.

Alexei obliges, thrusting into me up to the hilt and shoving me against the edge of the counter as his hips jerk erratically. The low, throaty groan that follows sends a heat racing up my spine. I shudder beneath him, my body so entirely spent that my knees grow weak with relief.

And with the tenderness of a man in love, he releases my hair and wrists, gently easing my hands back down to the counter as he supports me.

I can't seem to form words. I'm so deeply satisfied, I feel suddenly impossibly heavy, my contentment filling me with a wave of exhaustion. As if sensing my sudden change in energy, Alexei withdraws from my body to collect me in his arms.

Scooping my feet up off the floor, he cradles me against his strong chest. My cheek rests against his muscular shoulder, and I peer up at him with newfound appreciation.

Wordlessly, he carries me into his room. Wine completely forgotten, he lays me softly on the bed. I snuggle close to him as he joins me, pulling the blanket up over our naked bodies. Sighing contentedly, I look up at his gorgeous face. He leans in to press a soft kiss to my lips, and as soon as my cheek finds the firm plane of his chest, I'm asleep.

THE HEAVENLY SCENTS of cooking onions and hot coffee urge me from my dreams, and as I slowly wake, I hum appreciatively. I don't know when's the last time I'd slept so soundly—definitely sometime before I left New York.

Soft light filters through the large picture window of Alexei's bedroom, and I'm amazed that I managed to sleep later than him once again. I'm normally a very early riser. From the looks of the skyline, I would guess it's six, maybe seven o'clock.

Rolling contentedly onto my back, I take another deep breath of the mouth-watering scent. Then I sit up and take my time climbing out of bed.

Rather than going to the kitchen naked, where I know we left our clothes last night, I open Alexei's closet and step inside to find a soft button-down I like. Wearing it like a tunic, with just the bottom few buttons holding it closed, I pad softly down the hallway and into the open kitchen.

"Morning," Alexei says, his eyes observing me with silent appreciation.

"Morning," I agree, joining him at the stove to see just what he's cooking.

He pauses stirring the egg and vegetable scramble in the pan to lean down and kiss me. My stomach flutters involuntarily.

"Coffee's ready," he says, gesturing with his chin before he returns his attention to the stove. "Do you want toast?"

"That sounds nice," I say as I pour myself a steaming cup of joe. I leave mine without cream or sugar.

Though I enjoy the taste more with flavoring, it's important that I think about everything I put in my body, especially during performance season. I already splurged with clam chowder yesterday. Now, breakfast today. I suspect I'm going to have to watch my diet closely if I plan on spending time with Alexei.

While he seems to eat healthy, a body his size needs far more calories than I'm allowed if I want to maintain my optimal dancer's weight. Still, I can feel the pounds looming just from enjoying the delicious smell of sauteed vegetables.

Rather than stand back and watch him prepare a meal for me, I get to work on the toast. It takes a bit of searching, as I don't know my way around his kitchen, but he seems content to let me find my way.

It feels surprisingly natural to work together in the kitchen. We shift around each other as if we'd been cooking together for years, and it makes my stomach flip-flop in funny ways. I've never done a real relationship before, but I find I'm rather excited by the prospect of dipping my toes in to see how this goes.

23

ALEXEI

Nadia is stuck in my brain, and as I ride the elevator up to our office of the Federov Brothers Investments building, I keep replaying our date in my mind. I never fall for girls like this. But with Nadia, I feel addicted. The more I have of her, the more I want.

And after this morning, I think she just might be willing to stick around long enough to give it a try.

The elevator doors open into the reception area, and I step out. As I open my mouth to greet our receptionist, raised voices catch my ear, coming from Maksim's office. Quirking an eyebrow, I turn to look at Jacquie, our receptionist.

"Have they been at it long?" I ask. I'm a few minutes early for our weekly meeting, so I don't know why they're already arguing.

"For the last ten minutes, I'd say. Since Dimitri came in."

"Thanks, Jacquie," I say, heading toward Maksim's office. "And good morning," I add, patting the top of the half wall that surrounds her desk.

"You too." The sweet, bespectacled woman in her late sixties beamed.

Maksim made a good decision hiring her. At the time, Dimitri and I had griped that he ought to hire someone easy on the eyes, but Jacquie's proven to be a valuable asset. And my oldest brother was right. If we had hired a young, empty-headed bombshell, Dimitri and I probably would have spent too much time competing over her.

Now, especially after Nadia danced into my life, I can fully appreciate Jacquie's value.

"Isn't it a bit early to be fighting over who gets the last bowl of ice cream?" I tease, bursting into Maksim's office without knocking.

Both my older brothers level dark scowls at me, at least agreeing that they don't find me funny. But I think it's a very valid—if not entirely personally crafted—jibe, seeing as that was their most common argument growing up.

"What's got you two all wound up this morning?" I ask, flopping into one of the plush couches along the back wall of Maks's office.

If this is a business investment disagreement, I might just skip this week's meeting. I don't really care about which restaurants we acquire or don't, and I'm in far too good a mood to sit in here listening to them argue when I won't end up weighing in anyway.

Normally, they insist I attend our investment meetings, but it's not my area of expertise. I'm just here to ensure no one touches what belongs to us. That means managing the security and protection details required when people work for or sell their businesses to us.

"Vlad and some of his men ended up in a violent confrontation when they went to collect at the distillery yesterday," Dimitri says flatly, his eyes flashing as his anger spikes.

I sit up, suddenly interested in the conversation. My jurisdiction doesn't extend to the businesses that borrow money from our banks and fall behind on their payments. I protect what we own outright. But if someone's raising a fuss about paying off the money they're owed, I'm willing to lend a hand—or at least some men—to straighten it out.

"What kind of violent confrontation?" I ask.

"Several members of another Bay Area Bratva were already there trying to shake down Lupe Rasco for the money he owes us. They told him they were there to collect for us, but Lupe knows better after having dealt with me and Vlad for so many years. He refused, and when our boys showed up, it turned into an altercation," Dimitri stated, his anger apparent in his raised tone.

"What other Bratva?" I demand.

"That's the thing. Vlad thinks he recognized a few of the men as Aleksandr Volkov's."

The room falls into icy silence at the bomb Dimitri just dropped. Aleksandr Volkov has been something of a nemesis in my brother's eyes over the last few years. *Pakhan* to a Bratva that could almost rival our own, he's the owner of San Francisco's two biggest casinos.

And the man is notoriously unafraid of stepping on people's toes. But his clan and ours have never gone head to head. Despite their overlapping amenities, the casino industry and restaurants aren't really the same breed of horse.

But he put himself firmly on Dimitri's shit list a few years ago by purchasing multiple restaurants we had our eye on for investment. Whether he did it intentionally or not, I don't know. But Dimitri certainly seems to think so.

I glance toward my oldest brother, Maks, suddenly registering what their argument was about. He's always been the level-headed one, the voice of reason.

Dimitri's the one with the hot temper, willing to burst in, guns blazing, if he thinks anyone's caused our family offense. I'm sure he's been waiting for an excuse to get back at Aleksandr for how many times the toothpick of a man has outmaneuvered him on closing a deal.

So their debate is whether or not to confront Aleksandr directly, and I'm confident I know where they both stand.

"That's not all," Dimitri says, his voice coming out as more of a growl now.

Maksim sighs, the sound revealing his aggravation, and I cock my head as I turn to look at Dimitri.

"I believe these men might likely be associated with the Bratva that nearly killed Camille. The one that warned us war is coming..."

Dimitri's words sit heavily between us. It's a powerful statement, one that makes logical sense in my mind. *But confronting Aleksandr with that level of accusation?* If we're wrong, Aleksandr won't just let that slide.

And if he's right, then this most definitely means war, like the threatening message said. The man who attacked Camille nearly killed her and Dimitri's child with whom his wife was pregnant at the time. *And if that same group is the one fighting with our men over collections?* Whoever it is, they're deadly serious.

"We can't go accusing one of the largest Bratvas in the Bay area based on Vlad *thinking* he recognizes the men as members of the Volkov clan," Maks says, his scowl returning in full force.

"No one else would dare challenge our territory," Dimitri growls.

"I don't care. We can't afford to fight a war on two fronts, so we need to be absolutely certain who this is," Maksim counters, his tone authoritative as he closes the discussion.

As the eldest brother and leader of our clan, when Maksim puts his foot down, his word is law. Dimitri and I are more . . . consultants. I can see the reluctant acceptance in the slump of Dimitri's shoulders.

"We're wasting an opportunity to get ahead of his next move," he grumbles under his breath.

And I know their argument comes full circle as they scowl at each other once more.

After a tense moment of silence, Maks turns his attention to me. "You never did find who that man was tied to?"

He doesn't have to say which man he's referring to. I know he means the one Dimitri killed to protect his wife, Camille. We disposed of the body, but I spent weeks trying to track him down.

I shake my head. "Trail went cold. Whoever hired him did a very meticulous job of hiding any connections that might lead back to the source."

"I want you to dig further into the conflict at the distillery. Get me concrete evidence that it was Aleksandr's men," Maks says, his eyes flicking between me and Dimitri as if to say, *Does that settle it?*

I nod, rising from my chair, glad I have a mission.

"Alexei?"

I turn to meet Maks's steady gray gaze.

"Start adding security details to patrol all our assets. I don't want another one getting burned to the ground. And put a tail on Aleksandr Volkov—*discreetly*." He emphasizes the last word as Dimitri straightens in his chair.

"On it," I agree, heading for the door.

Neither of my brothers stops me to insist I stay for the weekly business meeting. This is more important. I rarely participate in the investment decisions, anyway. Dimitri can catch me up to speed later.

24

NADIA

I take my time blowing dry my hair and applying makeup for my date with Alexei tonight. My life feels almost strangely at peace right now, my performances going better than I ever could have dreamed, my time with Alexei more fun and entertaining than I could have imagined.

We've been dating for several weeks now, and each time he asks when he can see me again, I get a silent thrill. Because the attraction, the magnetic pull, doesn't seem to be waning even a little. If anything, it's only intensified.

As I stand, considering my outfit for tonight, my phone rings, and I head into my bedroom to answer it.

"Hey, Mom," I greet, putting her on speaker as I take her into the closet with me.

"Hi, honey, is this a good time? You're not getting ready for a performance, are you?"

"Anytime is a good time. No, I'm actually getting dressed for a date with Alexei," I say, unable to contain the smile that tugs at my lips when I say his name.

"How's that going? Are you two still doing well?"

"Yes," I admit, sorting through my dresses to find one that will suit our night in.

"He's comfortable with your crazy work hours and show schedule?" she presses.

It says a lot that my mom is concerned about the possible frustrations Alexei might find in dating me. It doesn't seem to bother her that he's considerably older than me. In truth, she's never seemed so invested in a relationship of mine working out before. He made a very good impression on her during our dinner while she was visiting.

"So far, so good," I admit. "We've both been very busy lately. And rather than demanding more of my time, he seems pretty content working with my schedule, grueling as it is."

"That's so nice," Mom says.

I agree distractedly as I pull a high-neck hunter-green dress off the rack. It's soft and flowy but also stylish and flattering. It'll be perfect. "He's seemed preoccupied enough by his work lately that he might just be as busy as I am," I joke lightly, heading back into my bedroom to get dressed.

"What does he do again?" she asks, making my stomach flip.

"He . . . works with his family. Heading their security team," I say delicately.

Fortunately, my mom doesn't seem to notice my moment of panic. "But he's finding time for you?" A hint of concern registers in her voice.

"Yes, Mom. Really, we're great."

"I'm happy to hear it."

"Were you calling for a reason?" I ask, scooping my hair over my shoulder so I can zip the back of my dress.

"Just checking in," she says. "I'll let you go so you and Alexei can enjoy your time together. Call me soon, okay?"

"Are you working tomorrow?" Digging through my drawer, I find a pair of thigh-high pantyhose and my garter belt. It doesn't take me long to decide to wear it—just for fun.

"No, feel free to call whenever. I love you, Nadia."

"Love you too!"

The phone beeps to signal the call ending, and I stoop to find a pair of black ankle boots. Then I head out my front door, heading to Alexei's penthouse. It seems I spend all my free nights there anymore.

And I thoroughly enjoy it.

While I love my little apartment near Chinatown, it's missing the person who has taken my life by storm. I can't seem to get enough of him.

The drive is short and sweet, and I park in the visitor's lot before heading into the elegant lobby of Alexei's building.

"He said to send you right up, Miss Lukyan," Alexei's doorman says with a polite smile as I stride in the door.

"Thanks, Gus." I keep walking, heading to the elevator to ride it all the way up, my heart thrumming an excited beat.

As soon as I reach the top floor and the doors open onto his beautifully decorated space, I recognize the low, masculine sound of Alexei's voice.

"*Mne vse ravno. Prosto sdelay eto,*" he says into his cell phone as he paces his living room—*I don't care. Just get it done.*

I pause at the agitation in his tone, my feet just inside the entryway of his luxurious penthouse. That he's speaking in Russian makes me think it must be business related—Bratva related. A detail of his life that still puts knots in my stomach. But I try not to think about what it means. Alexei is a very different man from the Bratva men I knew in Russia.

I worry my lip, wondering whether he would want me here if he knew I'd arrived. I feel as though I might be eavesdropping on an important conversation.

Then, his steps pause in the middle of a turn as he's pacing, and his eyes land on me. "I have to go. Call me once you find him," he commands in Russian, his voice authoritative, his eyes penetrating as he locks his gaze on mine.

Then he removes the phone from his ear and hangs up without another word.

"You look beautiful," he observes, stalking toward me.

The shift in his demeanor warms the chill trickling through my veins. Whatever had him so agitated on the phone he doesn't seem to carry into our time together. And while I'm curious, I also hesitate to ask. "Thanks."

"You're sure you don't want to go out? In a dress like that . . . you ought to be shown off."

Smiling coyly, I manage to unglue my feet from their frozen state on his floor. Giving a twirl to show off my dress, I approach him. Alexei meets me halfway, his strong hands finding my hips and pulling me firmly against him.

"You don't think this is a good dress to cook in?" I ask innocently. I won't give him the satisfaction of knowing I had a few other things in mind when I picked it.

How easily accessible my body is to him in this dress, for instance.

"I won't complain," he murmurs appreciatively, his eyes combing down my body and sending a shiver up my spine.

Then he leans in slowly to slant his lips over mine.

I melt into him, his broad shoulders and firm chest warming my body as I return the passionate embrace. He doesn't break away until we're both breathless and my heart is pounding with anticipation. He smiles down at me wolfishly, as if he can feel the force of my pulse hammering through my body and knows it's him doing that to me.

"So, what's for dinner?" I ask, trying to distract myself before we move on to dessert without actually eating.

"I thought we could make pasta," he says casually, interlacing our fingers to guide me into the kitchen.

Two wine glasses and a frost-glazed bottle of Sauvignon Blanc sit on the island where Alexei and I had sex several weeks ago, and my stomach flutters at the vivid memory.

"That sounds fun." Then I spot the range of ingredients waiting for us on the countertop. "Oh, you mean make-make pasta," I observe, breaking into a broad grin. I haven't made pasta from scratch since I was a child. After we fled Russia, Mom and I just never seemed to have the time to enjoy playing in the kitchen.

"Are you up for the challenge of homemade ravioli?"

"Definitely."

I head to the sink to wash my hands as Alexei pours us each a glass of white wine. Then he turns on music, the classy sound of Frank Sinatra trickling from his speakers.

"How was the performance last night?" he asks as we set up two separate stations to mix our flour and egg.

"Sold out and with another standing ovation at the end," I say. It's still a bit surreal to know I am the prima bringing in so many avid fans. After fighting for a role like this all my life, it's hard to think of it as really mine.

"Somehow, I'm not surprised. Watching you dance . . . it's mesmerizing."

The compliment sends a ripple of warmth through my body. I love that as powerful and dangerous and intimidating as Alexei might come across, he's both charming and a gentleman when it counts.

Pasta dough mixed, it's time for the rolling pins, and it's a pleasant sight to watch the brawny muscles of his strong arms flexing and bulging to flatten his pasta into a thin sheet. He's far more effective than I am, and I wonder how often he might do this.

Seeing him in the kitchen does odd things to my body. I like knowing that, even though his family probably owns half the restaurants in the Bay Area and he could go out to eat every night of the week, Alexei still took the time to learn the art of cooking. I'm not quite sure if I can think of something sexier.

The serenity of the moment is broken as his phone starts to buzz across the slab of granite countertop. A storm cloud overcomes his expression as Alexei glances down at the caller ID.

"*Blyat*," he curses under his breath. "I'll be right back," he says to me then, dusting off his hands and snatching up his phone.

I can hear the muffled sound of his voice as he leaves the main area of his home completely, vanishing into a room I would assume is his study. In the time he's gone, I finish rolling out my dough, then prepare our raviolis by taking the cheesy spinach mixture he prepared and placing small portions of it across the noodle's surface.

Next, I place his thin noodle sheet on top and gently press the pasta seams together, removing the air between them. I keep one ear on the muffled sound of his voice, my eyes darting toward the closed door every now and again.

Whatever he's on the phone about seems to be a problem. His tone is gruff, almost a growl, and he's never left our time together to deal with business before.

The sauce is simmering on the stove, and I'm just adding the raviolis to a boiling pot of water when he comes back out of the office, a deep frown creasing his strong brow. A look of frustration tightens his lips into a flat line.

"Something wrong?" I ask tentatively. Then I focus my eyes pointedly on my task so he won't see my unease.

"Sorry. I don't like work issues interrupting our night." His eyes assess my progress, and wordlessly, he steps up behind me to press a kiss below my ear.

I tip my head to expose my neck willingly to his attention, and goosebumps flash across my skin as he pulls me close, his arms wrapping around my waist.

"Do you want to talk about it?" I ask, stirring the creamy tomato sauce. Nerves fizzle in my stomach as I broach a topic I've been avoiding since we first started dating.

Alexei's quiet for long enough that I turn in his arms to peer up at his strained face. He seems lost in his own thoughts, and I'm tempted to press my thumbs between his brows to smooth the tension from his face.

As our eyes meet, the steel in his softens slightly, his shoulders dropping as he physically tries to shed his stress.

"My brothers and I run a company together, as you know. One that deals in lending and investment."

"Right," I agree.

Alexei sighs heavily. "We're the most prominent family in the Bay Area restaurant acquisitions industry, owning over thirty businesses outright between San Diego and Seattle. And we subsidize nearly a hundred more."

For a moment, I'm struck dumb by the sheer size of their production. I hadn't realized they were on that massive of a scale.

"But it's a cutthroat business with plenty of sharks looking to take a slice out of our business and profits. It means . . . it's not just growing our business but protecting the assets we own."

"Right," I agree slowly, spotting the point where Alexei's job comes into play but not quite sure how this ties in with what's eating at him.

"All this to say, some other . . . family has decided they would prefer a piece of our pie rather than being happy with the one they've cooked themselves."

Alexei releases me, turning his attention to straining the fully cooked ravioli. I step into action, pulling plates down and then pouring the sauce over our pasta after he serves them up.

"I'm sorry, I'm a little confused. Are you saying someone else has decided to buy into the restaurant industry on a mass scale?"

Considering California is a massive state and San Francisco is a mecca of culinary artists, this doesn't seem unreasonable to me. Even with how large Alexei's family business is, there are countless more restaurants to be had by someone who might want to invest.

We sit at the table, me across from Alexei, and from his expression, I gather he's struggling with a decision once again.

"Nadia, may I be frank with you?"

"Always."

"I've been chasing a Bratva that has been threatening war against my family for nearly a year now. My brother, Dimitri, has been facing minor aggravations in which he sets his sights on acquiring a specific location, only to find someone has swooped in and taken it—a dirty way of business, but still perfectly within a man's rights."

"Right," I agree as Alexei takes a bite.

"But we've had far more disturbing issues to contend with recently. The worst of which is that Dimitri's wife—the one who runs the French restaurant Le Fleur—she was attacked almost a year ago. Someone set fire to her restaurant, which nearly burned down. And at the same time, we received a note warning about an impending territory war. The note connected the violent acts done to Camille and her restaurant with this Bratva's intention to invade our territory. But they didn't identify themselves, and since then, the offenders have pretty much vanished. Until now."

Heart in my throat, I swallow hard, suddenly losing my appetite. "And you have no idea who's behind this?"

"At first, we didn't. But my job recently has been to find who it is. I'm closing in on them, which could mean trouble. And the more I dig, the less I like what I find. I'm starting to worry about my family's safety. If the evidence I'm uncovering is as big as it seems, we're facing a conflict unlike anything we've seen before."

25

ALEXEI

The stricken look on Nadia's face makes me question whether it was the right choice to tell her what's been troubling me. And the anxiety in her emerald eyes tells me all I've done is transfer my stress to her.

"Is this... something I should worry about?" she asks.

Dinner forgotten, I reach across the table to take her hand, brushing the pad of my thumb across her knuckles. "You have nothing to fear. I won't let anything happen to you. I would protect you with my own life," I say adamantly.

Nadia's features soften once again, and it warms my chest to know she trusts me enough to believe my conviction at this point. We've come a long way from the woman who wouldn't trust me as far as she could throw me when we first met.

Still, I'm troubled by the information my men and I have uncovered in the past few weeks. Particularly about Aleksandr Volkov. I suspect Dimitri's frustration with the casino owner may have more validation than I'd given my hot-tempered brother credit for.

Now that my men have been tracking him closely, it would seem he's definitively stepping from the world of gambling and casinos into restaurants. But more than that, it seems the number of new recruits he's initiated just in the last few weeks alone would say his expansion will be rather aggressive.

And the shipments of guns my men watched being unloaded into one of his casinos just tonight would very much make me think he's gearing up for a fight.

Where before, I had been more inclined to think Dimitri's hot-headed words were out of competitive frustration, I'm starting to think his instincts were spot on.

Still, I haven't found any concrete evidence connecting Aleksandr to the man who attacked Camille, the fire at her old establishment, or even the recent conflict at the distillery a few weeks ago.

Whatever Aleksandr has in store for those weapons, he's keeping it under wraps.

And that sets my teeth on edge.

"Alexei?" Nadia says, her soft voice calling me out of my reverie.

"Hmm?" I ask, looking up at her striking face as I realize I've been staring at her hand.

"I asked if you are worried they will target your brother's wife again."

"They won't get near her. Or her restaurant. I've seen to that. Besides, Dimitri is so fiercely protective of his wife and child that I would feel sorry for anyone who tried to touch either one of them. The last man who did is now in several different locations along the coast of California."

"I don't know whether to take that as a joke or not," Nadia observes dryly.

And her humor is just enough to lift me from my sour mood. I shouldn't be letting my troubles get in the way of a rare evening we get to spend together.

Smiling wolfishly, I reply, "I'll leave it up to you to decide."

Her sharp eyebrows rise in a look of surprised intrigue, but she doesn't press me further, and I'm grateful. I don't really want to tell her I was the one in charge of vanishing the man Dimitri killed to save Camille's life.

"I think this conflict has put a lot on your mind," Nadia observes, her eyes lighting as she says it. "You've been rather preoccupied, and I think you're in need of a distraction."

I had been thinking the same thing when I suggested cooking dinner together. Something to keep my hands and mind busy. But I sense that isn't where Nadia's going.

"And what, exactly, did you have in mind?" I ask, leaning back in my chair to cross my arms.

The dangerous smile that follows sets my veins on fire.

Without a word, Nadia takes our half-eaten plates and sets them aside on the kitchen island. She walks to my phone, resting facedown on the counter, and changes the song to something with a cool, sexy beat. Then she turns up the volume.

I watch with intense interest as she finds the rhythm of the song, her hips rocking as she nods along.

And when she turns to look at me, intense heat flashes in her eyes.

Whatever her intentions are, I know I'm going to like what she has in store for me.

Nadia walks slowly back to me, and her flowing green dress, which emphasizes the brilliant color of her eyes, sways and swishes enticingly around her body. I find my eyes drawn to the long, fit lines of her legs.

She's still wearing her black suede stiletto ankle boots she came in with, and they click softly against the marble floor until she's standing right before me.

She has my undivided attention now as she takes her chair and drags it around the corner of the table, setting the back against the table's edge.

"Hand," she demands, holding her own hand out, palm up as if I'm supposed to give her something.

I do as she says, placing my palm on top of hers as my fingers curl naturally around her slender hand. She then guides my arm up, flipping my palm over so my hand is more like a support. And she uses it as such to balance herself when she steps up onto the chair.

Then, the table.

From where I sit, I have the perfect view as Nadia releases my fingers and peers down at me over her shoulder. And from the fire in her eyes, I can guess she realizes just how enticing she looks right now.

Locking her knees, Nadia bends low to retrieve her glass of wine—and in the process, gives me a tantalizing peek of what lies beneath her mid-thigh-length dress. I suck a sharp breath in between my teeth at the garter straps that press into her milky thighs, the lace-lined pantyhose that I'd assumed was simply black until this point.

My cock comes immediately to life, swelling against my slacks at the momentary glimpse of what awaits me.

Nadia takes a slow sip of wine as she turns to face me, her hips forming provocative circles to the song's rhythm. Setting the glass out of the way, she gives herself a perfect platform to dance on, and I'm so intensely aroused by her bold display that I find it impossible not to sit and watch her.

And she watches me at the same time.

Her shocking green eyes dare me to think of anything but her as she runs her hands up and down her body, molding the flowing fabric against her perfect curves as she moves for me. My cock throbs when her lips part slightly in a look of pure temptation.

Then Nadia tilts her head, scooping her long, luscious black locks to one side and exposing her long neck, which I would love nothing more than to suck on. Her arms reach behind her as she rotates once more to show me the zipper she drags slowly down her back. As each inch parts, she exposes the sharp lines of her shoulder blades.

In a fluid, natural dance that matches the wonderfully suggestive song she put on, Nadia starts to strip for me. Her hands guide her dress up her body inch by inch, revealing first the tops of her pantyhose, then the lace-clad apex of her thighs. She turns in a constant rotation, showing me every angle as she uncovers the black satin-and-lace thong.

Then it's the smooth, flat surface of her stomach and the garter belt that rings it, delicate lace and ribbing wrapping around her hips before the straps extend down to connect to her stockings.

I groan as the dress rises up over her breasts to reveal her sexy cleavage and the balconet bra that scoops so low, it scarcely covers her nipples. I know because I can see the dark circles beneath the transparent black lace.

Christ, Nadia is the cheekiest woman I've ever met, dressing as if her sole purpose tonight was to taunt me with her perfection. She finishes taking her dress over her head with a sexy flourish, curving her body so the hunter-green fabric slides past her hair and drops to the floor in a soft pool of color.

Erection pulsing, I press against my zipper, threatening to tear straight through the fabric of my pants so I can get to Nadia, to feel her wet warmth wrapped around me. But I'm so consumed by her erotic dance that I can't bring myself to interrupt it.

I've never seen anyone dance the way she's dancing for me. Not strippers, not club girls, not ballet dancers. This is something entirely unique to Nadia. She's perfectly balanced on her heels, her muscular legs bending and stretching with impressively flexible dexterity. And her waist and chest seem to move as if entirely separate entities.

Her arms know just how to lure me in, forming beautiful shapes between provocative caresses that drive me mad with jealousy.

Nadia dips, sinking seductively onto her knees and leaning toward me, and I find myself drawn toward her, leaning forward in my chair, closing the distance between our lips.

Soft fingertips comb back into my hair and curve around my ear before stroking softly along the line of my chin, and the last inch of space between us vanishes as Nadia gives me a slow, soft taste of her lips.

I groan, leaning forward and reaching for her, unable to resist any longer.

I have to touch her.

But Nadia draws back, pulling away from me and rocking onto her heels as she rests her hips against them. Her knees spread automatically as she opens her thighs. It's the single best view I think I've seen in my life, every inch of her on display beneath the flimsy slip of fabric that covers her pussy and breasts.

Need pounding through my veins, I reach for her again, leaning against the table so I can cup one supple breast. Her nipple is hard and eager beneath my palm, telling me she's just as turned on by me watching her as I am.

Then a sharp snap accompanies the resulting sting on the back of my hand as Nadia swats it away.

"Naughty," she teases, rising to her feet and dancing out of reach. "This is my show. You can't touch until I'm good and ready for you to."

A low growl rumbles from my chest as I fight to contain my overwhelming urge to follow her onto the table. But I don't. Remaining seated, I sit tall, gripping the edge of the table to keep myself where I'm supposed to be.

And while I would love nothing more than to tie her up and punish her for teasing me, I want to see exactly what Nadia has in store for me because my feisty ballerina is proving far too enticing to want to subdue.

26

NADIA

I know from the heat in his gaze that I'm in for some serious punishment, and my panties moisten at the thought of the spanking coming my way. But I love the thrill of teasing Alexei. I never knew how exciting it could be to walk the line of pleasure and pain, danger and safety.

And he's always up for being playful—even after a bad day. He seemed so stressed tonight, I just want to bring him some relief. As I watch the desire smoldering in his eyes, I know my plan is working.

The music transitions into another song, and I match the new beat as I pick up where I left off, teasing my breasts as I torture Alexei with that fact that he doesn't get to touch me. Then I move slowly down my body.

Crouching, I spread my thighs again, loving the way Alexei's eyes covet my body as he openly appreciates me. Then I put one hand behind me, steadying myself as I arch my back. His agonized groan sends a jolt of arousal through my body, and I watch his hungry face as I reach between my thighs.

I rub my clit over the soft fabric of my panties, stimulating myself as I put on a show. I can feel my slick arousal, warm and wet, as it dampens the fabric covering me, pooling with my excitement.

As I play with myself in front of Alexei, teasing him as I touch myself, I roll my hips to the song's beat, turning it into a provocative dance.

"Fuck, Nadia," Alexei rasps, leaning forward in his chair.

"Fuck me?" I moan playfully, a wicked smile curving my lips.

"All night," he promises, his shoulders straining as he white-knuckles the edge of the table.

Shifting onto my hands and knees, I crawl across the table toward him once more.

"Deal," I breathe when my face is less than a foot from his.

His eyes flick down to my lips, the ravenous hunger there sending a shiver up my spine. And I know I'm not going to stay in charge for much longer if I don't do something about it.

Coming to sit on the edge of the table, my hips resting in the space between his hands, my legs dangling over the edge, I lean in to kiss Alexei deeply. Tongue delving between his teeth, I appreciate the flavor of him.

He responds eagerly, his tongue tangling with mine, his hands releasing the table to grip my exposed thighs. And I let him, the fire in my belly consuming me as I moan lustily against his lips.

Then, as his hands start to roam higher, exploring my body, I raise one foot, bringing it between us. And when my toe finds his sternum, I push him forcefully back into his chair. The heat of his expression comes with a scintillating warning.

I'm playing a dangerous game.

But in our weeks together, I've come to trust Alexei, to know that he would never actually hurt me. And I like pushing him when it comes to sexual play. Because he knows just how far to take the game. God, I love the way he plays it.

He grips his chair arms now as his eyes rake down my stocking-clad leg to the toe of my boot pinning him in his seat. His silver gaze flashes back up to my face.

"No touching," I remind him with impish authority.

He snarls, his arms flexing as he clenches the chair convulsively. But still, he obeys, remaining in place even when I remove the pressure of my foot from his chest. And because he's been exceedingly patient, I think it's time to reward him.

Sliding off the edge of the table, I come to stand before him. Then I sink onto my knees, my eyes never leaving his as my hands find his thighs. Slowly, I work my way up his thick, muscular legs.

"You're going to be the death of me," he rasps, his body nearly vibrating with the effort it takes him to hold still.

"Then you don't want a blowjob?" I ask innocently, pausing for a moment with my fingers on his belt.

"Nadia," he warns as the arms of his chair groan with the force with which he grips them.

My lips twitch with amusement as I get to work opening his pants. "I'm in charge tonight," I say. "All you get to do is sit back and enjoy."

I grip his hard length, guiding it out of his boxer briefs, and Alexei groans. The tendons of his jaw jump along his cheeks as he grinds his teeth, his eyes closing with the effort to restrain himself.

My clit throbs with fresh arousal at the intensity of his excitement. His cock is rock-hard and twitches in my grasp. I can't wait to have him inside me.

But first, I want to make him feel good.

Lowering my head, I take his silken tip between my lips, and as air hisses between Alexei's teeth, I lick and circle his cockhead with my tongue.

"Fucking Christ," he growls, his voice hoarse with lust.

Then I start to suck him, taking his impossibly thick girth into my mouth until he's pressing against the back of my throat. He's almost too big for me, his tip challenging my gag reflex before I can even swallow his entire length.

But he seems to enjoy the way I stroke the thick vein of his cock with my tongue as I ease him in and out of my mouth. Legs tense beneath my palms, Alexei gives a valiant effort trying to remain in his seat, to hold back for as long as he can.

In no time, I've completely soaked through my panties, my excitement so intense that all I want is for him to fuck me. Still, I swallow him again and again, slicking his hard length with saliva as I give him the best blowjob I can.

Twitching beneath me, Alexei can't seem to hold back for long.

My game is over in an instant as I push him too far.

Strong hands grip me as he pulls his cock from my mouth.

Then he lifts me up off the floor and back onto the table once more. I gasp as he spreads me across its length, lying me flat on my back, and he doesn't waste time stripping. Shoving his pants down around his knees, he joins me on the table a moment later.

His hips guide my knees apart, and as he hovers on top of me, one arm supporting his weight, his other hand reaches down to shove the soft fabric of my panties to the side.

I cry out as his cockhead finds my entrance and he slams inside me.

He fucks me hard, his thrusts powerful and deep, and he pounds me hard enough to make the sturdy table rock and groan beneath us.

All the while, his free hand explores my body, groping and kneading my flesh with a demanding greed. I gasp when he gets to my breasts and pinches my nipples mercilessly.

"You think you're funny, don't you?" he growls dangerously. "Making me watch you touch yourself, turning me on like you think I won't take what's mine. You're a naughty little tease, and you just earned yourself a very big punishment."

I shiver violently at the dark, sinful promise.

"What are you going to do to me?" I breathe, my question tapering into a moan as he shoves inside me.

"Whatever I want," he rasps, his hand gliding up my arm and raising it above my head.

He does the same to my other hand, pinning my wrists above my head with one firm grasp. His hips roll as he grinds against my clit with each thrust, penetrating me deeply. I arch into him, panting as I take the punishing pace with enthusiasm.

His free hand combs into my hair, and he takes a handful as he fists his fingers in my hair. Then he jerks my head back, exposing my neck.

"I hope you're good with makeup," he mocks darkly.

A violent shiver runs down my spine.

Taking my earlobe between his teeth, he bites it almost painfully. My clit throbs in response, my walls tightening as I grip his cock inside me. Then he moves lower, suctioning his lips behind my ear as he sucks on the tender flesh.

It drives me absolutely crazy.

Crying out, I buck beneath him, so intensely turned on that I almost don't care that he's marking me like one might mark their territory.

"Oh, God, I'm going to come," I gasp, shocked that he could drive me so quickly to this point.

"Don't you dare," he breathes against my flesh, and I know I'm not getting out of this without a thorough punishment.

I can't wait.

Alexei moves his lips a few inches lower and repeats the tantalizing punishment, sucking my skin between his lips with bruising force as he raises another hickey along my neck.

"Oh, fuck, please!" I beg, quivering with my effort to hold on.

My nipples are so hard and sensitive that even the lace covering them feels unbearably rough. I wish I'd taken the time to remove Alexei's shirt because I desperately want to feel his skin against mine.

"Please, what?" he teases, releasing my skin and letting his lips brush lightly against my neck.

"Please, let me come," I whimper, my hips rolling and grinding as the table rocks beneath us.

"That depends. Tell me, love, who's in charge?" He suctions against my neck for a third time, and as his tongue licks the bruising flesh, I can't hold on.

I cry out as my orgasm crashes through me like a tidal wave. Breath heaving from my lungs, I see stars behind my eyelids as my walls spasm around Alexei's hard length. My clit twitches, sending bursts of electric pleasure out from my core and tingling down to my toes.

Alexei snarls, fucking me harder.

"You're a disobedient little flirt, aren't you?" he rasps, releasing my wrists to wrap his fingers around my throat.

I gasp, shuddering against the threatening hold—though I know whatever he does next is only going to turn me on more.

He waits until the last of my aftershocks subsides before he executes my next punishment. He slides out of me, leaving a hollow ache deep inside my core. I whimper, missing his presence instantaneously as he shifts off the table.

But I don't have long to wait. Strong arms wrap around me as he lifts me off the table. Hoisting me over his shoulder, he carries me like a sack of potatoes.

"Alexei!" I protest, squirming in his grip as I brace against his strong back.

He answers me with a sharp spank across my ass, following it immediately with a matching one on my other ass cheek. I squeal even as my pussy throbs from the tantalizing punishment. When his fingers push my panties aside once more to spread my folds, intense excitement pools in my belly once more.

Two fingers delve inside me a moment later, and I pant as he fingers me, even as he carries me toward his bedroom.

"God, you're so fucking wet," he growls, fingering me more urgently before withdrawing them to circle my clit.

His fingertips are slick with my arousal, and I moan lustily at the intoxicating pleasure that radiates from my sensitive bundle of nerves. He pauses once we enter his bedroom, flicking on the light and moving to his dresser to withdraw something from the top drawer, even as he continues to hold me draped over his shoulder.

Then he takes me into his closet.

I shiver with excitement at this new adventure. We haven't had sex in here before. But when Alexei sets me lightly on my feet and spins me toward the rack that holds his ties, I'm more than a little intrigued.

Cool metal closes around my wrist a moment later, drawing my eyes downward, and my pulse quickens as Alexei tightens the handcuff with a soft click. Then he lifts my arm up to the top bar of his tie rack and loops the cuff's chain around it.

His warm fingers close around my other wrist a moment later, and he guides that hand up to the open manacle. I shiver as it latches snugly, trapping my arms securely above my head.

"This is what happens to naughty girls who don't do as they're told," he warns, his hands skimming down to my breasts as he gropes me from behind. Then he flicks my nipples, sending a sharp jolt to my core.

I moan, rocking my hips back against him involuntarily. I look over my shoulder to watch as he unbuttons his shirt and shrugs out of it. Next, he does his pants, pushing them down over his hips as he strips down.

Body heating at the gorgeous sight of his naked, tattooed body, I lightly bite my shoulder to keep silent. I crave Alexei with a need I never knew I could possess before him. The longer we're together, the more I yearn for him.

"This," he says, snapping one of my garter straps against my ass with a sharp bite of pain, "I like. These" —his hands reach around my hips, one palm sliding down the soft fabric of my panties to stroke across my clit— "have to go."

His fingers wrap around the fabric a moment later.

With a forceful jerk, he shreds the fabric, ripping them off my body, and I gasp from the tantalizing sting that accompanies his move. Bundling the panties, he then holds them in front of my lips.

"Open," he commands, and I shiver, a combination of arousal and horror burning inside me. "Open, Nadia," he repeats. "Bad girls get gags while they're spanked, and if you don't accept these, I promise you won't like the alternative."

My lips part on a gasp, and he takes the opportunity to press the balled-up fabric into my mouth.

"You don't get to spit them out until I say," he rasps as I taste the tang of my own arousal soaking the fabric. My pussy throbs in response.

"Good girl," he praises when I obediently close my lips. Then he guides my legs apart by placing one foot on the inside of my ankle and pushing it outward.

He reaches around me once more, his hands boldly exploring my body, and when his fingers stroke the seam of my slit, teasing my entrance, I shudder violently, moaning around the fabric that muffles my voice.

"I fucking love the sound of that," he purrs against my ear.

I roll my hips convulsively, throbbing to have his cock inside me. He releases a dark chuckle as he steps back. Continuing to cradle my clit with one hand, he runs his other hand over the curve of my ass, massaging and petting me.

Then he lifts his hand, bringing it down hard a moment later. I squeal around my panties, my hips jerking forward against his palm as my skin stings from the punishment. But his hand is back a moment later, soothing the burning after effect.

"Is this what you wanted, Nadia?" he rasps, his fingers stroking between my folds.

Air hisses between his teeth as he feels how wet I am. Then he presses two fingers inside my pussy.

"Do you think I can make you come just by spanking you?" he teases, sliding his fingers in and out of me until my walls tighten around him.

Then he brings his palm down on my other ass cheek, and I scream with mingled pain and pleasure, my skin burning as my clit pulses. I'm so close to coming, I can hardly breathe, and every time he moves his fingers inside me, I think I might just explode.

"Are you ready to come for me, love?" he asks, his voice low and full of erotic promise.

Whimpering, I nod.

"Good girl. When I spank you this time, I want to feel you gush all over my fingers. Understand?"

Again, I nod, shocked that I actually think I might climax from being spanked. But the way he's stimulating my clit intensifies each wave of euphoric relief that follows the sharp, stinging pain.

His hand lifts a third time, and I press my eyes tightly closed.

When his hand claps across my skin, I explode. Pussy pulsing, I tremble like a leaf as I fall apart with shocking intensity.

My knees buckle, but Alexei doesn't let me fall. Instead, his fingers continue to move inside me, the heel of his palm grinding against my clit as his other arm encircles me. Alexei holds me firmly against his chest.

I breathe heavily through my nose, panting with the force of my orgasm, my wrists straining against the cuffs holding my hands above my head. Then, one hand gliding up my body to cup my breast, Alexei eases his fingers out of me in order to guide his cockhead into my entrance.

I shiver violently at the ease with which he slides inside me, my pussy so wet that the friction is out of this world. And when he brushes his fingers across my clit, I nearly come undone.

27

ALEXEI

Nadia drives me absolutely crazy. I think she might just be the single sexiest woman I've ever met, and the fact that she would distract me with a strip tease after this trying day makes me want to give her the world.

And I'm going to do just that. I want to make her come all night, and I'm starting with a punishment because I know that's what she was hoping for. She was doing her very best to antagonize me.

And God damn, did she do a good job.

She would make a phenomenal dominatrix with a few of the moves she pulled on the kitchen table.

But I know she's a sub at heart.

Because it wasn't until I took control that she really let herself fall into the role.

And now, as I hold her close and fill her body, I can feel just how much she likes being punished.

"God, you're so wet," I groan as my cock slides in and out of her with tantalizing ease.

Nadia whimpers, the sound deliciously muffled by her panties, and my cock throbs at the reminder that she's tasting her own cum because of the makeshift gag. I want to punish her for hours, make her feel all the pain and pleasure her body can possibly handle.

But she's so intoxicating, so insanely irresistible that I'm barreling toward my own release. I know I won't be able to hold on much longer. Cock throbbing with need, I force myself to pull out of her, and I relish the sound of her agonized sob.

She doesn't like that I stopped fucking her.

But it's momentary.

Gripping Nadia's hips, I spin her around to face me. Her green eyes are dilated until they're nearly black, her face so strikingly sensual with her mouth full of black lace that I nearly lose it.

"Open," I command once again, pressing my arousal-slicked fingers against her lower lip.

She obeys immediately this time, and a smile curls the corners of my mouth.

I scoop the spent panties from between her teeth and toss them aside so I can kiss her deeply. Nadia groans in response, her back arching as she leans into me. I hold her firmly in my arms, craving her soft warmth.

"Are you ready to show me just how flexible you are, little ballerina?" I tease, running my hands over her round ass.

She nods against me, refusing to stop kissing me long enough to speak.

Supporting her with one hand, I let the other slide lower, down her thigh and to her knee. Slowly, I guide her leg upward, keeping her body flush against mine as I spread her legs. She lets me, following the motion with ease, and when her thighs are stretched as far as they will go, I move my hand down to her ankle.

She doesn't even bat an eye. Gripping the bar above her head, she relies on the strength of her arms and my hand for balance as she lets me lift her ankle up past my shoulder, my head, all the way until her toes are pointed toward the ceiling.

My balls tighten at the deep stretch she performs with ease. Her muscles don't even tremble with the effort of holding the compromising pose, and with one leg high in the air, she's fully exposed and waiting for me.

"You're something else, you know that?" I murmur and lean in to steal a kiss. Then I thrust inside her.

Nadia gasps, her head falling back as I stretch her slick pussy with my cock. She feels incredible, all tight and tense from her stretch and this new angle it creates. Wrapping both arms around her waist, I hold her close, bearing her weight as I move my hips to fuck her soft and slow.

She mewls, the sound sending an electric jolt through my core. I lean in to kiss her exposed neck, my tongue dancing lightly across her mottled flesh. Goosebumps rise across her back, beneath my palms, and I love how responsive she is to my every caress.

This new, slower pace is just as intensely pleasurable, and I revel in the heavenly feel of her pussy gripping me, begging me to stay inside her. I do, rocking in and out just enough to hit all the right spots.

"Oh, God!" she gasps, her arms jerking, making the cuffs clink against the metal pole. Her walls tighten, and I know she's on the edge of finding a third release.

"Come for me, Nadia," I command.

And she does just moments later. Trembling as her muscles tense with euphoria, Nadia orgasms for a third time. I groan with the intense concentration and self-control it takes to hold on any longer. But I manage, slowing my motion as I ride out her waves of ecstasy, my cock swollen and painfully hard inside her throbbing depths.

She gasps, her breaths washing over me as she seems too lost in the moment to think about much else. I love the way her leg muscles twitch against me. Not overextended, just twitching with pleasure.

Only after the last of her gripping spasms subside do I stop to admire the deep satisfaction on her face. Then slowly, gently, I ease her leg back down, placing her foot on the ground.

"You sure know how to take your punishment," I tease, my voice low and rasping.

Nadia releases a breathy giggle, leaning heavily against her handcuffs as I stoop to find the key in my discarded pants pocket. I retrieve it quickly and wrap one arm around her waist to support her weight. Then I release one wrist.

Her arms seem to weigh a hundred pounds as they drop like rocks, and Nadia sags against me. "You seemed like you needed a bit of stress relief," she observes quietly.

She rests her cheek against my chest as I scoop her up into my arms.

I chuckle softly. "Quite the philanthropist, aren't you?"

She hums softly. "I do what I can."

"Well, I hope you know the night isn't over yet," I warn, carrying her to my bed and setting her gently down.

Then I turn my attention to the remaining cuff on her wrist.

"Hmm, you promised me all night," she says, though her words are slightly slurred with lust and sleep.

"That's right," I agree, positioning myself between her thighs as I prepare to take her missionary style.

And as I ease inside her, inch by inch, I claim her lips in a fierce kiss. She groans, responding eagerly as her hips rock, grinding her clit against me. I press inside her up to the hilt. She feels sinfully good, her warm hole so wet and swollen from coming that it squeezes around my hard length, coaxing my orgasm with a tenacity that makes my balls ache.

"I want you to come inside me," Nadia breathes against my lips.

And though I've done just that numerous times before, hearing Nadia say it sets my soul on fire. I move sensually inside her, determined to ignite every nerve and stimulate her in ways that can only be reached when going nice.

And.

Slow.

"Oh, God, that feels so good," she whimpers, her clit fluttering with excitement, ready for release.

"You feel like heaven," I agree, determined to make her come one more time, though the agony of holding off any longer is almost excruciating.

I kiss her deeply, stroking my tongue between her lips and tangling with hers. And though I know she's lost in a sea of pleasure and contentment, Nadia responds with passionate intensity.

Her arms wrap around my neck, her fingers tangling in my hair as she holds me firmly against her. Demanding my lips, she consumes me greedily, her hips rolling and grinding at the same time, seemingly of their own accord.

"Oh, God, I'm coming," she whimpers, the sound torn between agony and disbelief.

And it undoes me completely. As the first wave of euphoria sweeps through her, tightening her pussy in a vise-like grip, I thrust deep and explode inside her. It feels ten times more thrilling, somehow, knowing that she wants me to fill her with my cum. Knowing that she's eager to take my seed.

Deep, possessive greed consumes me as I feel the intense need to protect Nadia. Wrapping her in a powerful embrace, I hold her close, relishing the feel of her lace-clad nipples crushed against my chest.

Her nylon stockings brush softly against my legs, reminding me of just how sexy she looks dressed in nothing but her cheeky lingerie. As we throb and pulse together, unraveling in each other's arms, I know this woman is the best thing that's ever happened to me.

I don't know what I would do without her. She fills my life with color and knows just how to brighten my day. I'm immersed in a deep, resounding desire to keep her safe and hold her close.

As we slow and still together, I know that's exactly what I will do for as long as she'll let me. Relishing the scent of her for a few more moments, I remain on top of her, crushing her into the bed with my body weight as I draw in a long breath.

Then, with a final kiss, I ease out of her.

Nadia releases a quiet, exceedingly adorable moan of disappointment when I do, and I have to admit, I'm with her. I would love to stay buried inside her forever. But her deep contentment is fading into silent exhaustion even as I study her breathtaking face.

And I feel it, too, that pull that promises to carry me into a long and dreamless sleep. Rolling onto the bed beside Nadia, I turn toward her and wrap an arm around her waist. Then I pull her snugly against my body.

Sinking into sleep has never been so easy, and as I drift into oblivion, I know that this is the perfect woman for me.

28

NADIA

"Good, ladies. McKenna, raise your chin," Stew says, moving his hand like a conductor in rhythm to the music.

As we practice our swan dance, spinning and leaping across the stage, I feel my dinner from last night lurch dangerously in my stomach. It was a late-night grab-and-go deal from my fridge, and I'm a little worried the leftover fried rice had been in there too long.

It would make sense, considering how many nights a week I've eaten with Alexei lately.

But that knowledge doesn't help me now.

I finish my set and know I'm in trouble.

Rather than waiting for the end of the song—or even the end of this bar—I sprint for the door, my hand over my mouth to try and hold back the vomit I know is coming.

"Nadia?"

I think the voice belongs to Stew, our director, but I'm hell-bent on getting to the bathroom in time, so I don't slow down to offer an explanation.

I barely make it, throwing myself onto my knees in front of a girl's restroom toilet before I purge my stomach in one violent go. As I throw up, cold sweat breaks out across my brow. Gripping the plastic seat like my life depends on it, I puke until there's nothing left.

Then I proceed to dry heave for several seconds longer.

Finally, I collapse, sitting heavily on the bathroom floor, utterly exhausted. Lifting a shaking hand, I wipe my sweaty brow with the back of it.

Well, shit. Food poisoning is the last thing I need right now. I have several more performances before my next day off, and I don't want to give up my spot because of some stupid stomach bug.

I remain on the bathroom floor for several minutes, trying to wrap my mind around what I ate that did this to me. The fried rice is all I can think of. I didn't even eat with Alexei last night, so I can't check in with him to see if he's feeling just as crummy.

I need to get back before Stew has a conniption. Still breathing heavily, I push myself back onto my feet and flush the toilet. Then I head to the sink to rinse my mouth.

Now that I'm done puking, I feel surprisingly better.

Maybe that was the end of it.

Just needed to get the bad food out.

I hope so.

Swishing water around my teeth, I check my coloring in the mirror. I'm flushed and sweaty, but I doubt anyone will notice since we're all working hard at practice. I spit my mouthful into the sink and wipe my face. Then I head back to the studio, sure I'm going to hear it from Stew for making a run for the bathroom mid-song.

Only, as I slip inside, the music is off and he's gone.

"What's going on?" I murmur as I approach McKenna.

She and Matteo are stretching along the back wall, keeping their muscles warm, which means practice isn't over.

"Stew got a call he said he needed to take," Matteo explains.

"You okay?" McKenna asks, studying me carefully, her brown eyes kind. "You bolted like your pants caught fire."

"I'm fine," I assure her quickly, my automatic go-to being to put up defensive walls. In the ballet world, it's better not to show any weakness if you want to survive the cutthroat inner circle. Ballet is an odd mix of competition and teamwork.

But McKenna has proven a good friend for a long time now, and she looks genuinely concerned.

"I think I might have eaten some fried rice that's been sitting in the fridge for too long. My stomach is not sitting well today. But I feel better now that I've thrown up." I give her a smile to show I appreciate her compassion.

"Ew, you're throwing up?" Candace asks, her sharp voice cutting through the room as she picks up the exact words I didn't want everyone to hear.

Not only is that harmful to the general cohesiveness of the group—no one wants to catch a bug from someone else in their troupe—but I'm sure Matteo and Ethan don't really want to anticipate me hurling on them every time they lift me over their heads, which I don't think I will.

"I'm fine now. Really, I feel much better. I think I just ate something that upset my stomach."

"You sure you're not pregnant with Boss Daddy Federov's baby?" Lina teases, her smug face telling me she's extra-proud of that joke at my expense.

Since the night we all went clubbing with Alexei, Lina and Candace have grown nearly intolerable. While the rest of the company seems to have let it go, those two prefer to get in digs about my hooking up with Alexei as often as they can.

"I assure you, that's impossible," I deadpan, irritated that I might have to confess something so personal as my infertility in front of everyone in the room. But that may end up being the only way if I want to get them off my back.

"Condoms aren't a hundred percent effective, honey," Candace pipes in, smirking.

"Thanks for the tip," I state, fighting the urge to snap at them.

"Oh, come on. Don't be so serious. We were only joking," Lina adds.

"Yeah, right," McKenna mutters under her breath as the two mean girls go about their business once again, ignoring me because I'm no fun to torment when I don't engage. "But, Nadia, in all honesty, you'd better not be. Or I mean, at least not if you want to keep your role. Getting pregnant is how you ruin your ballet career. Our previous principal was booted right after she told Stew she was pregnant last year. He has no sympathy for women who want to start a family."

Somehow, that doesn't surprise me. Stew does not strike me as the kind of man who would care to help a pregnant woman if it meant compromising his shows in any way. Then again, I can get why he wouldn't want a pregnant-bellied Odette. In a silent story, it kind of ruins the plot.

"Thanks for the heads-up," I say, giving McKenna a small smile.

I don't have it in me to explain why I know I'm not pregnant. Especially not with Candace and Lina within earshot.

Still, Matteo seems less confident about the concept of lifting me for the performance tonight, and I can't blame him. I imagine he would appreciate dancing with the understudy rather than being covered in vomit. But I'm confident I'll have it under control by tonight.

STANDING in the first-aid aisle of the grocery store, I contemplate what I could possibly take to help with the relentless upset stomach, heartburn, and vomiting I can't seem to get under control. I don't feel awful . . . I just don't seem to be doing a very good job of keeping things down, and it's leaving me weak and clumsier in my performance than usual.

Even if I've managed to hide it better from everyone since practice the other day.

I stroll up and down the aisles in an effort to spot something that I think will help.

Then I freeze.

Gaze landing on the colorful boxes of pregnancy tests, I hesitate. Despite my best attempts to get Candace and Lina's taunts from a few days ago out of my head, they've managed to set in a sliver of doubt that I can't seem to shake.

I can't be pregnant. I'm not even capable of it. But I'm tempted to take a test just to prove myself right. For peace of mind.

That's just silly, and I know it. Years ago, the doctor told me I'm infertile and would have to seek means outside my own body if I wanted children someday.

I shake my head as I start to leave the aisle. Then, at the last second, I turn and snatch one of the boxes off the shelf. Once I take a test, I'll be able to put their words out of my mind. *And what's fifteen dollars?*

I also grab a container of Tums before I leave the store. This time, I was more careful to go with less perishable items than veggies. Those, I can pick up night by night. For now, I grab some light, easy snacks—pickles, nuts, and protein bars, as well as a box of saltine crackers to calm my stomach—before heading home.

I know I'm being ridiculous, but I head for the bathroom first thing when I walk through my front door. I only stop to drop the groceries on the counter and dig out the pregnancy test. Then I close myself in and brace for a stressful few minutes.

Once I've followed the printed instructions, I wait, setting the test on the side of the tub and jittering nervously, though I know what it's going to say.

When my three minutes are up, I stare down at the results. I'm expecting one pink line, just like the box says, but a second one seems to be growing more prominent before my very eyes. Frowning, I look back at the box to ensure I have the reading instructions right.

Two lines means I'm pregnant.

Shocked, I stare in stunned silence as I try to make sense of it. I'm not supposed to be able to have children. To this day, I don't even have a consistent cycle. Partly why I haven't thought anything of my period not having come in months.

And yet there's the proof, in pink and white, telling me that I'm going to have a baby.

I don't know what to do.

I'd put away the idea of being a mom or having a family years ago. Back when I first went to the doctor for my horrible menstrual cramps and entirely erratic cycles, they told me then that my hormones were too far out of balance, that it would require considerable hormonal therapy if I ever hoped to have a child. And that would alter my body significantly, as well as cost a lot of money, without the guarantee of fertility.

At that time, back in high school, I'd traded the slim hope of having a child for my career as a ballerina. It was a conscious decision to pick something I had a better chance at achieving—and that's saying something, considering ballet was my only other passion besides being a mom.

The path to becoming a prima is both brutal and highly exclusive, so knowing that I had a better chance of that than of getting pregnant says everything when it comes to my odds now.

I care about dancing more than anything.

Or at least thought I did.

But having a baby?

It's too major of a bomb to wrap my head around.

I'll have to decide if I want to keep my position as principal ballerina or keep my baby. I know I can't have both. But the decision feels like such an obvious one.

Growing up, I'd always wanted to be a mom. It was a deep-seated truth that I'd known long before I became a woman, and the crushing blow of finding out I would never have that opportunity devastated me. I threw myself into my artistic passion because I thought if I couldn't have a family, then I wanted to create a legacy in some other way. And I have been living within that mindset ever since.

Hell, it's not like I haven't tested my infertility on multiple occasions. Even before Alexei. I found out I couldn't have children nearly five years ago, and it's not like I've been completely abstinent in that time—or particularly careful.

I have been far more sexually active with Alexei than I was with anyone else in my life, but I'm still shocked at the possibility that I'm having his child.

My heart flutters nervously as I think about Alexei.

I need to tell him, and I don't know how he might respond to the news. We haven't really discussed children much. On the few occasions it's come up, he hasn't given me the distinct impression that he wants to be a father—a fact I was thrilled about when I thought I couldn't have kids.

I still remember our first real date and talking about his brother's new baby—how he's excited to be the cool uncle, but he hadn't sounded envious of his brother's role as a father. I'd taken that as a good sign back then, that he might actually want to be with me for more than a quick fling. Now, I have no idea what he'll think, how he'll want me to handle it.

But as the reality of my condition finally starts to sink in, I look down at my flat stomach. It's not hard to know I want to keep my baby. I just have to find a way to tell Alexei—and my director, Stew.

Oh, God.

McKenna's words from the other day ring clearly in my head, following the taunting humor of Candace and Lina. If I tell Stew, he'll fire me in the blink of an eye. That's what he did to the previous prima. And from what I understand, she had far more tenure than I've had a chance to build.

No, I suspect that this baby will be the end of my ballet career. Or at least my role as prima at the Tapestry Dance Company. And while I'll miss it, I find the opportunity of being a mother makes the loss far more tolerable.

Still, I decide after a moment that I won't tell Stew until the end of the season. I love the opportunity I've had this year, and I think I can make it through at least the end of *Swan Lake*'s show dates before I break the news.

But if I don't want to tell the director, that means I can't tell anyone.

Not even Alexei.

Not just yet.

As the owner of Tapestry Dance Company, he would be obligated to make the right business decision over letting me have my way.

And it's just a few more weeks of performances.

Then the shows will be done, and I'll come clean.

29

ALEXEI

Maksim looks livid. Of the three of us, he's the one whose bad side I truly wouldn't want to get on. Because he's by far the most restrained and disciplined, keeping his temper in check all the way up until he snaps. But his breaking point is something to behold.

And right now, he looks like he's on the brink.

"We have the assets to take these kinds of hits, but why in fuck's name are we having to take them at all, Alexei?" he growls from the far side of his desk.

Being chastised by my older brother rankles, and I narrow my eyes at him darkly.

"You want to drum up the number of security details you're demanding of me? That many men with protection training don't exist in San Francisco, so I had to prioritize. Would you prefer I take men off Mom's estate? Or away from Le Fleur?"

"Not happening," Dimitri snarls, his temper rising at my suggestion.

I gesture toward Dimitri as if he's just proved my point. I wouldn't cut back on security for either of them even if Maksim told me to. On some things, I'm not willing to compromise, and protecting family comes before protecting our assets. Period. End of story.

"We've lost three more restaurants this week," Maksim states flatly.

"I've lost nine men," I counter. "You don't think I know? If you think you can do a better job, why don't you go stand watch each night? Or how about you find me more men? Mine are all pulling fourteen-hour shifts and fucking exhausted."

"Then why haven't you found who's doing this?"

"He has," Dimitri counters, cutting in to back me up.

"Don't start that again. We need evidence," Maksim argues, scowling fiercely at Dimitri. "Concrete evidence. And so far, Alexei's found nothing."

"A shipment of guns is not nothing," I disagree. I admit, it doesn't directly tie Aleksandr Volkov to the fires or the attack on Camille, but I've seen neither hide nor hair of anyone else acting suspicious in our town.

I've finally come around to Dimitri's side on that front. We should be doing something. I just don't know what. I understand Maksim's trepidation. But the longer we wait, the more businesses we lose. And being unable to stop the attack, to keep safe the people we swore to protect, it's wearing me down.

I'm not used to this kind of tension between me and my brothers—or concerning company decisions.

"A shipment of guns isn't proof that he's our enemy. So let's not unnecessarily make him one—especially if he's bulking up his reserves," Maksim says.

"What about guns tied with the fact that he keeps stepping on my toes?" Dimitri adds.

"It's business, Dimitri. If you don't like him taking the restaurants you set your sights on, get quicker on the draw."

Sometimes, Maksim is brutal. But he's right. And he's the right one to run our family—and the business. He's the level head we need when it comes to major decisions like this. I might agree with Dimitri that Aleksandr Volkov is the one behind all the attacks, but I'm not willing to put money down on that, let alone the lives of our men.

We're already bleeding. No point in turning it into a hemorrhage.

But Dimitri's hot temper won't allow him to see both sides. "We need to strike first, to get more aggressive before he catches us unprepared."

"What we need is proof before we go running head-first into a war. I refuse to bring your personal grudges into a decision this large. If you're wrong, you could end up costing us an ally, and it would definitely make him an enemy if he's not already." Maksim keeps his tone cool and even, his temper back under wraps, but I can see the frustration bubbling under the surface. He doesn't like that we're losing men any more than I do.

Throwing his hands up, Dimitri growls, "Fine." Then he storms from the room.

I watch in stunned silence as my brother slams the door behind himself as he goes. Normally, he leaves the door-slamming to show his irritation after I give him a hard time about something. So having him stomp off now means he must be thoroughly pissed.

"Alexei, I need proof," Maksim says, his tone less gruff and more openly worried now.

"I know," I agree with a heavy sigh. I scrub my face with my hands. It's been a long week of late nights, and I haven't had the opportunity to spend as much time with Nadia as I would like as a result. The strain is starting to wear me down. "I'm doing the best I can."

What I really need is to have my brothers on the same side. The infighting is doing nothing to help our cause. I know our mom would be furious if she found out how many times we've gone around with this same argument.

And the worst part is I'm trapped in the middle. I'm the reason neither of my brothers are on the same page. Because I can't find the asshole responsible for targeting our businesses. If I could just be sure, then I have no doubt we would join to create a united front, just like we always have.

Slapping the arms of my chair, I hoist myself out of the seat, heading for the door to get back at it.

"Alexei," Maksim says as I reach for the door handle.

"Hmm?" I ask, turning to face him, feeling the weight of my responsibility on my shoulders.

"Get some sleep," he says, his expression etched with genuine concern now.

"You're a wealth of contradictions today, aren't you?" I ask smartly, trying for humor to soften the blow.

Then an idea hits me, one that might help me ease my own tension and could bring my brothers back within a reasonable range of contention. "Maybe we ought to get the yacht back on the water this weekend. Just take a minute to unwind. Not a whole day. Maybe just an afternoon. If I don't do something to destress here soon, I just might lose my mind."

Maksim's eyebrow raises in an expression of mild amusement. Then he nods. "It's not a bad idea, Brother. I'll have the marina prep the boat."

"Perfect. I'll bring the ballerinas. You bring the booze—and Symphony, if she wants to come." Not that I necessarily want my brother's fiancée there, but if I plan on bringing Nadia—and I absolutely do—it wouldn't seem right to leave my brother's fiancée at home.

"Thanks, Alexei," Maksim says as I'm about to turn and go.

"For what?"

Maks jerks his chin toward the exit Dimitri left through. "Always knowing how to keep the family together."

I flash my oldest brother a cocky smile. "It's what I do."

Still, I appreciate his words of gratitude. I do end up being the peacemaker often, and I'm glad Maks both sees it and values it for what it is. Patting the doorframe, I signal that I'm heading out.

Dimitri, I know, will be the harder one to get on the yacht.

He's in his office, where I expect him to be, and I knock before entering, though the door is ajar.

"Hey," he says, glancing up from his computer momentarily.

"Thanks for having my back," I say, leaning against the doorframe.

"Yeah, well, you're right, and I don't like him shitting on you just because we're taking hits. If he'd stop playing defense and start playing offense, maybe we could stop losing assets."

"I hear you," I agree. "But he does have a point. If we lose sight of the big picture, we could easily walk ourselves into a trap we're not ready for."

Dimitri's gray eyes find mine, and he studies me silently for a moment. All three of us have the same prominent features—dark hair, gray eyes, we're each tall and on the muscular side, all lingering gifts imparted to us by our father. And right now, Dimitri has that same look Maksim gives me when he thinks I'm up to something.

"Look, I don't want to make you think I'm on his side because I definitely think this is Aleksandr Volkov, just like you. All I'm saying is he has the harder task of pulling the trigger on a pretty massive decision that could backfire and kill us all."

"I suppose," Dimitri agrees, his voice slow and reluctant.

"But that isn't why I came to talk to you." It is, but I know that the more I push, the more Dimitri will dig in his heels. "I'm thinking we need to take the boat out this weekend. Catch a breather, what with everything that's been going on lately. You and Camille should bring baby Leah and come."

"Who all will be going on this boat ride?" Dimitri asks, and I already know from his question that his answer will be no.

"Just the brothers . . . their women . . . and maybe the Tapestry Dance ballerinas. Come on. It'll be fun."

"I don't think a party boat with a bunch of ballerinas is the right place for my wife and newborn baby," he observes dryly.

"You don't have to spend time with the ballerinas," I point out. "The yacht is plenty big enough for everyone. Besides, we both know the reason you really don't want to go is that you hate Symphony."

Dimitri snorts, and the silent gesture tells me my accusation isn't far off. "Not this time, I think. But I do appreciate your effort. Maybe once Leah is a little older."

"Alright," I agree, letting my disappointment seep into my tone.

It would have been a good opportunity to see more of my brother and to get him and Maks talking rather than arguing. I'll need to find another way to get the heard-headed mules to call a truce.

But I do see Dimitri's point. I highly doubt Camille would enjoy a booze cruise with a baby, and Dimitri is all but glued to her side these days—particularly now that someone's been coming after our restaurants.

I can't say I blame him, seeing as he nearly lost Camille when she was the first target this enemy Bratva pinpointed. He's become a classic overprotective dad and husband. And since Camille owns and runs Le Fleur, she's far more at risk than Maks's fiancée, who's a model, or Nadia, as a ballerina.

Sighing heavily, I head to my own office, ready to get to work finding the bastard responsible for making my life hell.

30

NADIA

Dressed in a little black bikini and a coral-colored crocheted cover-up, I recline on the beach chair with my arm over my head, my sun hat shielding my face from the brilliant California rays. We didn't have to travel far down the coast to find a warm pocket of beach to anchor off, and if I weren't so riddled with guilt and anxiety, I might find myself enjoying the luxury yacht.

The rest of the Tapestry Dance crew are. That's for sure. The girls each hold a glass of champagne aloft as they sway to the music blasting from the speakers above us on the second-level deck.

But as I watch Alexei from the corner of my eye, I can't seem to find the party spirit I'll need to keep up my façade. It's been over a week. I've seen him multiple times—slept with him nearly every night—since I found out I'm pregnant, and keeping it a secret from him is slowly eating me from the inside.

"You're sure you don't want a glass?" Alexei offers, attempting to hand me his champagne flute for the fourth time.

"No really, I'm fine. Boats make me . . . nauseous," I explain as a bout of morning sickness threatens to rise up inside me.

It was a complete lie. I've never been motion sick in my life, but it's better to cover my bases, considering we're out on the water for enough hours that I'm bound to throw up at some point.

Alexei eyes me skeptically but doesn't press me further. Instead, he takes a swig of champagne and settles back on his chair once again. His oldest brother, Maksim, sits on the beach chair to his right, slathering sunscreen on his fiancée's shoulders.

"I'm glad you dragged us out here. I just wish Dimitri weren't being such a dad," he says.

Alexei laughs, and the sound is like a punch in the gut.

It makes me nervous to keep information from him, and I was just wondering if I begged Alexei to keep it a secret for a little while whether I might not be able to pull off my last few *Swan Lake* performances.

But that laugh triggers in me the doubt that has dogged my thoughts every time I'm tempted to say something. Because, in truth, I'm starting to realize that I'm using my final ballet performances as an excuse to maintain our happy relationship just as it is a little longer.

I don't know how Alexei might feel about having children.

And I'm more than a little terrified to find out.

My time with Alexei has been more than I could have dreamed. *What if he really doesn't want to start a family?*

My stomach knots painfully, and though I swallow hard, I can't quite hold back the wave of nausea that hits me this time.

In a flash, I'm up out of my chair and racing to the boat's railing. Leaning far over the side, I bring up my eggs and toast from this morning. I've yet to find something my stomach can keep down consistently, and I have to admit, being sick is not my favorite part of being pregnant.

Gasping as I finish my daily ritual of regurgitating my food, I lean heavily against the cool metal. From the corner of my eye, I can tell the girls are still dancing, too wrapped up in their party to notice I'm throwing up again. Thank God.

"You okay?"

Alexei's deep voice on my other side makes me jump, and I stand up straight as heat floods my cheeks.

"Yeah, I'm fine," I promise. "Just seasick."

It's a thin excuse in the tiny alcove where we've anchored. The edges of the surrounding land seem to be breaking the worst of the Pacific waves. Alexei scans the horizon as if taking note of that very thing. But if he's suspicious, he doesn't say anything.

"You should have told me. I could have picked another outing for the day," he says gently, his warm palm resting on the small of my back.

A fresh wave of guilt tightens my stomach as I consider how many times I might regret my lie. "Really, I'm fine," I promise. "Besides, everyone's having so much fun. I'll get over it."

"You want me to find you some Dramamine?" he offers.

I have no clue what that might do to the baby. "No, that will only make me sleepy." At least I think it will. I vaguely recall someone telling me that once.

But the concern in his eyes is tormenting me. I can't keep lying to him.

After over a week of hiding my pregnancy, I know it's time. I have to tell him.

"Alexei, will you . . . help me find a toothbrush? I would love to clean my teeth."

"Of course." His smile is knowing and kind, and he interlaces our fingers to guide me.

The simple gesture still makes my heart flutter, and my breath catches as I follow him along the side of the main-floor cabin toward the back of the yacht.

"Would you rather I take us back to San Francisco? Throwing up all afternoon does not sound like an ideal day out in my mind," he says, glancing at me from the corner of his eye.

"Really, Alexei, stop worrying. I'll be fine."

He shows me into the modest bedroom on the left side of the yacht, locking the door behind us as he explains that the boat actually has five rooms for people to sleep if they were so inclined. "But don't worry. We'll be back in port before sunset today," he adds when my expression grows pained.

Taking me into the sizable bathroom, complete with a jet tub and standing shower, he releases my hand to dig through the drawers until he finds my requested item. It's still wrapped in plastic and he hands it to me with a playful smile.

"Thanks," I murmur, my nerves roiling inside my belly. I wonder if he'll be wearing that expression much longer.

But I still need time to collect myself, so as Alexei leans against the doorframe, seeming content to wait while I brush my teeth, I give them a thorough scrubbing and try to collect my thoughts.

How does one go about telling their boyfriend that they got pregnant when they weren't supposed to be able to? Will he think I'm a liar? That I made up my infertility to entrap him?

Oh, God. I hadn't even thought about that until just now.

Coaching myself to breathe, I spit the toothpaste into the sink and rinse my mouth.

And as I bend over the sink, strong hands find my hips, massaging my skin as Alexei presses against me from behind.

"Even when you're seasick, you're still entirely too sexy," he observes darkly, his hands roaming slowly up and down my waist.

I turn in his arms, leaning back against the counter as I smile up at him. And I almost chicken out. That look in his eye tells me he wants me. That he's been thinking about what he could do to me now that we're alone.

And I'm sorely tempted to fall into that without question. Without bringing up the one very important piece of information I've been hiding for too long.

No, I need to tell him.

Biting my lip, I peer up at his strong features through my lashes. "Sit with me?" I suggest, my eyes darting to the bed behind him.

He steps aside, letting me lead the way back into the bedroom, and we settle on the edge of the bed as my nerves take a massive leap. I still don't know what to say. But I can't keep stalling. This isn't exactly something a person can put off until they finally feel ready.

Eventually, my body's going to tell him what I'm struggling so hard to get out.

Shifting nervously, I turn to face Alexei more fully and take his hand, interlacing our fingers and tracing the veins that stand out against the back of his palm.

"Nadia," he says gently, and my eyes automatically rise to meet his penetrating gray ones.

A flicker of amusement dances across his lips, then his thumb and forefinger come up to pinch my chin. My heart pounds as his eyes shift to my lips, and I know then that he's misread the situation.

But I can't stop him as he leans in slowly to kiss me.

"Let me take your mind off your queasiness," he suggests, his voice low and enticing as he pulls back for just a moment.

I gasp as my body responds with enthusiasm, my nausea vanishing as I'm suddenly filled with intense excitement. I don't know if the sudden shift is an indication of my changing hormones or if it's just because Alexei drives me wild.

And frankly, I don't care.

All thoughts of telling him my secret vanish beneath his kiss.

A growl of appreciation rumbles up his throat, and he deepens the kiss, his tongue stroking along the seam of my lips until I part them. Then he's tasting my freshly minty breath. His tongue tastes tart like champagne, and zinging pleasure ripples through my body as I let my mind go blank.

I can worry about telling him about the baby after this.

Tongues tangling, we shift closer together, Alexei's long fingers combing back into my hair. He consumes me with a heat that sets my stomach ablaze. When he guides me back onto the bed, I follow willingly, feeling like a teenager sneaking off with her boyfriend for a quick make-out session.

Leaning on one arm, Alexei lies beside me as he explores my body with the other. His hand makes its way up beneath the sheer crocheted beachwear to cradle my breast, and I moan at the new tenderness there. Not overwhelming, but more than I'm used to.

And it reminds me of what I'm stalling about as I let his touch distract me.

Maybe if I relax a little, it will be easier to say.

I gasp as he pushes aside the small black triangle of fabric to pinch my nipple lightly.

"Shh," he warns playfully, his lips curving against mine. "These walls aren't the thickest. And while I wouldn't mind everyone knowing what we slipped off to do, you're the one who has to work with the dancers on this boat."

"You're evil," I breathe and pull him firmly against my mouth to kiss him more deeply.

The rumbling chuckle that follows vibrates through my body, making my core tighten deliciously. I squirm closer to him, relishing the way he feels so warm and solid pressed against my side.

As his hand roams across the exposed skin of my chest, I shiver with anticipation.

31

ALEXEI

Nadia's clearly unsettled, and though she says it's from being on a boat, I'm not entirely sure that's true. She seemed fine through the choppiest of water. And now that we're anchored in a quiet cove, she threw up.

I had half a mind to question her about what's on her mind. She seems more tense than usual, her thoughts somewhere far away from the sunny day we found down the coast from San Francisco Bay.

And a toothbrush seemed like the perfect excuse to take a moment for a quiet conversation. But watching her bend over that sink, seeing her firm, round ass peeking out from beneath that cover-up, her little black bikini creeping provocatively up her butt cheeks, I couldn't help myself.

I can't resist Nadia.

She's the most beautiful woman I've ever seen, and now that I'm alone with her, all I can think about is finding ways to take her mind off her queasy stomach.

Gasping, Nadia arches her back as I make my way over to her second breast and give her taut nipple a light pinch. I know she's trying to be silent after my warning, but quiet sex isn't Nadia's forte, and I'm looking forward to seeing how much self-restraint she'll manage.

Teasing her nipples as I swallow the soft whimpers that issue from her mouth into mine, I soak up how responsive she is today. Like she's just been waiting for me to give her some relief.

Slowly, I trace a finger down the line of her stomach, circling her belly button and raising goosebumps along the way. Then I ease my fingers beneath the elastic of her black bikini bottoms.

God, I love this swimsuit she's wearing.

It's not just intensely flattering—and by that, I mean revealing—but it allows me easy access to all her most sensitive spots. When my fingers brush across Nadia's clit, she moans lasciviously.

My cock twitches in my swim trunks at the enticing sound.

I repeat the motion to be rewarded with her moan once again.

Though we've only just begun, she's already wet for me, and it makes my cock rock-hard in an instant to know how easily I turn her on. Teasing the soft velvet of her pussy lips with my fingers, I mirror the motion with my tongue, tasting the full cushion of her mouth's lips.

Nadia arches, her heels digging into the mattress as her body shows me what she wants. Me inside her. I fully intend to oblige, but first, I want to drive her wild with my fingers.

Quickening the circles with my fingers, I set her body to quivering before sliding between her folds to press inside her entrance. Nadia groans deep in her throat, the animalistic sound making my cock twitch.

I nip her lip in response and am rewarded with a gasp. Then she returns the favor, lifting her head up off the bed to consume my lips with verve. This insatiable, playful side of Nadia, the one that tells me she's not afraid to push back and take what she wants, it intoxicates me.

In a lifetime of living in a family of Federov brothers, where our name is synonymous with power and authority, I've grown tired of the meek women who think their life should be to serve me to have access to my money, and with Nadia, it's never that.

She holds her ground, demands what she wants, and I find I'm eager to please her, to know what makes her tick. I love turning her on, and now, as I finger her and feel her squirming beneath my palm, I want to feel her come on my hand.

"Hmm, feeling distracted?" I tease against her lips.

Nadia whimpers, nodding in response.

"I like watching you bend over things," I muse, talking dirty in low, playful tones as I continue to lavish her clit and pussy with attention. "Boat railings, sinks, tables. You have the best ass. I could bend you over and fuck this tight little pussy anywhere, you turn me on so much. Would you like that?"

"Yes," she gasps, her hips rolling as her walls tighten around my fingers.

A fresh wave of arousal slicks her walls, and I groan with the deep, carnal desire that makes me want to shove inside her raw.

"You like it when I talk dirty to you, Nadia?" I breathe, moving to kiss a trail down the curve of her neck.

Her hickeys have faded to soft pink circles now, easy to cover up. My lips pull into a smile as I remember the first morning she saw them, the mortification, asking how she's supposed to explain them at work.

"Tell them you're mine," I said, pulling her close as our eyes met in the mirror.

She shudders now as if reliving the experience with me. Then she bucks, her fingers curling convulsively as they press into my skin.

"Oh, God, Alexei," she moans.

"Shh." I chuckle against her throat, reminding her to be quiet as I finger her mercilessly.

And when I glance up at her as my lips find her collarbone, she's sucked the full pad of her lower lip between her teeth. Biting down hard enough to drain it of color, she struggles to keep herself quiet.

But I know I'm going to win this challenge.

She won't be able to hold it in once we start to fuck.

"Come for me, beautiful ballerina," I command, pinching her clit between my thumb and finger and rolling it lightly as I keep two fingers inside her slick entrance.

Sound vibrates against her forcibly sealed lips as Nadia obeys, her clit twitching against my fingers, her walls clamping down around me as she orgasms hard and fast. Panting, her breaths bursting from her nose, Nadia keeps her eyes pressed tightly closed.

Her delicate features look tortured with the intensity of her pleasure.

"Good girl," I praise, sliding my fingers in and out of her throbbing depths as I prolong her release.

Watching her unravel beneath my touch makes my balls tighten and throb. Nadia is so painfully sexy, her beauty almost painful as it takes my breath away. The healthy glow to her skin makes me want to kiss and lick every inch of it.

As she slowly comes down from her climax, Nadia trembles and twitches. Once the deep, reflexive groans subside, she releases her lip to let them softly part. Small indentations still mark the full, voluptuous pad, and I take it gently between mine, tracing it with the tip of my tongue to ease the abuse.

Humming appreciatively, Nadia curls her fingers into my hair at the nape of my neck, massaging and tugging as my reward for making her feel so good.

But now that I've made her come, there's no stopping me.

I need to feel her wrapped around me, to bury myself deep inside her core.

She looks calm now, the tension from earlier easing from her shoulders, and whether it's actually from seasickness or if something else is weighing on her mind, I like that I've relieved her from it if only for a small amount of time.

I intend to stretch that calm further, to blow her mind and perhaps make her forget about her troubles completely. Finding the hem of her cover-up, I work it slowly up her hips. She lifts them, making it easier for me.

When I reach her ribs, she grabs the fabric to pull it over her shoulders and head for me. I give a soft growl of appreciation as her lean muscles flex and stretch as she moves. Before she can lie back down, I reach behind her to take the thin strings of her bikini top.

She gives a girlish giggle as I remove the tiny triangles of fabric with a flourish, exposing her perfect breasts. I can't help myself as I lean in, capturing one taut nub between my lips. Nadia comes to life beneath me.

Her fingers scrabble at my T-shirt, raking it up my body to expose my chest and shoulders, and I lift my arms to let her strip me. She tosses the shirt carelessly aside, and her lips find the rigid line between my pecs as her hands immediately go to work on the lace of my swim trunks.

She shoves them down my hips and thighs a moment later, my hard cock springing free, eager to fill her wet depths. I kick free of my shorts then shift to kneel between her ankles. Hooking my fingers around the waist of her suit bottoms, I remove them completely this time.

And suddenly, nothing stands between us. Humming appreciatively at the glistening folds of her glorious pussy, I hook her knees around my elbows. Then I guide her thighs up and open, exposing her as I gain full access to her opening.

The look of pure, blazing heat in her gaze makes my heart pound. Sinking slowly on top of Nadia, I align my cockhead with her entrance. As I bend her in half, I ease inside her tight hole.

She groans, her lust-filled eyes fluttering closed as I fill her, penetrating her slow and deep. Fingers gripping the taut muscles of my back, Nadia pulls me closer, begging me to stay buried in her depths.

I oblige for several glorious seconds, relishing the way her wet heat enfolds me, her walls throbbing around my hard girth. I kiss her passionately, tasting her tongue with newfound appreciation.

She responds greedily, stroking her tongue between my teeth, dancing and tangling with my own. I'm surrounded by her in the best way, her thighs caging me between them as her hands cling to me with hungry anticipation.

Slowly, I rock my hips, my cock sliding in and out of her slick folds as I claim her body for my own. Nadia groans lasciviously, her intention to be quiet flying out the window. I chuckle, relishing the way I make her completely lose control.

Gradually, I increase my pace, thrusting faster, harder as I grind against her clit with my base. Gasping breaths escape her as she takes all of me inside her glorious depths.

I could stay here forever, torturing Nadia with pleasure, reveling in the soft cries of ecstasy. Her walls tighten around my cock, warning me that she's coming close to finding her release. And while I'm sorely tempted to let everyone know just how good she's getting it right now, I know she would hate it if her coworkers thought any less of her.

"You feel so fucking good," I growl, pounding inside her now.

With each stroke, I can feel her excitement building, her body humming with the anticipation of release.

"Oh fuuuu . . ." she groans, her head tipping back as her hips roll with unbridled need.

I chuckle, hushing her gently, but I'm not even sure she can hear me in her state of euphoric oblivion. So as I drive my cock home, hammering mercilessly into her G-spot, I release one knee with my arm.

I barely make it up in time, my palm clamping down over her mouth and chin just as she releases a cry of ecstasy, simultaneously falling apart beneath me.

32

NADIA

So lost in my intoxicating euphoria, I don't even notice I'm the one crying out until Alexei's hand covers my lips, forcing my mouth closed as he smothers the sound of my ecstasy. Deep gratitude blends with my throbbing release as I come hard and—thanks to Alexei—without my fellow dancers hearing.

I'm so far gone at this point, I almost don't care if they hear me. But I know, once the overpowering sense of bliss fades, I would be embarrassed if they did. So I silently count my blessings as I relish the way he imprisons my mouth with his palm.

It's surprisingly erotic, being so close to discovery, knowing I'm in here, being fucked into oblivion while my coworkers are outside dancing, completely unaware. The exhibitionist I didn't even know resided inside me comes to life, and once again, I find something new about myself that Alexei uncovers with natural ease.

He's so ridiculously sexy in his knowledge of erotic play that I don't quite know what to do with myself. I'm putty in his capable hands, an eager pupil wanting to learn all the ways he can turn me on and tease me into this carnal craving.

I find myself, somehow, even more aroused as Alexei manhandles me, one arm pinning my knee up by my breast as he punishes my pussy with powerful thrusts. His other hand continues to press my head into the soft mattress, keeping me from making a sound.

It's his way of showing me that my pleasure is at his will—and that he wants to make me feel it for as long and as deeply as I can.

All the while, his sexy chuckle vibrates through me as he revels in my complete lack of self-restraint. That he finds my lusty and entirely uncontrollable response to his attention amusing only makes him more appealing.

Like he can soak up pleasure from my body no matter what challenges I present.

And now, as I throb and pulse around his hard length, lost in the tingling ecstasy of my orgasm, I relish the way he lays claim to my body. He owns me so completely, the master of my pleasure, so willing to give it to me in every way.

Alexei releases a soft grunt as he continues to penetrate me deeply, forcing himself inside my hot depths, even when my walls clamp around him like a vise. My pussy throbs, begging him to stay buried inside me, to complete me as I milk him for his own reward.

It feels so good—the way he fills me, uses me, teases my body into submission. Being with Alexei is addicting. It's a punishing pleasure that leaves me coming back, time and again, for more.

Just being near him makes it impossible to think clearly, and when he kisses me, it's too easy to forget about telling him I'm pregnant. My mind goes completely blank, replaced by a white-hot euphoria that takes my breath away.

Lost in the moment, I'm filled with such intense desire, all I can think about is being with him, feeling him inside me. My attraction to Alexei has impacted my life permanently in so many ways. He's taught me so much about myself, about the limits of pleasure—or the lack thereof—about belonging to someone . . . about love.

And I never want this blissful connection to end.

A shiver runs down my spine as he traps my earlobe between his teeth, gently biting down until I whimper with my need for relief, and though the last of my aftershocks have only just subsided, I feel the heat of fresh excitement pooling in my belly.

Mewling against his warm, powerful hand, I quiver and jerk, my clit throbbing with the thought of him coming inside me. I want to take his cum again and again, to feel it filling me up with life.

It thrills me to know we work together not just physically or emotionally but on some deeper biological level. He fixed a part of me I thought was broken beyond repair.

He gave me a baby.

And I'm over the moon.

Knowing it as an undeniable truth makes sex so much more meaningful. I'm pregnant. I'm going to have a child. *I'm going to be a mom.* Overpowering excitement fills my chest.

Then a trickle of nerves slides down my spine, reminding me that I'm not the only new parent in this equation. I push the emotion down, determined to enjoy this time with Alexei.

Telling him about the baby could be the end of us, of this intoxicating connection, and I want to enjoy it while I still can.

"*Fuck,*" Alexei hisses next to my ear, and I can hear in the strain of his voice that he's close to coming.

The thought of it ratchets up my excitement, and I whimper.

"Are you ready to come for me, love?" he rasps.

"Yes," I moan, nodding against his palm, my muffled voice hardly distinguishable as a confirmation. "Yes, yes, please let me come," I beg, and though the words are impossible to make out, Alexei seems to grasp their meaning.

Pounding forcefully inside my pussy, he rocks with every forward motion, his hips grinding against my clit and demanding my release. And because he's still covering my mouth with a firm grip, I let myself go completely.

I sob euphorically, my cries vibrating against his palm with their intensity.

Muscles tensing deliciously, I tremble violently beneath him, savoring the heat of his strong chest pressed firmly against my own. The friction of our skin brushing together ignites a tantalizing arousal that ripples through my body, stemming from my overly sensitive nipples. I arch my back, intensifying the delicious sensation as I pant against his firm palm.

Alexei releases a low growl of approval as he slams deep inside my pussy, burying his cock up to the hilt in my folds. The commanding thrust sends me over the edge, and I come for a third time, my body quaking and twitching as I ride the waves of ecstasy.

Hot cum gushes inside me a moment later, filling me with a tingling relief that only Alexei can. I gasp, shuddering at the heavenly bliss of taking his seed deep inside my depths. As we slow together, breathing heavily, I find my brain foggy with the overwhelming strength of my relief.

I love the way we finish together, the sheer perfection of our mingled bliss, and as Alexei collapses on top of me, giving me the comfort of a weighted blanket, I take a moment to appreciate how good it feels to be in his arms.

His hand releases me now, allowing the air to rush between my lips as my chest heaves against his firm pecs. He peers deep into my eyes with his warm silver gaze, his fingertips brushing a soft trail along my cheek.

"You're so beautiful, Nadia," he breathes, his lips grazing mine a moment later in a tender kiss.

Tears sting the back of my eyes as emotion overwhelms me, and I can't quite be sure if it's my hormones speaking or the fact that Alexei is capable of being so insanely sensitive and kind. I love the way he makes me feel—so wanted and desired.

I wonder how drastically that might change when I tell him about the baby. Because revealing the truth will not only prove that I lied to his face, but it will change this dynamic completely. We haven't even discussed children, really. *What if he doesn't want to be a dad?*

It scares me to think I might lose my career and Alexei over this baby, trading my dream career and the dream relationship for something I thought I would never have.

I know it's what's right for me, even if it means losing two things I hold so dear.

All I can do is hope that Alexei might feel the same way—or at least come around to the idea of having a child with me.

Icy fear grips my chest as I know my time is almost up. I've stalled far longer than I ever should have. What I wouldn't give to just stay in this perfect space, the bliss of ignorance, but I can't keep it from him forever.

Just a few more minutes, I tell myself, holding him close as I breathe in his warm, spicy scent.

Right now, before we have the conversation that's long overdue, I just want to enjoy him a bit longer because I'm not sure where we'll end up once he knows I'm pregnant.

Alexei hums an appreciative sigh and eases out of me. Rolling onto the mattress next to me, he sprawls out, staring up at the ceiling as he revels in the moment.

I scoot closer, forming my body to his side as I rest my cheek on his muscular shoulder.

"I can see why you like boats," I tease lightly, running my fingers over the rippling lines of his abs.

Alexei chuckles, tightening his arm around my shoulders and leaning in to press a kiss to my forehead. "Your stomach feeling better?"

I nod, though it tightens and knots at his question.

Be brave, Nadia. Tell him.

Moving my hand up to his chest, I splay my fingers across his heart and feel the slow, powerful beat steadily thrumming against my palm. A tingle of excitement fills my chest as I wonder when I'll be able to hear my baby's heartbeat. I haven't been to the doctor yet.

I didn't want Alexei to miss the first appointment—if he even wants to be a part of it.

"Nadia, what's wrong?" he asks, his voice low and worried as he shifts to mimic my motion, his palm coming to rest between my breasts so he can feel my pulse.

It's hammering a mile a minute, reflecting my anxiety over telling him my secret.

"Your heart's beating so fast," he breathes, deep concern creasing his brow.

Oh, God. It's now or never.

I stare up into his striking silver eyes, my tongue darting out to wet my suddenly dry lips as I struggle to find the nerve to say what's going on. "I—"

A jarring rattle fills the air, cutting me off and stealing the oxygen from my lungs.

Is that gunfire?

The screams that follow a moment later turn my blood to ice.

33

ALEXEI

My anxiety spikes as the familiar sound of an automatic rifle splits the air, obliterating the intimate moment. Whatever Nadia was about to tell me will have to wait. The sudden panic on the other side of the wall tells me something is terribly wrong.

The muffled sounds of Russian commands tells me my men on duty are facing a serious threat.

"*Blyat!*" I curse, jumping up off the bed in a flash.

Snatching our clothes from the ground, I toss Nadia her suit and cover-up before yanking on my swim trunks. I don't bother with my shoes or shirt. Instead, I make a beeline for the safe hidden in one of the cabinets near the head of the bed.

"Hide," I command, keeping my voice low as I point Nadia in the direction of the bathroom. "Don't come out until I tell you it's safe. *Me*, Nadia. No one else."

She nods, her green eyes wide with fear.

I check my gun to make sure it's fully loaded, then I grasp her chin, giving her a quick, passionate kiss. The look of desperation on her face as we break apart tears at my heart.

"Be careful," she pleads.

But I'm already at the door, easing it open a crack so I can peer outside. Bare feet hammer across the deck as several ballerinas race from the back of the yacht, fleeing for their lives. Then everything falls silent as the coast clears.

I slip outside into the sunbaked air and make my way toward the outer deck. More shouted Russian greets me, and now that I'm outside, I know it's not one of my men barking commands.

Creeping toward the outside corner of the wall opposite the cabin where Nadia's hiding, I peer carefully around the edge to assess what's going on. Using the wall for cover, I only lean out far enough to look in the direction of the voice.

Three of my five men who had been standing on the upper deck lay dead, bleeding out across the planking at my feet. It seems they were shot and fell over the railing to find the floor beneath them. A few men I don't recognize lie not far beyond, their blood mingling in a gruesome red paint.

Several more armed gunmen have made their way off a small motorboat onto the back of our yacht. They appear to have climbed up the siding, rather than using the ladder, in order to catch my men by surprise. They must have killed the motor and rowed in to avoid drawing attention to themselves.

"Come out and play, Federov boys!" a bearded gunman taunts, silently gesturing for four of his men to slip around the far side of the deck while the rest of them come my way.

I count seven in all, and from the lack of return fire that would be coming from above, I suspect all five of my men are dead. I doubt any of the ballet company even knows how to hold a gun, let alone thought to bring one on board, which means it's up to me and Maks to take these assholes down.

Grinding my teeth, I press my back against the wall, staying hidden for as long as possible as I wait for my opportunity to attack. Holding my gun in one hand, I reach into the pocket of my swim trunks with my other to find my pocket knife.

A yacht really isn't ideal for taking down a handful of men armed with ARs. But that's the situation I find myself in. If I have to kill every last one of these bastards to keep Nadia and my brother safe, I will.

"What? Are you brothers just a bunch of cunts? Come out and greet me like men!" the leader mocks in Russian as he makes his way past the opening where I'm hiding.

Rapid gunfire bursts from the front of the yacht, followed by a revolting cocktail of terrified and agonized screams.

I catch the profile of his smile as the bastard in charge enjoys the sound of the massacre happening at the front of the yacht. I take advantage of the momentary distraction.

Bringing my gun up, I pause only a moment to aim before blasting a hole through the side of his head.

Then I turn as the second man shouts in surprise, bringing his gun up as he turns to face me.

Too late. I'm already ready for him.

I hit him with three bullets—two to the head, one to the chest—and send him toppling over the railing into the deep blue water.

The third guy is ready for me, jumping clear of the wall as he aims his rifle at my head. I don't have time to return fire. My ears ring as I duck, narrowly missing the shower of bullets that most definitely would have killed me.

Launching forward with explosive force, I drive my shoulder into his gut and carry him back until we collide with the railing. The air whooshes from his lungs, and his gun clatters to the deck. He sucks in a ragged breath, winded from having the wind knocked out of him.

I take advantage of his momentary incapacitation.

Firmly gripping the hilt of my knife, I drive it upward, stabbing beneath his ribs as I simultaneously disengage and come to a stand. The man's face pales, his eyes growing wide as he looks down at the blade protruding from his stomach.

Giving it a violent twist, I yank it back, and the man screams in agony.

Then, with a sharp slash, I silence him as I open his throat to the bone.

He follows the second man into the sea a moment later.

But the sound of bullets continues at the front of the boat. The rat-a-tat of rapid-fire intermingled with blood-curdling screams makes my pulse quicken. Wiping the man's blood off my palm and onto the shirt of his fallen leader, I then collect the remaining guns, slinging them across my back as I keep my more mobile handgun at the ready.

Then I creep forward, crouching low as I stay close to the wall. Knife gripped in one hand, I rest the base of my gun against my wrist, ready to aim and shoot at a moment's notice.

Where the hell is Maksim?

He'd better not be dead.

Horrible sobs rip through the air as the gunfire subsides, and my stomach knots painfully.

"A special message from Aleksandr Volkov," a man sneers in Russian. "War's here, asshole, so get ready to die."

My heart stops, and I throw caution to the wind as I sense my brother's life is in imminent danger. Rounding the corner, I take less than a second to assess the situation—my brother kneeling on the ground, his fiancée cradled in his arms, the gun lying uselessly on the ground at his side.

And one of Aleksandr's men leering over him, gun aimed squarely at Maksim's head.

"I don't think so," I growl, capturing his attention and having the intended effect.

As his eyes track toward my unexpected voice, the gunman's aim shifts slightly, the tip of his gun moving to point at the deck beside my brother. Without hesitation, I put a bullet between his eyes.

His gun misfires as his finger twitches in an involuntary spasm, and the deck beside Maksim's feet explodes, sending splinters into the air. Icy terror grips my heart as my brother doesn't even flinch.

I take stock of the situation on the deck now that all immediate threats seem to be subdued. Aside from the gunman I took down, two more must have fallen to Maksim's shots. They sit slumped and lifeless against the side of the boat.

Several of the ballet dancers appear to be bleeding, though none are grievously injured—from what I can tell at a glance. They huddle in the crevices between benches, hiding behind sun chairs or whatever cover they could find at the moment.

Tears stream down several of their faces as they sob openly, terrified for their lives.

But as my eyes track back to Maksim, my heart stops.

He's covered in blood, his eyes hauntingly hollow as he looks down at the woman in his arms. And for the first time, I register just how pale Symphony looks—too pale. Her skin is almost blue, it's so white.

As my eyes track down her body, I find the tiny, unassuming bullet hole on the inside of her left breast. Her breathing is so shallow that her chest rises and falls like a frightened rabbit's.

"I don't want to die, Maks," she breathes, her voice thin and high with terror.

Tears stream down her temples as she shakes uncontrollably, and she's bleeding out so fast, I know there's nothing we can do to save her.

"You're not going to die," my brother promises her, his large arms holding her close, cradling her in his lap.

And for a moment, he has me convinced that he believes his words. But when his eyes lift to find mine, I can see the haunting truth reflected there. He knows she has moments to live, and the pain on his face echoes inside my bones.

Then he releases me from his agonized gaze to turn his attention back to the woman he loves.

"Shh, you're fine," he murmurs, pressing his forehead to his fiancée's as he tries to calm her.

And that seems to have its intended effect. Symphony's breathing slows, and her face calms. Her limbs twitch. Then she goes limp in his arms.

Maksim releases a bone-chilling, agonized moan.

But before I can go to my brother, my senses tingle as my instincts kick into high gear.

There were seven gunmen.

We're missing one.

Though I want to focus on the grief incapacitating my oldest brother, I need to know where the last one went. Creeping carefully forward, I raise my gun to head around the far side of the yacht.

All eyes watch me from behind their respective forms of cover. All except Maksim's as he hunches protectively around the lifeless form of his fiancée, his loss overriding his concern for anyone's safety, including his own.

My pulse is steady, my hands even as I deal with this situation like I would any other security breach. Now that we have a lone gunman, I just need to weed him out. He probably saw his buddies dropping like flies and headed back toward the boat. But I'm not letting him get away.

I round the corner, gun raised and ready to shoot—only to find an empty deck.

Blood trickles over the railing from the yacht's open-air deck above, blood I'm sure is from my men, and my fury spikes. They're all dead because that greedy bastard Aleksandr Volkov decided he would like to have a piece of our pie.

I take a step toward the walkway running along the starboard side.

Then I freeze at the blood-curdling scream that comes from the stern.

Nadia.

34

NADIA

Tucked against the wall of the shower, I make myself as flat and inconsequential as I can, praying the intruder doesn't find me. Someone definitely just opened the door to the bedroom we were in, and it's not Alexei. He said he would tell me to come out when he came back.

No, this person treads lightly, but their heavy boots are different from the soft pad of Alexei's bare feet. My heart sprints in my chest, warning me that I should run. But I have nowhere to go. My only exit would take me straight into his line of sight.

Pressing my lips firmly together, I scarcely dare to breathe.

Something falls just on the other side of the wall, and my heart stops momentarily.

I think it's an item off the nightstand the intruder was just searching. Whether he's looking for something specific or just curious, I don't know. But the hair rises on the back of my neck as I pray he finds whatever it is and leaves.

The screams and gunfire outside are excruciating, the sound of people I know terrified and dying for some unknown cause. And I'm in here, cowering to save my life. *And the life of my unborn child.* That more than anything keeps me rooted to the spot.

What do these men want? I could hear them calling out, taunting Alexei and his brothers, daring them to engage. *But why? Some vendetta Alexei has never told me about? I have no clue what's going on.*

Shuddering, I close my eyes tight for one deep breath.

And as I open them again, the bathroom's sliding door whispers open.

My stomach drops, and a wave of terror sends bile racing up my throat.

Oh, God, not now. You cannot throw up right now, I command myself. It's the worst possible moment for my morning sickness to kick in.

Why do they even call it that when it comes at all times of the freaking day?

I could almost find my burst of frustration humorous if I weren't in such dire straits. One sound, and the intruder will find me for sure. At least the frosted glass of the shower door makes it less obvious that I'm here.

Fingers drum on the wall just feet from my head, and a moment later, I hear the lid to the toilet open with a *thunk*.

Is he seriously going to take a bathroom break in the middle of this massacre?

The sound of liquid splashing into the bowl confirms it, and I stand aghast as the intruder seems perfectly content to let his friends outside finish their job for him. My heart aches as the sound of gunfire peters to a stop, the screams dying down to nothing more than muffled sobs.

They can't have killed all the dancers because I hear a few female whimpers traveling through the walls. Alexei was right. They really are paper thin.

Is Alexei dead? All the armed men he brought on the boat "just as a precaution"?

The thought that Alexei might not come back—that he could have died trying to stop the men killing everyone—that hits me with an overwhelming dose of anxiety. My stomach turns violently at the possibility of his death. Before I can stop it, an audible gag escapes me.

I clap my hands over my mouth, trying to keep the motion as subtle as I can. Silently, I pray that the intruder's back is still toward the shower and that I managed to muffle the sound in time.

Too late, I realize that the bathroom is completely quiet. I close my eyes as terror grips my soul. Trembling, I wait with bated breath to see if he noticed me.

Then the shower door jerks open, and I release an involuntary squeak as I come face to face with the barrel of a gun.

"Look what I have here," the stocky Russian drawls in a lazy accent. "Come on, little mouse. Come out to play."

He reaches in and snatches my wrist, then yanks me forcefully against his chest.

"Let me go!" I shout, jerking as hard as I can to break his hold on me.

For a split second, I succeed.

I dart around him, desperate to escape. But the space is too narrow, and as large as he is, the man isn't slow. In a flash, his fingers grab a handful of my hair, and he hauls me backward with such force that I feel the roots giving way.

The scream of agony escapes my lips before I give it a thought, and I fall back against his sweaty chest as his arm wraps around my neck.

"Shut up," he growls, placing the cool metal of his gun's nose against my temple.

Sheer panic rises up inside me.

I'm terrified that this might be it. I'm going to die, and all I can think about is the baby growing inside me. How it will never have a chance at life?

"Please, please, don't kill me. I'll do anything. Just please . . ." Words flood me in a torrent of dread. I don't know what to say that might help me in this situation.

All I know is how desperately I need to live.

I'm shaking like a leaf, my heart roaring in my ears, and tears sting my eyes as I think about the innocent child who would be condemned to death if I die.

"Please," I whisper, gripping his forearm as it tightens, hindering my airway.

"Shut *up*," he snarls against my ear. "What you're going to do is walk outside with me like a good little girl so we can see just how many of your little ballet friends died with all those useless men the Federov brothers thought could protect you."

Biting back a sob, I nod. Together, his chest pressed firmly against my back, we creep through the bedroom. Then we head out the door and around the corner to the walkway on the right side of the ship.

My stomach plummets at the sight of blood dribbling down the yacht's white siding to coat the wood floor like wet paint. And when I look up the length of the boat, my heart skips a beat.

Alexei is already standing there, gun aimed pointedly in our direction, a bloody knife gripped in his free palm. I can feel my captor tense behind me. That wasn't what he had anticipated on finding when he came outside.

But he's ready for the confrontation as he shifts his face to hide more behind my head. "Don't even breathe without permission," he commands in a low, deadly voice. Then he shouts to Alexei, blasting my ear and making my head ring, "If you don't want me to put a bullet in her head, you'll lower your gun right now and back up!"

He pushes me forward, his head shifting against mine as if he's looking up and down the walkway, casting glances overhead.

I'm so filled with relief to see Alexei alive that it leaves me dizzy. *But why is his chest all covered in blood?* My stomach tightens. *Is he hurt?* He doesn't seem overly concerned about it as he hesitates before following my captor's command.

It makes my heart stop to watch him lower the gun, and a wave of overpowering helplessness follows as he steps back.

Then my captor pushes me forward, his arm around my neck tightening as if he thinks I might try to make a break for it. "Denka! Yuri! Mikhail!" he shouts, making my eardrum throb painfully once again. "Boss!"

No response.

As we reach the front corner of the yacht's enclosure, I can see why.

From the few that are within view now, I would assume they're all dead. The same thought seems to hit my captor at the same time, and the tip of the gun starts to tremble against my temple.

Oh, God, please don't shoot me by accident.

"Easy, comrade," Alexei says carefully, his hand reaching, palm down, fingers splayed in a calming gesture.

That's when my eyes land on Alexei's brother Maksim—and the lifeless figure cradled in his arms. Symphony looks so fragile compared to Maksim's impressive size, but she's entirely limp and deathly pale, which tells me it doesn't matter now. She's already gone.

This is the danger of dating a Federov brother. I knew it from the start. Bratva men are dangerous—it doesn't matter who's wielding the gun or why.

I shudder violently as I realize that I'm shortly going to follow the same fate as Maksim's fiancée because the man holding a gun to my head is losing it. I can feel it in the spastic way his arm tightens around my throat, truly choking me now.

But being pregnant puts my situation into a completely different perspective. I can't just stand idly by and expect Alexei to save me. If he tries to kill my aggressor, he could easily shoot me or hurt the baby.

And even if he does manage to shoot my captor, who's to say the gun pressed to my temple won't go off?

But if I do nothing, I'll pass out and die of oxygen deprivation.

I'm doomed no matter what I do, and I can't stand the thought of simply giving up.

Not when it would cost the life of my unborn child.

Desperation drives me to dig deep and do something reckless, anything that might save my baby.

So I go for the gun.

In one swift maneuver, I release my captor's arm to drive both palms toward the barrel of the gun. Relief floods me as I feel the metal slip from my temple. Without missing a beat, I lock my fingers together and drive my elbow into his gut, hoping the move might knock the wind out of him—or at least catch him off guard enough that he might release his chokehold.

It's just effective enough that I can suck in a desperate lungful of air, and I squirm, trying to escape my captor's hold. But he's clinging to me with the same life-and-death desperation that I feel in my drive to escape.

"Let me go!" I scream, wriggling desperately.

But he's getting his bearings back now that I've lost the element of surprise, and he's far stronger than I am simply because he's almost three times my size.

I fight like a wildcat, kicking and clawing, slapping and punching, lashing out at him in any way I can.

"I'll kill you, little bitch," he growls, jerking my wrist painfully as he brings me close and raises his gun.

My heart leaps into my throat as I see my death just moments before it happens.

And then the world freezes at the echoing blast of a gun.

35

ALEXEI

My heart stops, my blood turning to ice, and as Nadia's eyes grow wide in shock, the entire scene shifts into slow motion.

For one terrifying moment, I think I hit Nadia.

The bullet aimed for her captor was too bold. She was moving too much. My window was too small.

Then the man behind her drops like a ton of bricks.

The blood that seeps from the back of his head confirms it.

He's dead.

I close the distance between me and Nadia in three long strides, and she collapses against my chest, sobbing with fright. Trembling violently, she clings to me, her fingers pressing into the muscles of my back as she buries her face against my chest.

And it's all I can do to hold her in my arms.

"You're okay," I murmur, stroking her raven hair.

Then I glance over my shoulder. The same can't be said about my brother's fiancée—or my brother. Maksim appears to have morphed into some kind of grotesque, inconsolable statue, unable to look away from Symphony's lifeless face, his skin ashen, his lips so pale they might as well be drawn in chalk.

And it kills me to see him so devastated.

I can't imagine the pain of losing Nadia.

Just the thought of it makes my heart achingly hollow, and I pull her more firmly against me, needing to feel her safe and sound in my arms.

"Your skin is like ice," I observe as she shivers against me.

Nadia nods, and when she tips her chin up to look at me, her lips are almost purple. "I think I'm going into shock," she breathes, her green eyes round.

"Are you hurt?" I grip her shoulders to support her weight as I hold her at arm's length, scanning her body, but I can't see any obvious injury.

"I don't think so," she murmurs. Then her eyes fall to my chest, and she pales. "Are you?"

"I'm fine . . . It's not my blood," I say coarsely, my voice raspy with concern over her state.

"Mr. Federov." The white-haired captain, who must have been holed up in the yacht's cockpit during the violence, steps out now.

Several ballerinas step tentatively from the safety of the cockpit with him. Among them is the girl I recognize as Nadia's friend McKenna. I'm grateful to see he managed to keep a few of the girls out of harm's way.

His eyes seek orders from me—not Maksim, who is clearly unprepared to take charge at the moment.

"If the *Swan* can get us back to the Bay, then take us there," I say. "I'll have Dimitri meet us."

"Sir," he agrees with a dip of his head before vanishing back into the cockpit.

I'll need all the help I can get dealing with the mess Aleksandr has left us. Our boat, named after my mom's favorite ballet, is loaded with dead men from both sides of the fight, and while the police might see it our way when it comes to what happened today, we can't afford to be bogged down by an investigation.

Sighing, I take stock of our situation.

The ballet dancers seem to be gradually coming out of hiding and comforting each other or helping patch up minor injuries. Nadia, on the other hand, is shaking so hard her teeth are rattling. My brother refuses to accept help from the ballet director, Stew Lubox. He shoves the man roughly back when Lubox offers to help lay Symphony down.

Though it troubles me deeply to see my oldest brother so far gone, I can't think of anything to do for Maksim just now. Dimitri will know how to help, so calling him becomes my first priority. That and getting Nadia warm.

As I guide her gently toward the cabins once more, my arm wrapped snugly around her shoulders, I pull my phone from my back pocket and dial my middle brother's number.

"Man, you guys are getting old. Is the party over already?" he jokes by way of greeting, and the levity contrasts starkly with the gruesome truth of the day.

I tell him what happened, keeping my words short and to the point, not getting too graphic to spare Nadia.

"I'll have men ready to take care of the boat situation as soon as you make port . . . And I'll help Maksim lay Symphony to rest. I doubt he would let anyone but you or me touch her, and you need to take care of Nadia."

"Thanks, Dimitri."

"You're my brother," he says simply, as if that explains it all.

I don't know what I would do without him.

Hanging up, I toss the phone on the bed and guide Nadia into the bathroom to turn on the shower. She eyes it with silent contempt but doesn't say a thing. I wonder what happened in here when the gunman managed to take her captive, but I don't want to push her too hard.

As soon as the water's hot, I help Nadia across the shower threshold and bring her under the wet heat, hoping I can bring her temperature up. Slowly, her shivers ease, the color of her lips growing normal once again. Neither of us speaks as she silently turns her attention to washing the blood from my chest.

Forty-five minutes later, bundled in terry cloth towels and looking more like a boat of refugees than a ballet troupe coming off a party yacht, I guide the shaken dance crew onto the dock where Dimitri stands waiting.

"We've got cars to get the dancers home," he says as soon as I reach him.

"Good." I nod, pulling Nadia closer to my side, my hands kneading her arms compulsively. "We stacked the bodies." I jerk my head toward the back of the boat, where they're hidden from view on the land. "I hosed the decks. Maksim is with Symphony."

Dimitri nods, and I see reflected in his eyes the same gnawing guilt. We were both guilty of wishing our oldest brother and his fiancée would part ways for one reason or another. But neither of us would wish the girl ill to the point of wanting her dead. She just . . . hadn't had the same level of depth as Maksim.

But he loves her, and I don't know that there's a way back for him now.

Not from what I've seen today.

"I'll take it from here," Dimitri rasps, patting me on the shoulder and giving Nadia a perceptive scan.

"I'll call you later," I confirm, then guide the fragile dancer toward my car.

She hasn't said a word since the *Swan* turned for home, and I feel a sense of dread building in my chest. I think the worst of her physical reaction to being held at gunpoint and having her life threatened has passed. But something far heavier is weighing down her mind.

"Nadia!" her young, dark-skinned dancer friend calls.

Nadia attempts a brave smile as she stops and turns to find McKenna, and I stop with her, though I refuse to relinquish my hold.

"Hey, McKenna. You okay?" she asks, and the sound of her voice, shaky as it is, fills me with intense relief.

The younger ballerina nods. "I'm glad you are too. The way you took on that last gunman . . . you're so brave," she says, her voice airy with wonder. "I don't think I would have been able to move."

Nadia gives a shrill laugh that's very unlike her usual low, sultry sound. "You'd be amazed at how much it comes down to pure instinct. I don't think I had a plan in my head. I just panicked."

"Well, I'm glad we're all safe." She bites her lip as soon as the words are out, and I know she's thinking about Symphony—maybe even my men who gave their lives trying to stop Aleksandr's men.

"I'm grateful too," I cut in to ease her discomfort. "I assure you, when I invited the ballet out for a day on the yacht, I hadn't anticipated anything like this."

Her brown eyes grow round, and she nods shyly. Then she glances back at Nadia. "I'll see you tomorrow."

Nadia nods, and I take that as permission to lead her to the car.

But on our drive back to my penthouse, she's painfully silent in the passenger seat.

"Will you say something?" I ask gently, casting her a sidelong glance. The quiet between us has grown agonizing as I feel the blame for her trauma landing squarely on my shoulders.

She came so close—too close—to dying today. So easily, it could have been her instead of Symphony. And the longer I think about it, the closer I come to losing my mind. If Nadia thinks so, too, if she's weighing the risks of spending time with me, then all the hard work I've put into win her over these past few months will have vanished with a single boat ride.

She doesn't answer right away, and my stomach tightens when I see the troubled look on her face. When she finally does speak, it's not at all what I want to hear.

"We need to talk," she says gravely, the statement confirming my fears. She's going to end things. She doesn't want to be with me after the near-death experience that stemmed from her association with my family.

"Okay," I agree, fighting to keep my voice steady as my hands tighten on the steering wheel.

"Let's wait until we get back to your place."

I nod, the pressure in my chest too much to fit words around.

The silence that follows is stifling.

I know I shouldn't, but as we finally arrive at my apartment complex, park the car, and head toward the elevators, I reach for Nadia's hand. And to my surprise, she doesn't pull away, so I savor my last moments with her, contemplating whether there's anything I can do to change her mind.

The thought flits through my head that I could just *not* let her leave.

But she would hate me for that.

Finally, we step out of the elevator, into my flat, and I lead Nadia to the living room couch, my heart pounding a quick beat against my throat. We settle onto the seat, our knees bumping as we face each other, and the fear that tightens her features makes my stomach twist painfully.

Is she afraid of me?

I fight to rein in my impatience, to let her say it at her own pace, but the suspense is killing me. I want her to rip the Band-Aid off, and at the same time, I'm willing her to say anything besides that she doesn't want to see me anymore.

Nadia takes a deep breath, her green eyes wide and nervous, and I can feel her trembling once again through the connection of our palms. Her lips part, and her jaw works, but no sound comes out.

"For God's sake, Nadia, just say it," I plead, not sure I can stand another second.

"I'm pregnant," she blurts, and in the blaring silence that follows, her eyes start to brim with tears.

36

NADIA

Alexei looks beyond shocked, his face struck as he sits slack-jawed beside me. The horror hovering just beneath his surprise hits me like a freight train, and suddenly, I'm scrambling to give him a suitable explanation.

"I was scared to tell you since we haven't been using protection because I said I couldn't have kids, and we haven't even discussed something as serious as whether or not you even *want* to have children, and if Stew finds out, he might remove me from the ballet before the end of the season," I spew, my words coming out in one long, nonsensical sentence. "I know the baby will permanently affect my career, and I just—I wanted a little control over *when* my career ends. But I've also been worried about how it might affect us as a couple, and... and..."

A sob rips from my chest as Alexei sits frozen like a statue, his expression shifting from stunned to irate. In a flash, my worst fears are realized. He's mad because he thinks I did this on purpose. He thinks I lied to get pregnant, and he doesn't want this baby.

"How long have you known?" he growls, his hand tightening almost painfully around my fingers as his gray eyes flash with betrayal.

"A–About t–two weeks now . . ." I whisper, my voice abandoning me in the wake of his fury.

"You've known you were carrying my child for two weeks, and you never said a word? Two weeks we've been sleeping together, sharing intimate moments—fuck! I thought I was building your trust, and now it turns out you've been lying to me?" Alexei's up off the couch in a flash, pacing before me in his rage.

I tremble as his anger washes over me like a wave, stealing my breath away. His fingers rake into his dark hair, yanking violently at the roots and leaving it standing on end as he stops to face me.

"Are you serious right now, Nadia? Is that why you were throwing up on the boat today?"

I pale as he calls me out on my bold-faced lie, and as terrified as I am to admit it, I nod hesitantly.

He scoffs. "Seasick . . . that's rich . . ." The thunderstorm clouds gather across his face as he takes a moment—probably recalling all the other times I should have said something to him and chose not to.

Then, his jaw sets in a line of determination, and he strides toward me. Strong fingers wrap around my forearm, hauling me up off the couch with surprising ease, and he steers me back toward the elevator as if I weigh nothing.

"What are you doing?" I gasp, my stomach dropping. "Where are you taking me?"

But Alexei seethes silently beside me, never letting go of my arm as I struggle to break free of his hold. *Is he walking me out? Kicking me out of his apartment—his life?*

The agony that rips through me robs me of my will to fight. I knew it was a possibility. I knew he might not want me or the baby. I find it exceedingly ironic that I spent so many years thinking I would never find love because I couldn't be a mother—and now that I actually *can*, that's the very reason the man I love doesn't want me. But rather than taking me to the front door, we're right back in the parking garage, making a beeline for his sporty white Corvette.

"Alexei, please," I sob, wishing he would talk to me—say something.

But he seems beyond words. Opening the passenger-side door, he puts me inside. Then he moves around the front of the car and slips behind the wheel a moment later.

"Where are we going?" I murmur, my heart pounding, and I place a palm protectively over my abdomen.

The gesture doesn't seem lost on him as he catches it from the corner of his eye. He grinds his teeth visibly, the tendons of his jaw jumping beneath his skin as he throws the car in reverse and peels out in his haste to leave the parking lot.

It hits me then, why he might not want to say, and icy fear closes around my heart as I wonder for the first time if he might make me get rid of it.

"Please, Alexei," I breathe tearfully, imploring him to see reason.

But he simply flashes me a look that says he's in no mood to discuss things.

Crying silently, I turn to watch the world flash by outside the window. After fifteen minutes, as he takes us outside the city and onto the winding coastal highway, I frown.

Where is he taking me?

He's not making any sense. Unless he knows someone outside of town who's willing to perform emergency abortions against the mother's will. Terrified as I am right now, I don't know that I believe Alexei capable of that.

Then again, today I witnessed just how brutal and lethal he can be. At the time, I was more than grateful for it. Those men were going to kill us without mercy. I could feel the cold satisfaction it brought the man who took me captive.

He would have taken my life in an instant, no remorse.

But what about Alexei?

He wouldn't . . . kill me for getting pregnant, would he?

I shudder at the thought and almost feel bad for thinking it at all. But as I watch him from the corner of my eye, I don't think I've ever seen him this angry. Even when he shot the man behind me, he was calm, collected. He did it with deliberate and precise intention.

This Alexei, now, feels dangerously out of control. And though he steers his Corvette with flawless ease, it doesn't escape me that we're leaps and bounds above the speed limit and taking hairpin turns like we're on a Formula One speedway.

Anxiety washes through me as I think about our baby and what might happen if we crash. "Alexei, please slow down," I beg, my voice shaking uncontrollably.

And to my intense relief, he does, his foot easing off the pedal some to bring us within ten miles of the speed limit. His eyes flick down to the hand that protectively covers my stomach, and his expression grows inscrutable as his gaze moves back to the road ahead.

We drive like that for over an hour, the silence heavy between us. I worry my lip incessantly, not knowing what to expect as he takes me farther and farther into the countryside.

Finally, he slows to turn onto a gravel drive. The tires crunch across the road lined with tall Italian cypresses, and I look in awe as we follow the rolling drive toward a massive house. It looks almost as though he's brought me to a winery, with hills covered in vegetation sprawling out on either side of me—near impossible to make out clearly in the late dusk.

"Where are we?" I breathe, sitting up to peer more intently out the windshield now.

"Our family estate," he says, speaking for the first time since we got in the car. His voice is hoarse with tension, though slightly softer than it was when I first told him I was pregnant.

He circles the grand fountain that sits in the center of the mansion's courtyard, stopping right in front of the pillared front steps. Throwing the car into park, he comes around to open my door, and despite the tension in his face, he offers me his hand.

Heart skipping a beat, I take it, tentatively daring to believe the worst is over now that he's recovering from being completely blindsided. Guilt riddles me as I see it from his perspective. Not only did the woman he's with get knocked up when she said that was an impossibility, but she intentionally kept it from him for weeks, only to reveal it hours after everyone almost died.

Not cool, Nadia.

The air is cool and humid inside the vaulted entryway. Marble floors inlaid with beautiful mosaics decorate the open space, creating the image of an ornate compass with the seasons represented at the point of each cardinal direction.

Suspended above the floor art is a spectacular chandelier dripping with crystals that sparkle in the electric lighting.

"It's beautiful," I breathe, taken aback by the wealth demonstrated in every inch of the luxurious property.

I knew Alexei and his brothers had money. It's obvious from the view of his penthouse, the car he drives, the two-story yacht we spent the day on. But this is beyond anything I could possibly have fathomed.

Billionaire would be an understatement, I think. And while I make a comfortable living as a ballerina, I've never seen this kind of money before.

"I'm glad you like it," Alexei says plainly, leading me up the curving staircase to the second floor. "Because this is where you'll be staying until I figure out the mess with Aleksandr Volkov's Bratva. You and the baby will be safe here in the meantime. We can get married once things calm down, but you're not to leave the protection of my men."

"Excuse me?" I hiss, yanking my hand out of his before we're halfway up the stairs.

Alexei turns, his silver gaze steely and authoritative. "I won't lose you. Or our baby. And this is how I intend to ensure that."

A momentary flutter of excitement ripples through me at the sound of *our baby* passing between his lips. I could almost be flattered that he feels so protective of us. And I want our child to be safe, just like he does.

But I just told him at his penthouse that I didn't want to say anything about the baby because it might mean missing the rest of my ballet season. And now he's single-mindedly decided to take that option away from me. He just drove what would probably take a sane driver *hours* to cover, removing me from the city, my home, my job, *him*. And now he wants me to stay here "under the protection of his men"? I don't think so.

Not to mention, I think he just delivered the worst possible marriage proposal I've ever heard. In fact, it wasn't even a proposal. He didn't exactly give me a choice in the matter.

It feels like my freedom has been snatched from me in an instant. I'm not the woman he loves or the mother of his child. I'm the incubator to his spawn, and I will be kept out of sight or fear of harm until I've given birth to his progeny.

I want to have this child, and I love Alexei more than I know how to say. But I will not stand by and let him turn me into his property. I knew going into the relationship how dangerous it would be to be with Alexei.

It's not my problem if he's only just realized that being a prominent figure in a Bratva will put a target on his back as well as the people he loves.

That doesn't mean he gets to take control of my life, my fate.

I'm already giving up everything to have this child.

I know I won't be able to follow my dream of ballet.

How dare he drag me up here without a word of discussion and think he can just lock me away?

37

ALEXEI

"This is the only place I'm confident Aleksandr Volkov won't come after you, so you're staying here," I insist.

I can see the fierce rebellion on Nadia's face, the fire in her eyes. She doesn't like being told what to do, but I won't be moved in this regard.

She's the love of my life. And now the mother of my child. I've barely had time to wrap my mind around that monumental fact in the wake of today's events, but I refuse to let that slow me down. Not after I just watched Maksim's entire world implode upon Symphony's death.

I can't let that happen to Nadia. I won't survive it.

And now it's not just her safety I need to think about...

Intense, overwhelming feelings of protective possession tighten my muscles. I will do whatever it takes to keep that tiny, defenseless child safe inside her. I want them both out of harm's way, and she can fight me all she wants, but I won't risk losing them.

"You are a complete *ass*, Alexei!" Nadia screams, her face livid as she draws away from me. "I would never marry some misogynistic prick who doesn't have the common decency to at least talk this through with me. I told you why I was worried about telling you—told you how much finishing this season at Tapestry means to me. And now you're just proving my concerns were legitimate!"

"Talk it through with you? Are you fucking kidding me?" I growl, closing the distance between us to bring my face within inches of hers. "You lost the chance to have a civil conversation about what happens now when you kept your pregnancy from me for *weeks*."

Her choice once again demonstrates how little Nadia trusts me—to withhold something that important, that monumental. It hurts me deeply to know that she wouldn't trust me with her secrets, that she might think I wouldn't have her best interests at heart.

God, I'm going to be a father, and I don't even get the chance to be excited about it because I'm terrified for Nadia and our child's lives. And because of that, my words are gruff, harsh, far more scathing than I intend them to be.

I don't expect the slap. Nadia's hand comes out of left field, her palm colliding with my cheek and releasing a sharp snap. Heat radiates from the point, and it's a hard enough hit that it turns my face.

I'm more shocked than I am in pain.

When I turn to look at her again, I see a hint of remorse before her fury overrides it. And underneath it all, a hot desire that tells me, as angry as she is right now—even after she said she won't marry me—she still wants me.

And God, I want her too. I want her forever. I want to make a family with her, and I'll do anything to protect her, to keep her and our child alive and safe.

She's the love of my life.

Nadia can hate me all she wants right now, but I won't risk her life. Not after Maksim lost his fiancée.

Before she can object, I grab her by the nape of her neck and pull her roughly to me. Our lips collide in a passionate kiss. All of my suppressed fear and anxiety over seeing a gun pressed to Nadia's head come flooding through my body and into my embrace.

She tenses in my arms, her palms flat against my chest as if to shove me away, but holding her is the only thing keeping me from losing my mind completely in this instant. I've held it together as long as I can, the pressure of the day's violence combined with such a life-changing revelation all culminating in a fierce need to keep her close.

After a second of hesitation, Nadia melts into me, her hands sliding up my chest to snake around my neck, her back arching so every possible inch of our bodies might connect.

I groan, curving around her as I tighten my hold, deepening the kiss until I'm entirely surrounded by her, filled with her intoxicating presence. She drives me crazy, this fiery Russian ballerina who is so dead set on living life the way she intends to. I love that about her, even if it turns me into something of a madman.

Straightening, I lift Nadia off her feet, and her legs wrap around me. I can't bring myself to break away from her lips long enough to watch where I'm going. Blindly finding the banister with one hand, I use it to guide me the rest of the way up the stairs as I carry her, one arm circled around her waist.

I make it just far enough down the upstairs hall to find the first guest bedroom, and I open it by touch. It takes every measure of self-control I can find to wait that long to ravish her. To punish her for being so obstinate. And to reward her for saving the life of our child.

I knew from the first night we had sex that Nadia meant what she said—she truly didn't believe herself capable of having children. I could see it in the agony of her face when she told me. And I hadn't wanted to press her on the matter, to open a wound that was clearly so raw and painful.

It'd been a disappointment to know that being with her would mean we couldn't have children together. But that never would have stopped me from being with her. I'm so drawn to Nadia, so enraptured by her, that I wanted her no matter the price.

And now?

It fills me with a deep and thrilling pride to know I'll be the father of her child.

And to know that she wants our child without question.

What hurts is to know that I'm what she doubts. Not just whether

I might be willing to share this secret with her. She doubted that I would want the child. She thought I might be mad about it. She was scared to tell me.

Anger flares up amid the pain, and I'm a tumult of emotion as we fall onto the bed together. Nadia seems to meet me point for point, her kisses desperate and passionate, greedy and grateful, furious and hurt.

But overriding it all is an overwhelming desire that blazes like an inferno as it mingles with my own.

She tears at my T-shirt, dragging it over my head impatiently as I rip the crocheted cover-up that forms a pattern across her chest. Still dressed in our beachwear, neither of us seems to care. My only goal is to get us out of it as quickly as possible.

Nadia seems to be on the same page. Her firm breasts heave as she arches her back to untie her swimsuit top, and I take advantage of the moment to pull her bottoms down over her hips and thighs.

She's naked in a matter of moments, her body still as slender and fit as the day I met her. A deep, aching longing settles into my balls at the thought of seeing her swollen and big-bellied with our child.

Christ, the thought is sexy.

As Nadia settles onto the bed, I trail kisses between her breasts, kneading them with my palms as I make my way down to her abdomen. I linger there, worshiping her skin as I think about the tiny life growing there.

When she went wild on her captor today, the thought had flashed through my head that she looked like a mother bear willing to stop at nothing to protect her cub. In the moment, I'd thought it an odd comparison to make.

But now, it feels just right.

She's going to make a spectacular mom.

Nadia's breaths grow shallow and ragged as I take my time to properly greet the little life we've made, and when I look up the length of her body to meet her eyes, they shine with a heat that tells me all her fear and anxiety have been burned away.

I creep lower, down her body, my hands shifting from her breasts to her hips. I cradle them with my palms, lifting them up off the mattress until her slick moisture finds my lips. Nadia groans, her head falling back as her clit twitches with pleasure, and I lick her wet folds, collecting her tang on my tongue.

Hips jerking with her excitement, Nadia curls her toes, and I know that she's ready for angry sex—to take out her pent-up frustration and aggression on my cock. I can't wait to see it.

I suck her clit between my lips, suctioning it mercilessly until Nadia cries out. Then I release it. The look of pure fire that she levels on me draws a devilish grin to my lips. She sits up, closing the distance between our mouths, and kisses me violently, her fingers tangling in my hair as her tongue delves between my teeth.

Groaning hungrily as she takes control, I grip her hips with my fingers, steadying her as she climbs onto my lap. Then she grinds against me. I can feel her warm wetness through my swim trunks, and I just about lose my mind as she uses my throbbing erection to stimulate herself.

"I want you inside me," she murmurs against my lips, leaning her bare breasts against my pecs so I can feel the hard peaks of her nipples.

I lift her off my lap, bringing us both to our knees as I strip my trunks quickly and my cock springs free. The tip grazes along the soft flesh of her stomach, and she falls into me, aligning our bodies as she silently urges me onto my back.

Fully appreciating this fierce, demanding side of Nadia, I obey. I lie back, pulling her on top of me at the same time. She straddles me, resting her hips on top of mine as she rocks, her pussy lips wrapping around my cock as she humps me without putting me inside.

"Fuck, Nadia," I breathe, my fingers spasming against her hips.

She gives me a playful smile and scoops her raven locks over her head so they cascade down one shoulder. Head tilted in the sexiest of innocent poses, she arches her back to showcase just how beautiful her tits are, how firm her stomach.

Then she reaches between us to grasp my cock in a powerful grip.

I groan, my cock throbbing from the punishing pleasure, and she strokes me with slow, deliberate confidence, using her own arousal as lube.

"Tell me you want me," she commands, and the order both fills me with intense desire and makes my heart ache from the hint of vulnerability that lies beneath.

"Always," I rasp. *How could she not know that by now?*

Her lips part with sensual relief, her excitement coloring her cheeks rosy pink. Then she guides my tip along her slick seam until I find her entrance, and slowly, so deliciously slowly, she sinks down on top of me.

Snarling as she comes to a stop only after I'm balls deep inside her tight hole, I lick the pad of my thumb, then reach between us to press it to her clit. Nadia gasps, her hips rocking forward as I connect with the tiny bundle of nerves.

And then she starts to ride me. Hard.

Hips rolling as she grinds against my thumb, Nadia slides up and down the length of my cock, driving the tip deep inside her every time she sits. The sexy vixen is going to make me blow my load if she doesn't pace herself.

I'm sorely tempted to let her because I don't think I've ever seen something so captivating as Nadia riding me into bliss. When her eyes roll into the back of her head and her walls swell and tighten around my hard length, I know she's close, and I'm mesmerized by her unbridled desire, her willingness to use me for her own satisfaction.

I fucking love it.

Releasing her hip with my unencumbered hand, I reach up to pinch her nipple. She gasps as I give it a slight twist, then I tug at it until she leans toward me. She keeps her brutal pace as her body shifts forward, her skin grazing against mine as I bring her close.

Without relinquishing her taut nub, I steal a kiss from her lips.

She finds her release as I suck her full lower lip between my teeth, and I greedily swallow her cry as I refuse to let her go. She feels so mind-blowingly incredible, her walls clamping down around me like a vise before breaking into a full-on sprint.

Her clit flutters as she gives me a climax so intense, it takes everything in me not to follow her into oblivion. Groaning with the agony of holding on, I release her nipple and remove my thumb from her clit so I can roll on top of her once more.

38

NADIA

Arguing with Alexei was going to get me nowhere. I could see the iron strength of his will in his eyes, and it left no room for compromise. But the heat of his touch lights me on fire in a way I hadn't known I needed in this moment.

The agonizing vulnerability stemming from the question of whether he might reject me for getting pregnant vanishes with the desperation in his touch. This overprotective hard-headedness that comes from wanting to keep me—or at the very least his baby—safe somehow fills me with an intense relief.

It moves me deeply to know that he would do whatever it takes to protect and care for me and our baby.

His touch gives me a sense of belonging I hadn't known I was so terrified of losing until now. And knowing that he wants me *always* creates a fiery passion within my soul that burns like an inferno.

I want him desperately. I want this desperately. I want to feel this bottomless connection that draws me to him like a moth to the flame.

And at the same time, I'm still furious with Alexei for being such a tyrant. It feels good to unleash all that frustration on his body, to take what I want from him rather than letting him control my body.

How is it that he can find the give and take in the bedroom, but when it comes to my freedom, he won't give an inch?

I'm giving up my life, my future as a ballerina to have this child. And I would do so willingly, every day of the week. *So why can't he let me have this?*

I let my fury stoke my desire as I ride my climax well beyond its usual extreme. Even as he rolls on top of me, trapping me against the sheets, I'm lost in a sea of euphoria, my body tingling with such intense relief that I can hardly recall the terror of today.

"God, I love you, Nadia," Alexei rasps, his voice floating on a fog of ecstasy as he starts to move on top of me.

My heart swells at his words, and it doesn't matter that I'm still mad about being imprisoned on his family estate. Despite everything, Alexei still wants to be with me. He wants our baby who's growing inside me. And he just said those three magical words that somehow alter my world.

"I love you too," I breathe, unable to say it louder than a whisper, even though I feel it's true with every fiber of my being. I love Alexei to the moon and back. I love him relentlessly. And I can't believe we're going to have a baby together.

"Swear to me you won't ever keep something like that from me again," he rasps, rolling his hips to entice me into agreement.

"I won't." Keeping it from him in the first place had left me riddled with guilt, constantly questioning my fortitude, sure I would blurt something because it took all I had not to say something. I hadn't even made it half the time I'd initially intended to keep my secret.

And if those men hadn't attacked our boat today, I would have told him about the baby in the yacht's cabin. But I don't have to say all that.

His lips come crushing down on mine, and I need the bruising passion of his touch, the fury with which he claims my lips and body for his own.

With his cock driving into my depths with punishing force, Alexei fills me with every scintillating stroke, demanding my pleasure as he takes his own. I know he's still mad at me for keeping our child a secret for so long, and frankly, I feel more justified in my decision than I did from the start.

Because he spirited me away to the middle of nowhere the moment he found out.

And because the angry sex is out of this world.

I'm sorely tempted to piss him off more regularly if it means feeling the level of furious passion with which he fucks me now.

"Oh, God, I'm coming," I gasp, the realization hitting me just moments before I fall apart.

I groan low and long as my pussy throbs, pulsing around Alexei's impossibly large erection, begging him to follow me into oblivion. He grunts, his shoulders bunching as his head falls onto the pillow beside my ear. He slams home, driving inside me to the hilt before releasing deep in my depths.

I shudder with that erotic feel of his seed filling me up. Heart fluttering with the aftershocks of my own release, I wrap my arms around him, holding him against my body. He settles on top of me, his hips spreading my thighs farther until I let them fall open completely.

Nuzzling my hair away from my ear, Alexei takes the lobe gently between his teeth and nibbles, teasing a few more shiver-inducing spasms from my pussy.

"We're having a baby?" he murmurs, the revelation vibrating through my chest in his deep baritone.

I nod, a smile spreading across my face.

Then his head rises off the pillow so his silver eyes can meet mine. "You were worried that getting pregnant would affect us as a couple?"

"Well . . . yeah. I mean, I've always thought that especially by your age, guys want to find women to settle down and have a family with, so from the start, I thought you might just want a fling."

Alexei quirks an eyebrow, donning an expression of amused offense, but he remains silent, letting me finish digging my grave.

"And then, when we started dating, I kind of got the impression that you weren't interested in being anything more than the 'cool uncle', and since I was told my low body weight necessary for being a ballerina combined with my already wacky hormonal imbalance would make me infertile, I didn't think starting a family would be in the cards for me..."

His eyes soften in the most beautiful way, as if he can feel the lingering sadness that has haunted me for years. My heart flutters as I wonder for the first time if he already knew about my struggle—because he doesn't seem surprised to hear it in my voice now.

"I really thought I couldn't get pregnant," I breathe, my eyes stinging with unshed tears as I relive my grief.

"I know, love. I could see it in your body language when you told me. It hurt you deeply to think you wouldn't have a child."

Alexei brushes such a tender kiss across my lips that my heart throbs. And suddenly, a weight lifts from my chest as I realize all that crushing sadness is over. I am capable of getting pregnant.

"I also knew that I wanted you no matter the circumstances. I can't wait to have a family with you. But I would have loved you regardless. You're unlike any woman I've ever met, Nadia. You captivate me. You intoxicate me with your mere presence, and I would give up children to be with you. But I want this baby just as much as you do."

Tears spill openly from my eyes now, and I sob as I bury my face in Alexei's shoulder. Somewhere along the line, I convinced myself that I was unlovable, undeserving of a man or a family because I couldn't have a child.

Hearing that Alexei would want me either way, it overcomes me. His words are not just empty. He made love to me just as passionately on our first night together as he did tonight.

And I find that truth earth-shattering.

Alexei's rumbling chuckle soothes my heart.

"Why are you crying, love?" he murmurs.

I laugh with him. "Because... you love me."

Alexei laughs harder, the amusement breaking across his chiseled, masculine face. "I don't know what I'm going to do with you," he says, his tone gently admonishing.

"Let me perform tomorrow?" I suggest, opening my eyes wide in a pleading expression.

His mirth is gone in a flash, his face growing stormy. "No."

Biting my lip, I fight the urge to argue my case. We've made enough good headway for the night. I don't want to push my luck by making demands. But I'm not about to give up dancing my last week of *Swan Lake* performances because he's being irrational.

It's late afternoon as Alexei leaves me on the front steps of his family estate with nothing but a searing kiss to remind me of what I'll be missing and the promise to return as soon as he can.

Then he climbs into the front seat of his flashy white Corvette and drives off into the sunset to put an end to a Bratva war that some man named Aleksandr Volkov just started.

He has business to do, and I'm to stay put, safe and sound, and a prisoner in all but name because I'm carrying his child.

I don't think so.

I love Alexei, but after an argument-filled morning—along with a momentary break in which I got to meet his lovely mom—I know he's dead wrong on this one.

He's taken away my choice, my freedom, and completely unromanticized his proposal by *telling* me we're getting married—no ifs, ands, or buts about it—something which he failed to rectify despite the considerable opportunities I gave him throughout the day.

Well, I refuse to just roll over and accept my fate. I *do* want to have his child. And I could definitely see marrying him someday. But I refuse to say my vows without a proper proposal—one in which he *asks* me to marry him. Preferably, while he's down on one knee.

And I will have my way about the ending to my one and only season as a principal ballerina. He's being overprotective, worrying about my safety when no one could possibly be willing to come after me in the middle of a sold-out public performance.

I'll take a ride into the city, go home to collect some clothes and my car, then come straight back. I'm even willing to give up practice—which Stew has said on multiple occasions is mandatory.

See? Compromise. It's not that hard.

I wait until Alexei's car vanishes down the long drive before I even order my Uber. My stomach knots when I see that it's going to be forty-five minutes before a driver can come get me. I suppose that's fair, considering I'm in the middle of nowhere.

But I'm going to be cutting it close to get to my performance on time. Chewing my lip, I contemplate my options, slapping my phone against my palm as I debate whether or not I can pull this off.

Then I scroll to McKenna's number and hit the green phone.

"Nadia, where are you? Are you okay? I got worried when you missed practice today."

"I'm fine," I assure her. "It's . . . been a crazy twelve hours. I kind of got stranded at Alexei's estate. But I'm on my way. Will you please let Stew know that I'll be there for curtain call?"

"Yeah, of course. No problem, but . . . you're sure you're okay?"

"Really, I'm fine," I insist. "I'll see you tonight."

I'd better pull this off.

39

NADIA

Brow sweaty, I race into the Curran Theater with less than fifteen minutes to spare.

"Nadia!" McKenna calls, her smile brilliant as her shoulders relax visibly. "You made it."

"Yes, I'm sorry I'm so late," I say as Stew glowers at me from the near side of the stage.

"You're not dressed. Go, go!" he barks, shooing me toward the dressing rooms.

"Want help?" McKenna offers.

"Please," I gush, the air whooshing from me in my frantic desperation.

I had time to pin my hair up in a tight bun while I was waiting for my ride, but I didn't have any of my stage makeup or my outfit to put on, and that usually takes me at least half an hour. This is going to be the fastest wardrobe change of my life.

Together, we race toward the back hall, catching a glare from Candace, who stands with haughty contempt, wearing her own version of an Odette costume. I hadn't thought about how she's my understudy. Coming in last-minute means she'll be back in the corps de ballet tonight.

"I'm so glad you're here," McKenna says in a low voice, leaning close so only I can hear.

"Really? Why?" Something in her voice tells me it's more than just a friendly statement.

"Candace was practicing as Odette all morning because Mr. Federov called to inform Stew that you wouldn't make the performance..."

I bristle at the revelation, learning just how far Alexei went to keep me from being here tonight. He sure is confident in his control over my life. Too bad he underestimated my determination to be here.

"Anyway, she couldn't get the lifts right. And she's off on the steps for her dance as Odile," McKenna says, flinching visibly.

That's one of the most important moments in the performance. Falling short on Odile could easily destroy the entire show.

"Anyway, I'm positive Ethan and Matteo are grateful you're here after today. And Stew's never looked more relieved to see you."

I snort, recalling his furious expression.

"Believe me, that was pleased," McKenna reiterates.

As we enter my dressing room, I don't waste time with modesty, stripping right in front of McKenna to don my tights and corset as she sets out the makeup. It's a joint effort, me stooping as I hook the eyes of my top while she smears paint across my face.

Then we pause momentarily so I can pull my flowing skirt up around my hips. My tutu will be waiting for me backstage—for when I'll need to make a quick change to show my transformation into a swan.

"Eyes," McKenna commands, her face laser focused as she holds the black liner brush before my face.

I close them obediently, trying to stay steady as I close the back of my skirt.

By some miracle and the grace of God for sending me McKenna, we manage to get me outfitted with three minutes to spare. Then we race back up the walkway to the side of the stage.

"Cutting it close, aren't we, Lukyan?" Stew growls as I breathe deeply.

"Sorry," I murmur, but I can't stop the smile from spreading across my face.

And when I meet Ethan's eye, he reflects my emotion—the gratitude for being a part of such a meaningful production, the opportunity to make art come to life. This is what I was made for, and though I'm willing to give it up to be a mom, I wouldn't miss tonight for the world.

The disembodied greeting welcoming guests to the theater and requesting they silence their cell phones before inviting them to enjoy the show brings me a sense of calm I feel in few other places. Taking a steadying breath in through my nose, I release it slowly between my lips.

And then the music starts.

Heart fluttering in my chest, I make my way onstage, dancing across it in a greeting to my audience. Representing all the light-hearted innocence of a young woman just risen from her youth, I move with energy and excitement. Each leap is a reminder of the joy of childhood—something I will get to witness firsthand as my own child grows.

My feet carry me across the stage with well-practiced ease, and despite not having made practice this morning, I can feel the music flowing through me. This role is one I've dreamed of performing all my life, and now here I am, dancing it to a sold-out audience.

I can hear the hush that falls over the crowd, the stillness with which they watch me. And when Matteo comes on stage, his face solemn and dramatic in the makeup of the villainous Baron von Rothbart, there comes a collective gasp.

Tonight, his expression is less disciplined, and I can feel the anticipation with which he takes my hand in our first pass. We complete it with flawless execution, me spinning around him to flit across to the far side of the stage.

Again, we come together, his presence this time looming more dangerously over my Odette. The ominous energy radiates from him, so convincing, I could almost believe it's real—and for Odette, it's too late.

I feel the moment deeply, reliving my own escape from St. Petersburg as if it were yesterday, the fear on my mom's face, the haunting shadows of the night that threatened to swallow us if we dared close our eyes.

And as Matteo transforms me into a swan for the first time, I vanish backstage, stripping my skirt as soon as I'm hidden and stepping into my tutu. I have only seconds to pin the feathered crown to my hair.

Then it's my cue to return—a beautiful white bird that floats seamlessly across the floor.

Rising onto my toes in a soft en pointe, I circle sadly, arching my back and curving my arms as I follow the solemn notes of the song.

This is my home. This is where I belong.

And I love it here.

The music moves me, transforming me into something greater than a dancer or a swan, and I'm so glad I came tonight—even if Alexei's going to be furious with me afterward.

But as I dance, I also know that I'll be okay with letting my career go because the idea of starting a family fills me with excitement I've never known before. So I intend to cherish this night—my last week of performances, if I can—before I start my grand new adventure into motherhood.

During intermission, I trade out my lighter, more innocent white makeup for the darker look of Odile, and a soft knock comes at my dressing room door. I don't know why, but I half expect it to be Alexei, and my heart sputters nervously.

"Come in," I call, bracing myself for an argument.

Instead, it's Stew who enters, his scowl telling me I'm in for a tongue lashing. "I don't know why Mr. Federov changed his mind, but I'm glad you're here," he states, catching me completely by surprise.

"Changed his mind?"

"Yes, he told me you wouldn't be back this week. I've been in a panic all morning. Candace made such a mess of practice, I was sure the performance would be a disaster. So, whatever you did to change his mind... good work."

I flash Stew a forced smile in my mirror, though my stomach knots. The likelihood that I'll be able to come back tomorrow doesn't seem very high—unless I can manage to slip back into Alexei's estate unnoticed. But I doubt it.

"You know, McKenna might be young, but she's a hard worker. You could consider her for an understudy," I point out. I've seen her dance a few shorter sections of Odette's part, and she's good.

Stew waves me off. "She's not a natural like you. And besides, you're back, so we don't need to talk about understudies."

"I assure you, Mr. Lubox, I was not a natural either. She has the drive for it that Candace doesn't—if you want my humble opinion."

"I'll take it into account," he grumbles. "Anyway, I'll let you get back to it. Just wanted to say I'm glad you're back."

Those might be the nicest words he's ever said to me, and I smile for real as the door shuts behind him.

Then the break is over, and I take my place on stage, waiting for my entrance to Odile's solo. The heavy curtains rise, slow and steady, as the music crescendos into the introductory notes.

And when I look out this time, I can just make out the faces of my audience, pale, almost glowing in the dim light. I stride forward, arms extended, to show off just how alluring I can be, weaving a bewitching dance for Ethan to succumb to.

But something doesn't feel right. The atmosphere of the theater hall feels dark, ominous. I break out in a cold sweat as a shiver runs down my spine.

Standing there, in the center aisle of the audience, is a dark figure. He wears shadows like a cloak, hiding his face. And I can't distinguish his lines because the stage lights are too bright.

But I know. I can feel it. He's watching me with silent, deadly eyes.

Faltering, I miss a step in my rotation, and the audience gasps as I fall out of step for the first time this season. My gut clenches, and I rip my eyes from the haunting figure, unsure of why he frightens me so terribly.

He's probably an usher or an audience member who came in late and doesn't want to interrupt people to get to his seat. It takes everything I have to focus on my performance, to set aside the unnerving sense of foreboding that haunts my every step.

But when the music stops and I freeze in my arrogant Odile position, the one that says the prince should have eyes only for me, my eyes immediately find him.

And my heart stops.

My breath catches in my throat.

He reaches slowly behind him, his pale hands vanishing behind his back for only a moment.

I've made a terrible mistake.

I never should have come tonight.

Alexei was right.

This man is here to kill me.

In a flash, he pulls out a gun, aiming it at me as he stalks down the aisle, and I freeze. I don't think anyone else has noticed the gunman.

But he's all I can think about as he aims squarely for my chest, prepared to steal my life away. And that of my unborn child.

There's no fighting him off this time. He's too far away. And he's not the lazy, slothful man I took on last time. This man is laser focused, his eyes full of malicious glee.

The music flares up around me, telling me to move, but I can't. I'm frozen in place.

Then everything goes into slow motion as the gun goes off.

40

ALEXEI

I've never run so fast in my life.

But as I sprint across the theater stage, all I can do is pray I'll make it in time.

As the crack of the gun goes off, I turn my back to the audience, enfolding Nadia in my arms and rotating to cushion her fall as I take her heavily down to the floor.

She gasps, the sound like a jolt of adrenaline straight to my heart. For a split second, our eyes meet before I hit the ground, and I can see in her emerald depths all the fear, the regret, the pain, the devastation.

I'd heard about her coming to the theater against my wishes. One of the security men I used to work with called to inform me during intermission. And though I was livid, my fear for Nadia's safety overrode it all. I dropped everything to get here before something bad could happen, calling in all my men as I drove because I had a gut feeling that something would go wrong.

We barely made it in time.

I was still sprinting up the gangplank as I watched the curtains go up. Only then did I stop to catch my breath at the side of the stage.

Nadia would have been furious if I'd interrupted her number, and

I let my guard down, allowing her to have her moment—not to mention, I was captivated by her dance as soon as she began.

She is truly something to behold, a work of art with her body, and I couldn't bring myself to ruin it. Not when she'd put in so much effort to defy me.

And then she'd stumbled. I knew something was wrong because Nadia never makes mistakes. In the countless times I've been to see her show since that night we first met, she hasn't once faltered. But tonight, her unstable footing was noticeable enough to make the audience react.

Their collective gasp made me look.

That's when I saw him. The shadowed figure standing in the aisle, looming ominously, like the grim reaper. Over the security radio nestled in my ear, I sent my men around back to cut him off and subdue him before he could cause any harm.

And then, like an idiot, I waited and watched him to see what he would do.

I should have gone with my instincts.

I should have pulled Nadia off the stage right then and there.

Screw the ballet. The audience could have their money back.

But I didn't.

I hesitated.

I wanted to give Nadia her moment.

And now, as pain explodes through my chest, the bullet finding me, not her, all I can feel is relief.

Screams ring through the massive theater, the audience panicking from the loud crack of the bullet leaving the gun.

I wince as Nadia and I hit the stage floor hard, me on bottom. A second burst of agony erupts through my chest as the impact is followed by Nadia's light weight colliding with my wound.

I cradle her close, shielding her with my body as best I can.

But I'm not about to relax until I know she's out of danger. Jerking my head in the direction of the audience, I watch as two of my men tackle the gunman, bringing him forcefully to the ground and wrenching the weapon from his hand.

And like a sea parting, the audience floods toward the doors, avoiding the center aisle by any means as they stampede toward safety.

"Alexei, you've been shot," Nadia says, her voice filled with horror as she removes her weight from my chest.

I turn to look at her, momentarily mesmerized by the soft glow of her black feather crown that shines like raven feathers atop her black hair. She looks like an angel of death come to deliver me to my final resting place. And if Nadia were who was meant to carry me to the afterlife, I would go without a second thought.

But the devastation that consumes her beautiful face calls me back to the reality of my situation.

"*Blyat*," I groan as crushing pain follows, and I reach for my chest.

"Alexei," she breathes, her eyes widening as I grow suddenly lightheaded. "Oh, God, you're losing so much blood."

The panic in her voice tells me it's bad, and I clench my teeth as her delicate hands put an impressive amount of pressure on the center point of my wound.

"That fucking hurts, woman," I growl, pointing out the obvious as I try to make light of the situation, then my head thumps heavily back onto the stage.

The tears streaming down her cheeks, drawing black rivulets of mascara down to her sharp chin, tells me she's beyond the point of finding humor in the situation.

"Someone call an ambulance!" she screams before turning her face back to me. "I'm so sorry," she sobs. "God, I'm so sorry, Alexei. I was so stupid."

Other faces crowd above us, and I think I hear someone say help is on the way, but my ears are starting to ring, and the pain is making it hard to focus.

"Stay with me, Alexei. Please. Please don't leave me."

I find the request rather funny when I can't seem to get up off the floor. All of me is far too heavy as my weight seems to be pinning me against the floor. I chuckle, and the amusement ends as a sharp pain cuts through my torso. I groan with the reminder that I have a bullet residing somewhere in my chest.

Nadia sobs harder, wrapping one arm around me, holding me close as she tries to staunch the bleeding as best she can. "Don't die on me, Alexei. Please," she cries, her voice broken. "I'll do anything. Just don't die."

"Anything? Even marry me?" I tease despite the world spinning dangerously around me. "Because you sounded pretty dead set against it last night."

I finally get a tearful laugh from her. "Of course I'll marry you, you big, dumb idiot," she says. "All you had to do was ask."

I chuckle again and wince as the pain sears through my chest.

Then her lips find mine as she kisses me passionately, and nothing else matters because she's here, she's safe, and she agreed to marry me.

Though my hand feels like lead, I reach up to cradle the back of her head, holding her lips to mine. I savor the taste of her mouth, the hint of salt there from her hard work during the performance.

I kiss her for as long as I can. And she kisses me back just as furiously, her soft sobs interrupting our rhythm and making my heart twinge. I don't like to hear her grief. It hurts me physically to know she's suffering.

"I'm okay, Nadia," I promise, and the pain is lessening as my body starts to go numb.

"I'm so sorry, Alexei," Nadia repeats. "I never should have come. I should have listened to you. It was so stupid, and ... and ... this is all my fault." She sobs harder as she presses her forehead to mine.

Hearing her say she should have listened to me brings a smile to my face. I can't imagine this girl ever willingly obeying me. Then I flinch as the gesture makes my bullet hole ache. "Why didn't you? Listen, I mean," I grit out, breathing heavily as the numbness recedes just in time for the agony to return.

Nadia pulls back to look at me, sniffling as she works to get her breathing under control. "Because I'm stupid and hard-headed, and with the baby coming, I knew this would be the end of my career, that

I couldn't get away with more than these last performances. I just wanted to enjoy the feeling a few more times."

I swallow convulsively, fighting down a wave of nausea that hits me after the pain. I press my eyes closed tightly until I'm sure I have my stomach under control.

"Alexei?" Nadia breathes, her voice filled with horror.

"I'm here," I promise, opening my eyes to find her emerald ones once more. "Just trying not to throw up. And now who's the big, dumb idiot? Why would your career be over?"

"Because . . . primas can't be moms. No one ever hires a pregnant ballerina, and it's not like you can just take a year off and expect a dance troupe to hold your spot."

Her logic seems so irrational, I'm starting to wonder if I've lost too much blood. *Why would anyone want a world without Nadia in the spotlight?* She's the most beautiful dancer this city has ever seen. She's going to take the world by storm. So I say the only thing I can think of to make sense of it all.

"Nadia, I own this dance company. You can do whatever the fuck you want."

That draws a startled laugh from her, and though she's still crying, she rewards me with a brilliant smile. "I love you so much." She sniffles, pressing another kiss to my lips.

I groan, a sound that mingles both my pleasure and pain. "I love you too," I rasp when she pulls away.

The paramedics arrive a moment later, and Nadia reluctantly releases me so they can administer first aid. They lift me immediately onto a gurney, patching me up even as they cart me toward the ambulance.

"Nadia," I command, letting my hand fall to my side, fingers extended to show her I need her nearby.

"I'm right here," she promises, her delicate fingers closing around mine, and I can feel the slick wetness of my blood on her palm.

"Stay close. And call Dimitri. He'll protect you."

"You've already done that," she assures me, her grip tightening on my hand as the lights above me flash by.

I curl my fingers, trapping her in my grasp and clinging to her to reassure myself that the danger has passed.

Then we're outside, the crisp bay breeze washing through the city streets and over my face, bringing me intense relief. In the background, I can hear Nadia speaking with Dimitri as the paramedics load me into the ambulance.

And once Nadia climbs in to sit beside me, the doors close securely, I know everything will be alright.

EPILOGUE
NADIA

Six Months Later

"You look beautiful, honey," Mom says, her eyes brimming with tears as our gazes meet in the mirror.

"Thanks, Mom." I beam as I smooth the soft white organza layers over my growing baby belly. My heart warms as I think about little Liam growing inside me.

I don't care that I look immensely pregnant. This is the best day of my life, and I'm excited to share it with Alexei and our unborn child.

"Knock-knock," McKenna's bright voice says from the doorway, and I turn to smile at her as she peeks inside the room.

She gasps, her jaw dropping, and she steps fully inside. "You're perfect," she breathes, her brown eyes growing wide with appreciation.

"I should go see if everyone's ready," Mom says shrewdly. "I'll be right back."

Looking as young and vibrant as ever in her shiny rose gold dress, my mom scoots past McKenna and slips out the door.

"Thank you for coming," I say to McKenna as soon as we're alone.

"Are you kidding? I wouldn't miss it!" she gushes, stepping closer to admire my dress. "Man, it fits you perfectly," she observes, marveling at the white buttons that run up the sheer back.

I laugh. "It wasn't my original dress. I had to pick one three weeks ago that would fit my belly. I thought I would have a bit more time before I got this big."

"Oh, please. You're still so tiny."

"So . . . ?" I ask, turning to face her fully.

McKenna bites her lip, and the hesitation makes my heart sink. Stew decided to have open auditions for the temporary position of prima—that could become a permanent one someday, when I'm ready to give up the spotlight. But I won't be back for this upcoming season. I need time to heal, get back in shape, be a mom.

And in the meantime, Candace has definitely forfeited her spot. I've been rooting hard for McKenna, but I know she wants to earn it on her own merit, and it breaks my heart if she didn't get it.

"I got the spot!" she gushes after a moment, doing an excited dance in her high heels.

I laugh, stepping down from my stool to pull her into a hug. "You deserve it," I say warmly.

It's amazing how far I've come, opening my heart to these kinds of relationships now that I'm not intent on keeping everyone out. And McKenna's a good friend, a true friend who's been nothing but sweet to me from the very start.

"Thanks, Nadia," she says, her brilliant smile shy.

"Okay, we're ready for you," Mom says, entering the room once more.

"Eek!" McKenna gives an excited squeak. "I'll go find my seat. See you after!"

Then she scampers from the room.

"Ready?" Mom asks, her smile warm and filled with emotion.

"Don't start crying," I warn her. "You'll make me cry."

"I'm not crying," she promises, even as she sniffles and dabs under her eyes.

I can't help but hug her, pulling her tight against my round belly for a moment of shared excitement. Then we loop arms as we make our way out of the bedroom.

Music filters up to us from the grand entry, a grand piano filling one corner of the Federov brothers' foyer. I've fallen in love with the estate their family owns, acres and acres of nature and beauty out in the middle of nowhere wine country.

And the beautiful mosaic floor is as impactful as it was the day I first saw it. The compass showing true north will guide me toward my groom, showing me the way to happiness. I love that we're having a winter wedding right inside the family home.

We only invited family and our very closest friends, which means, for me, my mom and McKenna. I think our wedding involves twenty people in all—including the pianist.

I take a deep, steadying breath as Mom and I pause just around the corner of the stairs.

When the wedding march begins, we walk together in a slow, deliberate march down the ornate, curving staircase. The guests rise —Alexei's brothers, Camille, and their little baby cradled affectionately in her arms. Alexei's mom, whom I've only come to adore more over time.

She and my mom have proven to be a force of nature when they put their heads together to help me plan this wedding. And though it's a small ceremony done quickly so I might enjoy a bit of married time with Alexei before baby Liam comes, it's been planned to perfection.

Alexei comes into view last of all. He's turned to watch me make my slow, steady descent. He looks debonair in his black tux with a splash of emerald green coming from his silk cummerbund. Hair slicked back and styled to perfection, he looks every bit the gentleman.

He stands proudly, his shoulders square, his hands clasped in front of him.

It fills my heart with relief to know he's fully recovered from the gunshot wound to his shoulder. And though he'll always bear the scar that shows just how far he'll go to protect me, he's as fit and healthy as ever.

Tears sting my eyes as Mom and I reach the makeshift altar, a podium decorated with flowers and a curving archway that stands behind our officiant.

Alexei graciously accepts my hands from my mom, giving her a kiss on either cheek as she hands me over. The symbolism of the moment nearly overcomes me. My mom has always been my best friend, the person who has looked out for me and sacrificed so much to take care of me.

Now, she's passing that responsibility on to Alexei, and I love that I'm not only marrying the love of my life but also a new best friend, someone I want to do everything with, a man I want to build a family with, a life, a home.

"Hi," Alexei murmurs, his gray eyes dancing as he flashes me a devilish smile.

"Hi," I breathe, releasing a soft giggle as he helps break the tension of this moment.

"Welcome, everyone, to this momentous occasion of the marriage between Nadia Lukyan and Alexei Federov. Please be seated," our officiant says.

I scarcely hear a word of the pastor's speech as I stare deep into Alexei's loving eyes, astonished that this is the man I get to spend the rest of my life with. And when it's time to say our vows, he delivers his flawlessly, sprinkling the perfect amount of levity to help me avoid crying.

But when it comes to my turn, I can scarcely catch my breath. "I vow to love you, Alexei, from this day until our last. To cherish the time we spend together, to value every time you make me laugh. I vow to listen to you as best I can—"

Alexei gives a playful snort, drawing laughter from our family and friends, and I glare at him even as a smile tugs mercilessly at the corners of my lips.

"And I vow to question you always," I add.

"Now that's the woman I know and love," he growls appreciatively.

My heart warms to know he values my fiery obstinance, even if it means I make mistakes sometimes.

"I love you, Alexei, with all my heart. I feel so blessed to be a part of your family. And I'm over the moon that we're starting a little family of our own."

I release one of his hands to smooth my palm over my tummy, and Alexei's eyes flash with a passionate tenderness as he rests his hand over my belly button.

"These rings symbolize your never-ending love for each other," the officiant says. "Take them and repeat after me."

We do, collecting the rings and simultaneously sliding them onto each other's ring fingers. My skin tingles deliciously as our voices blend together as we say, "You are more precious to me today than yesterday, and you will be more cherished tomorrow than you are today. Please wear this ring as a symbol of my eternal love for you, a love that transcends all our yesterdays, all our todays, and all our tomorrows."

"Alexei, Nadia, I now pronounce you man and wife. You may kiss your bride."

Heart brimming with happiness, I melt into Alexei as he pulls me close, fingers combing into my hair as his other arm wraps around the small of my back. And when his lips meet mine, electric sparks of anticipation crackle through me, searing away all my pre-wedding nerves.

This is where I'm meant to be, wrapped in Alexei's powerful arms.

A war still looms on the horizon, the threat of Aleksandr Volkov never far from my or Alexei's minds. But today, right now, I intend to enjoy every second I have with the man I love.

What follows is a bit less conventional, seeing as our wedding is small enough that the reception is going to be closer to a dinner party and an early night. So as we make our way to the spacious dining room, Alexei and I are bombarded with congratulations and well-wishes.

"I can't believe my baby brother is all grown up and getting married. You sure you want him to be the father of your child?" Dimitri jokes, gripping Alexei's shoulder and giving him a playful shake.

I laugh, smiling at my new brother-in-law. The constant banter between him and Alexei was a bit to wrap my mind around at first, but now I understand how my husband can be so playful and carefree. He has an older brother to tease and torment constantly.

"I don't think I have a choice at this point, do I? The deed is done," I joke back cheekily.

"Hey, I think what you mean to say is you couldn't dream of having any other man be the father of your child," Alexei growls, wrapping his arm around my waist and kissing me greedily.

I giggle as Dimitri and Camille keep walking, giving us a moment alone.

"Isn't that what I said?" I ask quietly, pressing my forehead to his. "That's definitely what I meant."

Alexei hums appreciatively and gives me another gentle kiss before letting me go.

"Congratulations." The deep, solemn voice of Alexei's older brother cuts through the happy atmosphere like a knife, and as we turn to face him, my heart twinges with sympathy.

Maksim has changed a lot since I met him that day on the yacht. His already-serious demeanor has become almost sullen, his eyes sad and haunted no matter the occasion.

"Thanks, Maks," Alexei says softly, his own joy dimming in the wake of his brother's overshadowing grief. He takes my hand, giving it a reassuring squeeze as we pause to speak with Alexei's oldest brother.

"I'm sorry, but I can't stay for the reception. I have some pressing work to finish," Maksim says after a long pause.

I can see the flash of disappointment that flickers across Alexei's face, but he covers it well. "Of course, no need to apologize. I'm sure we'll see you again soon," he agrees.

And I know he's being gentle because he understands that his brother is hurting. While Alexei and Dimitri are happy and starting families, Maksim just lost the woman he was supposed to marry. A wedding right now must be torture for him.

"Thanks, Alexei. And really, I'm very happy for the both of you." Maksim meets his brother's eyes, then mine, and the depth of pain I see there steals my breath away.

Then he's gone, shoulders hunching as he turns for the front door and leaves without a backward glance.

"You think he'll be okay?" I breathe, anxiety gripping me as I look up at Alexei's worried face.

He peers down at me and offers a sad smile. Then he brushes a kiss across the back of my palm. "I hope so."

Dinner is exquisite, the accompanying music divine, and after hours of laughter and celebration, Alexei and I finally make our way upstairs for the night. We leave for our honeymoon vacation tomorrow. But tonight, I just want to spend some time wrapped in Alexei's arms.

I groan appreciatively as I close the door behind us, happy to have a moment alone with my husband. Tingling excitement races up my spine to think the word.

"How are you feeling, Mrs. Federov?" Alexei asks playfully, scooping me up off my sore, swollen feet and carrying me to the bed as if I weigh nothing.

I moan, wrapping my arms around his neck. "Much better now, thanks, husband."

The word sounds even better when I say it out loud, and Alexei rewards me with a wolfish grin.

"I could get used to that," he rumbles, then he gently lays me down on the bed.

I roll into him, resting against the length of his solid warmth. "I love you," I breathe, peering up through my lashes at his gorgeous face.

"I love you too, Nadia." Alexei cups my cheek.

Then he leans in, slow and smooth, his eyes flicking down to my lips. They part in anticipation, my breath hitching as we come together for a passionate kiss.

I can't believe after so many years of struggles, fear, and self-doubt, I'm here with Alexei, our baby growing in my belly, a life of joy and laughter sprawling before me as far as the eye can see. I have everything I've ever wanted in the world. And I couldn't be happier.

EXTENDED EPILOGUE
MAKSIM

Stepping out onto the pillared front steps of our family estate, I breathe in the crisp January air like a drowning man who only just surfaced. I'm still lost at sea, unable to spot a life raft or even some driftwood to offer me a momentary reprieve.

Since Symphony died, I feel as though I'm struggling to keep my head above water. I know Dimitri and Alexei never particularly cared for my choice. They told me on more than one occasion that she wasn't good enough for me.

But she was mine, the only thing I've chosen for me. Not the good of my family. And now she's gone, a light snuffed out too soon because I couldn't pull the trigger.

I should have listened to my brothers—to Dimitri's incessant warnings. Alexei told me Aleksandr Volkov had guns, that he was likely the one targeting us. That we should be ready. But I deal in facts and numbers. I drive our success by making confident decisions based on the proof I have in hand.

And this time, I chose wrong.

For that, I cost Symphony her life.

I deserve this pain I feel. Let my brothers celebrate their futures. Let them find the happiness they have earned. I'm doomed to suffer a different fate. If this year has taught me anything, it's these two cold, hard truths. Mercy is for the weak, and there's no room for love when you're on top.

As the oldest brother and the head of our family, I should have known that from the start. My father gave his life building this empire we've amassed. And as the *pakhan* of our Bratva now, I'll more than likely follow in his footsteps.

There's no room for mistakes, no window for weakness, and now that I've lost the woman I love, I can see that my life does not belong to me. It belongs to my family. I can't make selfish decisions. I don't have the freedom to fall in love.

If I'm going to steer us through the storm ahead, I need to stay focused.

And Aleksandr Volkov is going to pay for what he's done.

Now that my brothers are both happily married and starting their families, the real work begins.

Tomorrow, I will find a way to crush my enemy, to wipe him from the face of the earth.

But tonight, I need something to numb the pain, to help me forget about what I've lost.

Driving like a bat out of hell, I make my way back into the city and park my car in the garage beneath my penthouse in Pacific Heights. Then I head straight for the strip club down the street. It's unlimited alcohol within walking distance, and I intend to get obliterated, maybe find some mindless sex before the end of my night.

I pay the cover charge then find a seat along the catwalk, slumping into my chair and unbuttoning my black suit I didn't bother to change out of.

"What can I get you, handsome?" one of the bar girls dressed in tight booty shorts asks, her tone appreciative as she places a hand on my shoulder.

I look at it for a long moment, contemplating the gesture. Then I shift my gaze up to her heavily made-up eyes. "Jewel of Russia, Ultra Black. Chilled. You can bring the bottle."

"S–Sure," she stutters, her glitter-hooded eyes growing wide.

She lifts the credit card from my fingers and departs quickly, leaving me to watch the girl who just strutted fiercely onto the stage. Wearing little more than dental floss that glitters in the strobe lights, she flaunts her body with practiced ease, making her way down to the pole at the far end of the stage.

A second girl comes on, her waves of blonde hair catching the light and shining like liquid gold. This girl moves differently. Though her body is just as perfect as the one before, she doesn't prance but rather sways. Her movement is almost naturally sensual, capturing my attention and holding it, even as she reaches the pole right before me.

Our eyes meet. Her hazel ones, each rimmed with a dark circle of brown before bursting into a seafoam green, read me, seeing deep into my tortured soul. And rather than the pity I've seen for months now, I find a deep sadness there that reflects my own.

"Your vodka, Mr. Federov," my waitress says, setting down an ice bucket and pouring me two fingers of chilled alcohol before setting the bottle in the silver holder.

I accept the glass with a casual glance before turning my eyes back to the strikingly beautiful stripper before me.

She's turned her attention to the pole now, gripping it confidently with one hand as she spins in a slow circle, showing me every curve and angle of her perfect curves. And suddenly, I'm less inclined to drink myself into a stupor.

This woman might just be all the distraction I need from the pain —at least for tonight.

Though it's sipping vodka, I take the drink like a shot and pour myself another. Then I settle back to watch the beautiful blonde dance. Entranced by her movement, the emotion with which she rocks and sways, wrapping her body around the pole, I feel compelled to watch her.

And I do, my eyes fixed to her tantalizing hips and long legs. Then the song ends, and the girls rotate. Anxiety spikes in my chest as the blonde heads off stage, her heels clicking softly against the hard catwalk.

Flagging down my server, I point out the stripper just before she vanishes around the corner. "I want a private dance with her," I state.

"Of course," the server says, her smile tight. Then she straightens to her full height and makes her way toward the back of the house.

A moment later, my glittery-eyed server is collecting my ice bucket of vodka and showing me back to my private room. It's a small enclosure, the circular booth-like bench backlit with soft red light. Crimson vinyl covers the seat, and small end tables occupy each end of the curving bench. The platform that fills the center of the room is clearly meant for my dancer.

"Angel will be right with you," my server says. Then she pulls the black velvet curtains closed, leaving me alone in the small room.

Music trickles from the walls and ceiling, surrounding me with the slow, scintillating sound of sex in the form of art. The comparison immediately makes me think of Symphony—her unusual name and how often I'd drawn the connection. It used to drive her crazy. My chest aches hollowly at the memory.

A moment later, my attention is captured by the curtain sliding back, and Angel enters the room. She's dressed in a new outfit now—thigh-high fishnet stockings attached to her small waist by a lacy garter belt. A floral lace bra that barely comes high enough to cover her nipples and a matching thong, all as white as freshly fallen snow.

"Evening, Mr. Federov," she says in a soft, feminine voice.

It has the hint of a Southern drawl that piques my interest. As she approaches, she captures her lower lip between her teeth—either a coy gesture or a hint of trepidation in being alone with me.

"You know my name?" I ask, my voice sounding coarse in the softer atmosphere of our private space.

Angel smiles gently, the gesture forcing her to release her lower lip, and she climbs up onto the red vinyl bench, placing one knee on either side of my thighs as she straddles me. "We make a point of knowing all our high-paying customers' names."

My hands twitch with the urge to touch her, to grip her thighs and pull her closer, but I know I'm not allowed. Not here, at the strip club.

I lose track of our conversation as Angel starts to dance on top of me, her hips rolling in time to the sensual rhythm of the music. Her arms fall gently over my shoulders as she grips the back of the seat.

And when she leans in to gently graze her breasts across my chest, I can smell the rich, enticing scent of honeysuckle.

"Where are you from?" I rasp as I feel my arousal consuming me rapidly. I haven't been here for more than a half hour, and already, I'm throbbing to get out of my pants.

"Not here" is all she says, and the breathy sound of her voice combined with her cheeky comment leaves me aching for more.

"Have you been in the city long?"

"Mm-hmm."

"Then how come I've never seen you here before?"

Angel releases a soft laugh that sounds shockingly devoid of humor. "You are full of questions, aren't you Mr. Federov?"

"I want to get to know you," I confess. This girl intrigues me. She seems so . . . out of place despite her natural sexuality that's driving me wild.

"You didn't pay to get to know me," she points out, and she changes her position then, turning to face away from me so she can gently grind her ass against my lap.

I swallow hard as she takes my hands and guides them slowly up her body—a rare treat seldom offered in a paid lap dance.

"What if I did?" I ask, the ragged sound of my voice revealing my intense excitement. "What if I paid you to spend the night with me?"

Angel freezes, her fingers tightening around the backs of my hands. Then she shoves them away from her body as she jerks away from me. "I'm not a whore," she says, her voice sharp and cutting as she turns to face me.

Her countenance has changed completely, her soft hazel eyes flashing with deep insult.

"Fifty thousand dollars," I offer boldly because I don't want her to leave just yet.

I haven't been this excited in a long time, and I'm curious to see if there's a number she'll accept. I know it's against the strip club's policy. But everyone has a price.

"I can't," she says, though her face twists as if the offer is painful to reject.

She needs money.

"I need this job."

"A hundred thousand," I offer, watching her closely.

Her breasts rise and fall rapidly as she quickly climbs to the edge of hyperventilating, and a visible tremble racks her body. She closes her eyes, cutting off my main source of information.

I wait, my hands clenched as I force myself to be patient. Pushing her won't make it more likely that I'll get a yes.

"Okay," she breathes, her answer hardly more than a whisper. Then she glances over her shoulder, as if afraid someone might overhear.

A dark smile of satisfaction spreads across my face, and I stand. "Good. Tell your boss you're feeling sick and need to go home. I'll meet you out front in fifteen."

Continue reading Maksim and Angel's story here.

SEASON OF MALICE
(PREVIEW)

DESCRIPTION

**He's old enough to be my father.
He might be the one who killed my boyfriend.
And I can't resist him any longer.**

Not only is my boyfriend dead, he left me with a sizable loan in my name to a mafia boss.
When Dimitri Federov, a handsome, loaded Russian playboy, appears on my doorstep, I panic.

He wants money to repay the debt. Money I don't have.

The prick offers me a solution - pay with my body. I turn him down flat, but the indecent proposal remains in my thoughts, forever reminding me of what could have been...

But when Dimitri turns on his charms, it gets even harder to resist him, and much easier to forget he's a ruthless kingpin... a *killer*.

And once I let him have what he so desperately wants, give into our desires and follow this basic instinct to its heady climax... There will be no stopping Dimitri's dark desires.

One night leaves me with the biggest secret of my life... and I have to make sure Dimitri never finds out he got me *pregnant*.

1

Camille

"No, no that's way too hot!" I shout, snatching the saucepan from the stove as I watch the creamy beurre blanc break before my eyes. Then I burst into tears.

Poor Louis looks like I might as well have slapped him across the face as his eyes widen with fear. "I'm sorry, Chef. I just turned away for a moment..."

He looks utterly crestfallen as my tears come hard and fast, spilling down my cheeks in a torrent. I can't help myself. Normally, I wouldn't cry over something so minor as broken sauce—even in the middle of the dinner rush—not when it's a simple fix of adding water while whisking to re-emulsify the butter. But the last two weeks have been some of the worst of my life. And that's saying something.

"It's f-fine," I stutter, wiping brusquely at my cheeks. "You know how to fix it?"

Louis nods his head vigorously.

Hannah, my best friend and front-of-house manager, steps into the kitchen at the commotion, and when her eyes find mine, her shoulders drop.

"Cami, go home," she insists for what must be the hundredth time.

But I can't. I'm the head chef—the only head chef at my restaurant, Le Fleur—and I have an obligation to see us through the Friday night rush, no matter what state I'm in.

Sniffling, I shake my head and step back up to the grill. "I'm fine," I insist, avoiding Hannah's stern hazel gaze.

She plants her hands on her hips and steps close to speak in a low voice. "You've suffered a major personal loss, honey. Nobody would hold it against you if you closed the restaurant for a few days—hell, even a week—if you need to. And I'm sure we would survive—broken sauces and all—even if you left us to run the restaurant without a head chef."

"I didn't *suffer a loss*, Hannah. Roy was murdered. Why else would the police ask if he had any enemies?" Fresh tears threaten to spill at the memory of that call notifying me that my boyfriend of two years had been found dead in a house fire.

The term 'suspicious circumstances' had been thrown around more than once while I'd bawled my eyes out, but no one had been willing to tell me what those suspicious circumstances were because of the pending investigation. Therefore, I'd been left to speculate and grieve all in one fell swoop.

"I know what you think, Cami. And I totally get it. I just think you're putting yourself under a lot of pressure trying to cook and run a business seven days a week when you haven't even had the time to process."

Sliding the pan-fried sol from the stove and plating it, I keep my hands busy. "I don't need time to process. Cooking helps clear my mind, and right now, the less thinking I do, the better. Besides, Daddy never took a day off, and I don't need to either."

"You're not helping your case with that last statement, hon," Hannah says dryly.

When I shoot her a withering glare, she puts her hands up in surrender. But I suppose she's right. My dad died of a massive heart attack before his forty-fifth birthday—probably due in part to the amount of stress he endured from working so many hours to raise me on his own and put me through college.

But opening this restaurant was Daddy's and my dream, and I won't let it fall apart just because my personal life has.

"I'm fine," I state definitively. "I'll be fine. You just go back out there and win over our customers. I'll get my act together in here."

Hannah releases a heavy sigh, then gives my shoulder a squeeze before heading back through the swinging door to the front of the house, her honey-blond ponytail swishing.

"The beurre blanc is ready, Chef," Louis says apologetically, stepping up beside me.

"Good, good. Thank you, Louis." I take the saucepan from him with a forced smile and finish plating the sol.

It's a long night of grueling work as the rush never seems to end, and after my meltdown, my eyes feel tired, my body heavy with grief. But we make it. At ten o'clock, I glance around the kitchen at my staff. They're cleaning up for the night, hauling dirty dishes toward Marie, our dishwasher, and sanitizing the stainless steel surfaces.

Wiping the sweat from my brow, I turn back to my own station to ensure it's spotless.

"Um, Cami?" Hannah says tentatively from the kitchen doorway.

"Hmm?" I glance up and immediately stop my cleaning from the look of apprehension that scrunches my best friend's face.

"There's a man out front who asked to speak with the owner."

"At this time of night?" I'm baffled. Usually, food critics would alert me to their presence before the kitchen closes, and I can't think of anyone I had an appointment with. "I'll be right out," I add, wiping my hands on my apron.

I scan my station to ensure I've turned everything off—a habit my father drilled into me as a child—then follow Hannah into the dining area.

It's empty and still, the soft jazz music trickling through the speakers sounding almost too loud without the din of customers eating and talking and laughing.

Brushing the stray wisps of auburn hair back from my face, I approach the host stand, and my heart skips a beat. The gentleman waiting there—a businessman from the looks of him in his fine-tailored suit and dark, wavy hair styled to perfection—is gorgeous. He must be over six feet tall with a trim, muscular physique. A healthy amount of facial hair shadows his strong jaw, calling attention to his lips.

Gray eyes meet mine as I approach, and a predatory smile lifts the corners of his mouth as he looks me up and down in a way that leaves me feeling exposed, almost naked. And though he looks nearly old enough to be my father, the appreciative gaze that comes to rest on my face once more makes my stomach quiver.

"Hi, I'm Camille Anderson," I state, my voice sounding more confident than I feel in this stranger's presence. Extending my hand as I close the distance between us, I strive for professionalism, even though he's asking for me at such a late hour.

"Dimitri Federov," he introduces himself, the hint of a Russian accent rolling off his tongue.

He accepts my hand, and rather than shaking it, draws my knuckles to his lips. His gray eyes never leave mine as he brushes a soft kiss over the back of my hand.

Gasping in shock, I pull my hand back quickly, balling my fist in an attempt to subdue the tingles that race up my arm. "How can I help you, Mr. Federov?" This time, my voice wavers slightly.

"Please, call me Dimitri," he insists, his low voice making my stomach quiver. Then the businessman's smile creeps higher as his eyes flash dangerously. "And I've come because your loan payment is overdue. I'm here to collect."

His soft, inviting tone is an utter contradiction to the words that leave his mouth, and for a moment, I stand frozen, not quite sure I heard him right.

"I'm-I'm sorry? You must have the wrong person. I don't have a loan," I state when I finally find my voice.

His dark eyebrows raise as if in mild surprise, but that smile never falters. "No? Then why does my paperwork put your business as collateral for a significant personal loan that is now overdue?"

Is that amusement in his voice? He must be joking. Irritation flares inside me. Whatever stunt he thinks he's pulling, I don't have the time for it. Or the energy. All I want to do is put on my comfiest pair of pajamas, curl up on my couch with my favorite chick flick, and mourn my dead boyfriend. But this jerk thinks tonight's the night to pull one over on me? I don't think so.

"I already told you I haven't put a lien on my business, nor would I ever. So, you need to leave." I force as much authority into my voice as I can muster, though my still-trembling stomach does nothing to help me.

"I have paperwork that would disagree with you, Miss Anderson," the handsome stranger states.

Scoffing, I plant my hands on my hips. "Alright then. Why don't you show me this supposed paperwork?"

"Gladly," Dimitri says. Then he gestures to a nearby booth. "May I?"

"Be my guest." I wave him toward it, though my tone would say he's anything but welcome in my restaurant.

The tall businessman sets his briefcase on the table and pops the clasps before withdrawing a document from inside. I take the opportunity to study his chiseled face, the hint of silver at his temples, looking for any underlying motive he might have. I can find nothing in his expression.

He skims the document as if to ensure it's the right one before flipping it to face me and handing it over. I snatch it from him with unnecessary sass and slowly lower my eyes from his to read the paper's contents.

The document looks official enough. And it outlines a loan for half a million dollars, putting *my* restaurant up as collateral. My blood turns to ice in my veins as I reach the bottom of the page and find a rather adept forgery of my signature. And next to it. Roy's. My boyfriend of two years betrayed me. Used me.

It appears he granted a lien on my business six months ago without telling me. Though what he needed half a million dollars for, I haven't the slightest clue. He never mentioned anything about needing a loan.

"This is my boyfriend, Roy. Not me. And he did this without my knowledge," I state flatly, shoving the condemning paperwork back toward Dimitri Federov.

"Yes, well, your boyfriend stopped making payments a few months ago, and my men have informed me that he was spending a lot of time at the casinos before that, so he probably gambled it away," he explains casually. "The contract states that failure to make payment entitles me to claim this restaurant as collateral. So, seeing as your boyfriend has stopped returning my calls, I've come to collect. You have two options, Miss Anderson."

He steps close to me, invading my personal space and forcing me to look up at him. My heart hammers in my chest. The masculine scent of leather and pine fills my nose as I inhale sharply, and I swallow hard.

A mere foot from me now, the man feels far more intimidating than I had realized upon first meeting him, and a shiver races down my spine. But I refuse to back up.

"Either you can pay me back in full, or I'll take your business," he states softly, his voice almost a caress, even as he threatens to take away my entire life.

"You can't do that," I say firmly, standing my ground. I lick my suddenly dry lips and glare up into Dimitri Federov's penetrating gaze. "I didn't even know about the lien, and besides, my boyfriend is... dead." My voice cracks on the last word.

Dimitri's face maintains the same calm, watchful expression, and I slowly realize with growing horror that he already knows. Cold terror seeps into my bones as a new thought comes to mind. If he already knows Roy is dead, does that mean this is the man who killed him?

As soon as the thought occurs, it solidifies as an undeniable fact inside me. Roy lost the money. He couldn't pay back what he owed, so Dimitri killed him. And now he's here to collect. If I'm not careful, he might just do the same to me.

2

Dimitri

The fear in Camille Anderson's striking features tells me she doesn't have the money. Who would? I'm not surprised that Roy Lochte went behind his girlfriend's back and took out a loan he couldn't afford. He seemed like a slimy git from the start.

But now that we're in this situation, I can't simply rip up the contract and walk away. My brothers and I don't make the kind of money we do by forgiving unpaid debts. We always collect, and that's why they send me.

Still, I have a few alternatives I could suggest for this alluring, voluptuous beauty if she doesn't think she can pay. Though I know my brothers would be pissed, I feel inclined to cut this enticing and fiery young chef a break.

"If you don't think you can pay the debt in full, I might be willing to let you pay it off in installments..." I suggest.

Immediately, the worry lines around her blue eyes soften, telling me her greatest fear is losing her business.

"You could compensate me with sexual favors," I suggest playfully, reaching out to touch a stray lock of auburn hair that falls from her messy bun. I mean it more as a joke. The stunning young woman looks nearly half my age. But still, the idea *does* appeal to me. If she were interested.

"How dare you," she demands, her cheeks turning a delicious shade of red as she takes a step back from me and bumps into the wall behind her. "I would never sell my body to you."

That last statement burrows under my skin in a way comments don't usually, posing a challenge that makes me eager to change her mind. "Not to me?" I press, moving closer once again.

"To anyone," she clarifies forcefully, her eyes snapping with cold fire. "And my business is perfectly capable of paying off the lien if you'll just give me more time."

"Hmm," I hum, considering the offer.

Camille takes a step to the side, moving away from the wall before retreating farther. "I can prove it to you," she offers, her voice growing urgent. "Just… just let me prepare something for you, and you can judge for yourself if my business is worthy of a long-term loan."

Amused by the suggestion, I shrug. "Alright. Impress me."

Camille releases a breath of relief, calling attention to her generous breasts, and I trace my eyes down her body once more. She's on the shorter side, with curves in all the right places, and when she turns to retreat into the kitchen, I can't help but follow the sway of her hips.

Unwilling to let her out of my sight, I join her in the kitchen, stepping through the swinging door a beat after she does. The staff members, dressed in chef's robes, cast curious glances in my direction, but none say anything as they go about cleaning the pristine space.

"How long have you been in business?" I ask, coming to rest beside the stove as Camille turns it on.

A startled squeak bursts from her as she jumps away from me and presses a palm to her ample breasts. "You scared me. What are you doing in here?"

"I want to see you work, watch the magic, know that my investment would be worth my while." My lips tug up into a wicked grin as she throws a thunderous scowl in my direction.

"Fine. Just don't touch anything... please." She seems to second guess her harsh tone and tack on the please at the last minute.

Lifting my hands to show I'll keep them to myself, I lean back against the counter so I can watch her cook. "You didn't answer my question," I state after several moments of silence.

Camille bustles around the kitchen, collecting supplies with a confidence she didn't have when we first met. And the sight of her in her element makes her that much more attractive.

"What question?" she asks, casting me a sidelong glance.

"How long have you been in business?"

"Oh, um, a little over a year."

Impressive. I'm aware of how well her restaurant has been doing in the culinary mecca of San Francisco. I did a bit of digging to learn its value when Roy first took out his loan—to ensure it would make appropriate collateral. But to rise so quickly after just a year in business? That takes talent.

Falling silent once more, I watch with interest as she pounds a piece of meat, her intent expression making me wonder if she's picturing my face beneath her tenderizer. After it's been thoroughly pounded, she seasons the meat before putting it on the grill. Then she moves on to the stove to start a sauce.

As soon as Camille appears to accept my presence, the rest of the staff do as well. I respect that. They seem to trust her as their employer and demonstrate that her opinion is both valued and taken without question. The kitchen staff swiftly finish their work and trickle out the back door, wishing the restaurant owner and chef a tentative good night as they go.

She goes the whole nine yards, cooking me a lamb cutlet drizzled with what looks like a cranberry sauce, adding caramelized carrots and fingerling potatoes as my side. She plates the whole thing like an artist, adding rosemary for garnish.

Then she gestures toward the swinging door, indicating I should lead the way.

I pick a table in the center of the room, one that still has silverware set, waiting for its next customer. Rather than following me directly, Camille stops at the bar, speaking in hushed tones to the bartender, who had been busy restocking a moment before.

He pauses to uncork a bottle of red wine and pours a glass.

With familiar ease, Camille approaches the table with my meal, and the sight of her makes my mouth water. Not just from the fact that my long day at the office delayed my dinner but also the way her blue eyes trap me in a daring gaze.

"Your dinner, Mr. Federov," she says smartly, emphasizing my last name as she sets my plate and glass of wine before me. "Lamb cutlet with a cranberry balsamic drizzle, glazed carrots, fresh from our garden, and roasted fingerling potatoes; paired with a 2016 cabernet sauvignon, for your pleasure."

She takes a step back and clasps her hands behind her, as if waiting for my verdict. And suddenly, I know she's dangerous. Because I find her entirely too appealing. And I'm supposed to be here on business, acquiring another restaurant for my family's considerable empire.

"Come sit," I say, pulling out the chair to my right and refusing to touch my food until she obeys.

After several seconds of hesitation, Camille slides into the seat beside me. Only then do I cut into the impressively tender meat and place a bite in my mouth. The explosion of flavor stuns me momentarily, and my chewing slows as I savor the best bite I think I've ever tasted.

Flicking my eyes toward the heart-shaped face beside me, I find a smile tugging at her bee-stung lips. She knows just how good she is. And that proud smirk might be the sexiest thing I've ever seen.

Following my bite with a sip of wine, I take my time relishing the culinary masterpiece she's put before me. I don't know how she can be so young and so talented all at once, but I would eat here every single day of the week.

"Well?" she asks nervously as I continue to sample my plate without a word.

"How old are you, Miss Anderson?" I ask, and though it's a forward question, I'm dying to know.

Color stains her porcelain cheeks. "Don't you know it's rude to ask women that?" she demands, her eyes flashing.

I chuckle, low and soft, enjoying her consternation. "I only ask because this is some of the best lamb I have ever tasted, and I've never met a chef with this level of skill at such a young age."

Her blush intensifies, and Camille drops her eyes to the table. "Well, thank you."

"You are... I'm going to guess twenty-five." She looks younger, but a man can hope.

Blue eyes snap up to meet mine, and then she narrows them. "I'll be twenty-five in June," she says slowly, her voice laced with suspicion. "How did you know?"

I shrug. "Lucky guess."

Camille purses her lips but doesn't argue. Instead, she watches as I eat another bite.

I swallow deliberately and turn to face her. "And you opened this restaurant by yourself?"

She shrugs one shoulder. "My friend Hannah helps me run it. She hires and manages the restaurant staff while I manage the kitchen. But yes, Le Fleur is *my* restaurant." She says the last almost possessively, reminding me of why I'm here.

Now that I've indulged in what's proven to be one of the best meals of my life, I need to get back to business. But before I do, I have to try something.

Turning to face the young chef, I take her hand and pull her close, moving Camille from her chair to my lap in one swift move. She has time to release a startled yelp before I capture her lips with mine.

Electric attraction sizzles like a live wire between us. She tastes faintly of balsamic glaze, tangy and crisp. And her soft lips yield to mine, molding to my kiss as if made for me. Her rigid body demonstrates her shock, and yet, as I tease her lower lip with the tip of my tongue, she does not pull away.

Instead, she seems to relax, her muscles releasing as I hold her close. Her lips part on a sigh, and I take the opportunity to deepen the kiss, so tempted by her sultry figure and delicious flavor that I have to try more.

We kiss for a long moment, and when Camille finally pulls back, she looks flustered in the best way. Her cheeks are flush with excitement, her lips red and swollen from my exploring touch.

She scrambles back into her seat, her blue eyes wide with confusion and shock. "What was that for?" she gasps, her breaths coming hard, her breasts rising and falling dramatically.

"I've decided to make you a new offer," I say calmly, ignoring her question. My brothers won't like the bold move, but I can't let Camille slip through my fingers. "Rather than taking your restaurant from you or making you pay back the loan in full, I'll buy your restaurant outright. I believe it is worth enough that I can pay you $1.5 million. Cash. We can take the amount of the loan from that. And then you and I will be business partners."

Her look of utter horror tells me her answer long before she manages to regain her voice. Her lips move silently for several seconds, opening and closing as if trying to formulate a sentence.

Finally, she gasps, "How is that in any way a business partnership? That sounds like you're just taking my business from me!"

"Only you would be a million dollars richer," I counter logically. "And you would stay on as head chef, managing your restaurant exactly as you have been for the last year. I would be a silent investor of sorts."

Camille's expression brews with a storm of fury, her eyes flashing like lightning, and her beauty in that moment is breathtaking.

End of preview. *Continue reading this sizzling hot, Bratva romance here.*

Ready for ALL books in the series?

Season of Malice (Dimitri and Camille)

Season of Desire (Alexei and Nadia)

Season of Wrath (Maksim and Angel)

Made in United States
Troutdale, OR
12/27/2023